SOMETHING IN THE AIR

The management of Sparrow Flyways wants to expand and offer coast-to-coast service, and to finance the project they have approached the Sloan Guaranty Trust. Sparrow Flyways is unique in that there are no unions, each employee buys ten shares in the company, thus becoming part of the management. But many of them are unhappy about going trans-continental—and when a Sparrow pilot who is especially against the expansion is found dead, John Putnam Thatcher, executive vice-president of the Sloan, finds himself in the midst of mergers—and murder . . .

SOMETHING IN THE AIR

EMMA LATHEN

A New Portway Large Print Book

CHIVERS PRESS
BATH

First published in Great Britain 1988
by
Simon & Schuster Ltd
This Large Print edition published by
Chivers Press
by arrangement with
Simon & Schuster Ltd
at the request of
The London & Home Counties Branch
of
The Library Association
1990

ISBN 0 7451 7246 6

British Library Cataloguing in Publication Data

Lathen, Emma
  Something in the air.
  I. Title
  813.54

  ISBN 0–7451–7246–6

CONTENTS

SOMETHING IN THE AIR

CHAPTER ONE

OFTEN SOARS VERY HIGH

On Wall Street, immortality belongs to the institutions. Individuals only attain fleeting fame—usually for the wrong reasons. Sooner or later, all the Jay Goulds lay down their proxies; holding companies can last forever.

Bank holding companies always do.

The Sloan Guaranty Trust has not only survived, it has flourished. The third-largest bank in the world, it now dwarfs the thousands of men and women who hurry past its portals or work within them.

John Putnam Thatcher, executive vice-president, was technically answerable to the Board of Directors for staff performance at the Sloan. In reality, there was a frightening amount of signing power in hands other than his. So, outside his own power base on the sixth floor where he commanded the Trust and Investment Divisions, he braced himself for the worst whenever he saw another Sloan bigwig beckoning. Even if it was simply a chance encounter in the down elevator with Kyle Yetter.

'John, just the man!' Yetter exclaimed, beaming. 'Here's somebody I'd like you to meet.'

Only a customer brought out the sunshine in Kyle Yetter, one of the pillars of Commercial Credit, where a million dollars was small change. Naturally, Thatcher inspected Yetter's companion with interest.

The youthful, solidly built man with brilliant blue eyes and a mat of thick brown hair was, it developed, more than a would-be borrower. He was a celebrity.

'Mitchell Scovil, president of Sparrow Flyways up in Boston. That's the commuter line that's one of the few remaining successes of deregulation, you recall,' Yetter was saying when the doors opened on the executive lobby.

Thatcher always appreciated helpful introductions, although no reader of the daily paper, let alone the financial press, could have missed Sparrow Flyways. A dollar for every time it was described as no-frills would mop up the national debt.

Scovil barely let Yetter finish.

'Sparrow's commuter days are about to become a thing of the past,' he said confidently. 'Once we line up the right backing, we're busting out of the northeast corridor and offering coast-to-coast service. We'll be the high-tech link between Route 128 and Silicon Valley.'

Thatcher recognized a born salesman when he heard one. He could only hope that Kyle Yetter did too.

Meanwhile Scovil was forging ahead. 'Kyle and I are just going out to lunch. Why don't you come along, too? Then I could tell you all about Sparrow, and what we're planning.'

His persuasiveness, reputed to perform miracles at Sparrow, was misplaced. At the Sloan, trying to go over Yetter's head could lead the enterprising Mr. Scovil out the door.

'Yes, John, join us if you're free,' Yetter said, signaling his lack of objection.

2

'I'm afraid I have another engagement,' said Thatcher. Then, incautiously, he added that it, too, was Boston-based.

'Does that mean you'll be coming up to Boston?' Scovil asked alertly. 'Why don't you come and look Sparrow over? A picture's worth a thousand words, and ten minutes watching us run the shop will explain how Sparrow beat the competition.'

Thatcher reminded himself that Commercial Credit paid Kyle Yetter a substantial salary. Let him earn it!

'I'm sure it would, but I see I'm running late. It was a pleasure meeting you, Scovil. I know Yetter here will take good care of the best interests of Sparrow—amd the Sloan.'

By the time Thatcher was on the sidewalk, Scovil and Sparrow were fast slipping from his mind. If he could remember them long enough to quiz Kyle Yetter, he would be doing well.

Since his fool's paradise included a chill November drizzle, he turned up his collar and headed north to other, more demanding, matters.

Kyle Yetter was not the only authority on Mitchell Scovil. What the other experts had to say depended on where they sat.

'He was a goddam nuisance from the beginning.'

'And now he's a menace.'

The site was St. Louis, Missouri, a few miles west of Lambert Airport where Atlantic & Pacific Airlines (known familiarly as A&P) maintained corporate headquarters. The voices raised in anger belonged to vice-presidents who had been abusing Scovil since the Airline Deregulation Act of 1978. Sparrow had started with twenty-five employees and three secondhand planes. Now this Mickey Mouse operation had thousands on the payroll, served the whole East Coast, and was rumored to be eyeing California.

'That cheap SOB's got a nerve,' said Wilfred Merrick, longtime president of A&P. Savaging his Jamaican cigar, he rumbled: 'He made a quick killing because he wasn't saddled with unions. Now he thinks he's ready for the big time.'

The big time, it went without saying, belonged exclusively to Atlantic & Pacific Airlines and its few peers. After all, A&P had roots stretching back to the dawn of commercial aviation. Photographs on the boardroom walls celebrated early fragile biplanes, historic deliveries of the U.S. Mail, and rugged pioneers in leather helmets.

A&P had still been pointing to this illustrious past when it was sandbagged by deregulation, oil crises, and competition. Costs ballooned, revenues plummeted, and yesterday's muscle became today's flab.

The inevitable call for new blood had produced Fritz Diehl, the youngest vice-president at the table and the last to speak.

'There's no future for the commuters. Either they expand, or they go under,' he said dispassionately. 'Sooner or later one of them is bound to go coast-to-coast against us. But my guess is that they'll do it by acquisition—buying somebody else out. Whether or not it will be Sparrow—that's another proposition altogether.'

'You should know,' Merrick told him sourly.

The credentials that had brought Diehl to A&P included a stint at Sparrow Flyways. In fact, like Mitchell Scovil, he was one of its founders. This

4

meant guilt by association to A&P's old guard. Everybody else envied him his profits.

Ignoring the crosscurrents, Diehl said: 'Sparrow's innovations were perfect for the time . . .'

'Grr!' Merrick growled reflexively.

'. . . but trying to expand them to California now would be damned near impossible. They're already having trouble keeping their profit margins up. Any more pressure and the whole system will crumble.'

'What about Toronto?' challenged a rival. 'Scovil's showing a profit after just three months, isn't he?'

'Toronto is the past,' said Fritz Diehl coolly. 'I'm talking about the future.'

If Norman Pitts had anything to say about it, the future was pure gold. In East Boston, Massachusetts, home of Logan Airport and Sparrow Flyways, young Pitts was ready to do or die for Sparrow.

He had been on the payroll for exactly one week. And crowning the orientation course, here was Mitchell ('Call me Mitch!') Scovil himself.

'At Sparrow we're proud of our record, and we owe it to the very programs that people told us would never work. I know you've had it drilled into you all week, but if you've got any questions—I'm here to answer them.'

Scovil's sessions with the new recruits were always informal, but he did not take them lightly. To meet this batch, he had rushed up from New York as soon as he left Kyle Yetter.

'Nothing bugging you?' he asked, when silence continued. 'You're not shrinking violets, are you? If

5

so, Sparrow's no place for you.'

Laughter broke the ice for one bespectacled young woman. 'Mitch,' she said, taking a deep breath. 'I know about the team system, but will you explain why that means that Sparrow doesn't need a union.'

Norman Pitts shuddered, afraid that the love feast was going to end. But Scovil was glad she had asked.

'Sure,' he said. 'The team system—and I'll bet you're tired of hearing us say so—is the real heart of Sparrow. When we have a problem like opening up a new facility, we pull a group, form them into a team, and let them handle the whole thing. The people we sent to Toronto set up banking facilities, hired a starter set of local people, and arranged everything from customs inspections to supplies. And all the team members got whopping stock bonuses. That's why we don't have unions. All of us are management.'

His audience was starry-eyed.

'Is that why you make us all buy ten shares?' asked one of them admiringly.

Scovil scrubbed the heel of his hand across his hair, searching for the right words. 'You see, we're trying to blast you into a new way of thinking. Sparrow is your company as much as it is mine. But unless you put out a hundred and ten percent, you won't cut it here. Lie down on the job and you're out. We don't carry deadweight, and we don't want it in our profit-sharing scheme. So if you're the kind who's happy going through the motions, look for another job.'

He paused for effect.

'Now don't worry about not fitting in,' Scovil

resumed. 'The real no-shows don't get as far as you have. If you hit any trouble adjusting, It probably means you're in the wrong slot. Just talk to Eleanor Gough—and she'll fix you up. Then, when you find the right niche, go to work. We want your brains and your energy and your creativity. As far as Sparrow's concerned, the sky's the limit. Welcome aboard—and God bless!'

With a wave of his tanned arm, he left the room. Before he was out the door, Eleanor Gough was on her feet.

'Now, I just want to explain how the profit-sharing system works...'

Norman Pitts, still dazzled, could barely listen.

There, he would have gladly told John Thatcher, is a man in a million.

A&P and Norman Pitts covered the extremes. The truth about Mitchell Scovil lay somewhere in between, as his closer associates agreed.

Eleanor Gough and Clay Batchelder had been watching their partner perform for five years. When Fritz Diehl walked out of Sparrow, they had remained to form two parts of the management triumvirate. Scovil was the front man, occupying any and all spotlights, while the other two ran the store.

Batchelder, only a few years older than Scovil, was big and stolid, with the weathered skin of an outdoorsman. His background included buying planes and leasing equipment, and, at Sparrow, he functioned as chief of operations. He and Scovil complemented each other neatly.

Mrs. Gough, however, was another proposition altogether. From the beginning, she had been

7

Sparrow's all-purpose troubleshooter, dealing with everything from FAA compliance to employee relations. She was competent, attractive, and unmistakably older than either of her companions. With two adult children, she qualified as a grandmother in the Sparrow youth culture. Just now, she sounded like one.

'Clay, when will you talk sense to Mitch about Pittsburgh?' she said as they trailed out of the conference room. 'Conditions there are deteriorating every day.'

Batchelder straight-armed a swinging door, waiting for her to precede him.

'Mitch doesn't like talking about failures,' he said, as if she needed reminding. 'The trouble is that Pittsburgh's not top priority.'

'Well, it should be,' she said tartly as they reached the so-called executive suite.

In keeping with Sparrow's stripped-down image, this consisted of a few cubbyholes opening off the larger space used to accommodate group efforts. Scovil stood at his desk, examining the mail.

'How do you think the talk went?' he said, looking up expectantly.

'The way it always does,' said Batchelder, poker-faced. 'After all, it's the same speech.'

'Hey!' Scovil protested. 'I cover the same topics, but I do it off the cuff.'

With some impatience, Mrs. Gough ended the banter. 'How did things go in New York?'

'It couldn't have been better,' Scovil said, launching on an exuberant recital.

Both Batchelder and Mrs. Gough listened intently.

'And the Sloan isn't surprised that Sparrow wants

8

to go transcontinental?' Mrs Gough asked, when Scovil finally finished.

'How could they be surprised, Eleanor?' Batchelder asked reasonably. 'Mitch has been leaking hints for months. He likes letting the competition know that we're nipping at their heels.'

Scovil grinned, but Eleanor Gough remained thoughtful. 'Scaring A&P is one thing, scaring our own people is another. Do you two realize that half the employees are on the verge of mutiny?'

'Don't exaggerate,' said Scovil. 'This is our biggest leap forward, so there's the most static. But once I explain—'

'Sure,' said Batchelder, seizing his moment. 'All you have to do is explain it to the employees' committee. I've set up a meeting with them next Thursday.'

'Employees' committee?' Scovil said blankly. 'Don't tell me, let me guess. It has to be Phoebe Fournier, stirring things up. That kid is something else!'

'Which is why we chose her to run the Toronto team,' Eleanor pointed out. 'Besides, lots of people are nervous. That's why so many of them have been signing petitions.'

But Scovil had moved on to the next stage of his thinking. 'Tell you what—let's not make a federal case out of this. I'll calm Phoebe down tonight. She's coming to the party.'

Sparrow, only five years old, was already encrusted with traditions. One was a lavish party at Mitch Scovil's waterfront condominium to reward successful team efforts.

'It won't be as easy as you think,' said Mrs. Gough. 'It's not just the expansion that's worrying

9

people, it's Pittsburgh. We're losing money on every plane we fly there. That's a drain on the profit-sharing fund, and that gets everybody upset. Don't you realize how closely they follow our financial reports? For heaven's sake, Mitch, you just told them they're all stockholders.'

His determined good humor faltered. 'Listen up,' he said sharply. Then, with an effort: 'I'll tell you what, you get on the phone to Pittsburgh. Tell Reardon we want results, or else. And, in the meantime, I'll fill Clay in about New York.'

Eleanor Gough studied her two partners. Then, with a slight shrug, she turned, going off to do what had to be done.

CHAPTER TWO

YOUNG BIRDS IN TRANSITION

At six twenty-seven that evening, personable young women all over the United States were smiling into television cameras. In Boston, one of them was saying: '. . . so be sure to join us tomorrow night when we visit Plymouth Plantation, where Thanksgiving all began.'

Then, leaving exactly two minutes for commercials, Kate McDermott unclipped her microphone.

'Want to come along for a quick one, Katie?' a colleague asked.

'Thanks, but I've got to get home,' she replied, moving off the set. 'You haven't forgotten the party tonight, have you, Dave?'

Dave had not, and neither had any other staffer on Channel Three's award-winning news team.

'I wouldn't miss it for the world.'

'Good,' she said, disappearing into a minimal makeup room. There she made a dive for the phone. 'Mitch? I'm on my way.'

'Who cares?' her husband replied affectionately. 'I'm here—and so are the caterers. That's all that matters.'

'Is that your way of telling me that things went well in New York?' she replied.

'Better than you'd believe,' Scovil said. 'I think I may have the Sloan hooked.'

Even allowing for his inveterate optimism, this sounded promising and Kate said so. But, at the moment, other details took precedence. 'Tell the caterers to make sure there's some place for all those toothpicks, will you?'

Everything else was being taken care of, if the caterers knew what was good for them. The setting was already perfect. The Scovil duplex on India Wharf combined expensive space with casual comfort. At the right time of year, their rooftop terrace overlooking Boston Harbor was a showplace. The other requisite for successful entertaining was no problem. The Sparrow side of the guest list was always ready to party. And, for her part, Kate provided touches of glamour in the form of the touring personalities like rock superstars, best-selling doctors, and presidential candidates, who paraded endlessly through Channel Three.

Her catch tonight was Number One on the charts.

'Straight home this time, Phil,' she told her

11

regular cabby. 'Mitch and I have people coming in.'

'Just like you or me,' Phil later told his long-suffering wife. 'I mean not jittery or uptight or anything.'

Phil's wife was a fan of Kate McDermott's, but she was not a doormat. 'Give me the kind of money they have, and I wouldn't worry either.'

If the hostess was carefree, the same could not be said of all her guests.

'Maybe I should have gone home to change,' said the young lawyer, still dressed for success.

'Oh, for heaven's sake,' laughed Phoebe Fournier, although she had done just that.

The home they shared was an apartment in nearby Brookline and it had taken Phoebe less than an hour to shed her Sparrow uniform and hurry downtown to join Bryan Kiley for dinner.

'But should it have been a tux—or my leather jacket?' he mused. 'You never can tell who you'll meet at the Scovils'. Judge Grayson was there last time.'

'Oh, just relax,' she said, reminding them both that she was the real authority on the subject. Phoebe Fournier had been to so many Scovil celebrations that she had lost count. A small, dark-haired bundle of energy, she was also Sparrow's role model par excellence. Starting out as a raw recruit the day Sparrow opened its doors, she had soared. Today, aged twenty-eight, she was an expert on airline finance, and the owner of ten thousand shares of Sparrow common.

'. . . which has been losing ground for months,' she said a few minutes later. 'If Mitch seriously pushes California, the bottom could drop out. As if

12

Pittsburgh isn't bad enough.'

Bryan winced. 'I hope you're not planning to bring that up tonight?'

'Who me?' she replied, confirming his worst fears.

Alan Whetmore *was* wearing his leather jacket. Like Phoebe Fournier, he worked at Sparrow, but there the resemblance ended. Whetmore was advertising's Older Man, complete with deep tan and full head of hair. Even so, he was a Sparrow newcomer, one of the many pilots who had been laid off elsewhere. Far from being a jubilant team member, he was attending Scovil's party as the escort of one of Kate's Channel Three colleagues. Nevertheless, he whistled happily as he set forth to collect Mary Lou. Tonight, he felt sure, was going to be wonderful. His tomorrows looked damned good too.

At ten-thirty, Kate knew she had another winner. bar and buffet were doing land-office business. In the greenhouse, people sat cross-legged, singing country music with the star attraction, while everybody else ate, drank, laughed, and talked.

'Who could ask for anything more?' she hummed to herself. Then she came face to face with her husband and had no trouble deciphering his expression.

'Why so hot and bothered? You were the life and soul of the party ten minutes ago.'

With a broad smile for public consumption, Scovil muttered under his breath: 'I've just come off a tough round with Phoebe.'

'Oh dear,' said Kate, glancing toward the

13

animated group in the corner. 'But she looks as if she's having fun.'

'You can say that again,' replied Scovil bitterly.

Phoebe Fournier gave group fun five more minutes, then detached a lanky young black man and took him aside.

'Joe, I've got to talk to you. Mitch is losing his mind.'

Joe Cleveland was a mechanic, not a lawyer, but he shared some of the instincts of Phoebe's Bryan. 'You shouldn't tackle Mitch at his own party.'

'I didn't tackle him,' she retorted. 'He tackled me. Mitch seems to think I'm the only one who's worried about Sparrow.'

'How can he?' Cleveland objected. 'Clay has already agreed to a meeting because we represent a majority of the employees.'

'According to Mitch, I'm stirring everybody up,' she responded. 'Otherwise people would be happy as clams.'

After some thought, Cleveland said, 'I guess we've got to set him straight, only I don't see how. Mitch is a great guy, but he can be stubborn as a mule.'

'Don't I know it!' she said. 'But I've had a brilliant idea. If I do all the talking, Mitch will know that he was right. So, we should get someone else to speak for the committee.'

'Don't look at me,' said Cleveland hastily. 'I understand the numbers when you lay them out, but if I tried explaining them, I'd just mess up.'

Phoebe already knew he was not her man. 'What about Alan Whetmore?' she suggested.

Joe gaped. 'Whetmore? But, Phoebe, he's a pilot.'

It was a legitimate objection. As a group, pilots were the least enthusiastic converts to the Sparrow system. Like Whetmore, most of them came from elsewhere, and Sparrow meant smaller paychecks and one week each month doing lowly ground work.

'Besides,' Cleveland continued, 'Whetmore's never even signed any of our petitions.'

'That's what makes it so neat,' she argued. 'This committee would be the first time Alan moved his butt. When Mitch sees that, he'll realize everybody is up in arms.'

Cleveland still had reservations. 'Maybe,' he said reluctantly. 'I suppose it's worth a try. But you and I have to be there, to sit on Whetmore if we have to. He's got a pretty good opinion of himself.'

'He's a loudmouth,' she agreed. 'Just what Mitch deserves. C'mon.'

Before Joe knew it, they had Whetmore cornered.

Looking bored, he let Phoebe rattle through the preliminaries. 'Yes, I heard that some of you are going to meet with Clay and Mitch,' he said. 'Frankly, I doubt—'

'We were wondering if you'd act as our spokesman,' Phoebe broke in.

There was a pause, then Whetmore brightened. 'That never occurred to me. But, you know, you may be right. I have had twenty years' experience, and I've handled executives before.'

Cleveland had to swallow hard as Alan Whetmore rolled on: 'In fact, the more I think about it, the better I like it. And you know what? I might draw

15

up a written list of demands. That way we could take care of everything at once.'

'I suppose that would be all right,' said Phoebe hesitantly. Then, warming to his proposal, she went on: 'You could use the backgropund material I've already developed. And, while you're working on that, I'll check the stockholder list again. We might do something with that, too.'

Whetmore was judicious. 'I'll have to decide what kind of approach to take.'

Before Phoebe could reply, Mary Lou emerged, demanding attention. She did not remove Alan Whetmore one minute too soon.

'How you can stand that conceited jerk, beats me!' Cleveland exploded. 'Did you hear him? *He's* going to have to decide!'

'Alan's doing what we want, isn't he?' Phoebe replied.

'He's planning to give us the benefit of his guidance,' Cleveland said. 'Christ, he's so dumb it's unbelievable.'

'Well, thank God for that,' she said. 'If Alan wasn't so dumb, he'd realize that all we want is a figurehead.'

Her plot was beginning to confuse Cleveland. 'What was that about the stockholder list that you just happened to slip in?' he demanded. 'You've got something up your sleeve, don't you, Phoebe?'

'Boy, do I!' she said, pleased with herself. 'This morning I did a computer printout of employee stockholdings. Guess what I found?'

Furrowing his brow, he said, 'Well, I suppose we control a fair amount, between stock bonuses and the payroll plan. Even those initial purchases have to add up.'

16

'To thirty percent of Sparrow,' she said. But her triumph was yet to come. 'Then I asked who owned the rest. And guess what?'

'You're losing me,' Cleveland confessed. 'Mitch and Clay and Eleanor each own ten percent. The rest must be spread around.'

'Wrong!' Phoebe crowed. 'The biggest stockholder of all is some bank in New York. And they own a big, fat twenty percent.'

When Cleveland did not break into cheers, she prompted him.

'Thirty plus twenty equals fifty, Joe.'

As he had said earlier, if somebody laid the numbers out, he understood their significance. 'But, Phoebe, that means you're talking about control of Sparrow!'

His awe made her laugh aloud. 'And just wait until we slide that one past Mitch!'

CHAPTER THREE

SPORADIC WANDERER

'Mr. Thatcher,' said his incomparable secretary early the following week, 'is out of town.'

Miss Corsa's formula was not good enough for some of Thatcher's senior staff. Charles F. Trinkam, fearlessly risking a snub, elicited more detail.

'Boston, eh?' said Walter Bowman, chief of research. He considered every Sloan client north of the Bronx, then said: 'There's that Cetonix secondary.'

Charlie inclined toward software. 'John wouldn't

17

bother about them. I bet he's huddling with Crocus.'

Their colleague, Everett Gabler, was too conservative to evince any enthusiasm for biomedicine or computers.

Miss Corsa ended the suspense by announcing: 'Mr. Thatcher is meeting with Rupert Vernon—from Edinburgh.'

On the whole, Gabler would have preferred the frontiers of science. Rupert Vernon headed the Scotch real estate developers who operated shopping centers in the Midlands, industrial parks in Kuwait, and resort hotels on islands previously unlisted in any atlas.

'And what,' Everett demanded with patriotic indignation, 'is Vernon doing in Boston, of all places?'

He was, at that very moment, massing an all-out assault. On a windy downtown corner within sight of the Public Garden, he stood gesturing broadly. 'They've barely scratched the surface here,' he announced with a drumroll of R's. Around him, young people ducked into boutiques, fur-coated matrons swept out of Elizabeth Arden, and business groups descended on upscale restaurants. 'Just look!'

'Yes, Rupert,' said Thatcher. 'I can see this is Gold Coast territory, but how much of it is available?'

Too much, it developed, as Vernon's tour was designed to illustrate. Taking Thatcher in tow, he plunged up Commonwealth Avenue, along Clarendon Street, down Marlborough Street, pausing only to draw attention to clusters of old-fashioned town houses. His grand finale was a group of larger buildings occupying a complete city block.

'And all this belongs to some college I've never heard of?' Thatcher asked when they finished their trek.

'Correct!' said Vernon. 'They're cash poor and land rich, so the intention is for Gauthier College to move to the suburbs. It's a wise solution for them.'

'And a windfall for you,' Thatcher observed.

Vernon certainly hoped so. 'Of course, I'll be doing this again tomorrow when my chaps arrive, but I particularly wanted to show it to you today.'

Thatcher, who had done business with Rupert Vernon before, recognized the technique. He was being primed so that when the investors from the UK disembarked, they would wade straight into a sea of euphoria.

'But why bother, Rupert?' he asked frankly. 'This Gauthier property speaks for itself.'

'I want all the support I can get,' Vernon confided. 'You see, on Thursday afternoon, I am taking this proposal to His Honor the mayor.'

He was considerably understating his need for allies, as Thatcher discovered that evening upon studying the proposal's fine print. Apparently Vernon intended to treat the Back Bay like some squalid corner of the Third World, bulldozing everything in sight. Omitted from consideration were the protesting hordes of community activists, environmentalists, and local politicians. But Thatcher could see them, in their serried ranks, and he had no doubt that His Honor would be able to do so as well.

This presentiment was so vivid that when the

19

hotel phone rang, Thatcher thought it might be Rupert Vernon raising the clans. But the voice belonged to someone much younger.

'Thatcher? This is Mitch Scovil, from Sparrow. We met last week when I was down talking to Kyle Yetter. I called him today and he mentioned that you're in town.'

Thatcher could scarcely deny it.

'You remember we said it would be a good idea for you to look at Sparrow?' Scovil continued. 'I was wondering if you could make it tomorrow.'

Thatcher recalled that the idea had been exclusively Scovil's. Then an incautious movement tumbled Rupert Vernon's folio from the desk, and produced an inspiration.

'I'm busy tomorrow, but I could be free on Thursday,' he said, seizing the lesser of two evils.

'That's okay with me, except that I've got a noon meeting,' Scovil said. 'How about two o'clock?'

'Fine,' said Thatcher.

Sparrow Flyways could not be worse than round one at City Hall.

Mitchell Scovil and Rupert Vernon were not the only ones revving up for Thursday.

Alan Whetmore, clipboard in hand, arrived at Clay Batchelder's office the following morning ready to roll. 'If you and I can get the ground rules straight, the meeting will go that much better,' he announced.

'I'll never understand why they picked you for the job,' Batchelder replied.

'Experience,' Whetmore said, busying himself with a file folder. 'I knew about labor negotiations before they were born.'

20

'Labor negotiations? Is that what you're calling this?' Batchelder said sourly. He knew for a fact that Whetmore's participation in the Pilots' Association had been limited to paying his dues and doing what he was told.

'Sparrow's employees do have legitimate demands,' Whetmore replied complacently.

'Okay, shoot,' said Batchelder, rumpling his hair with an oil-stained hand.

Whetmore, just off a flight from Chicago, was the neater of the two, as well as the more articulate.

'Now, Clay, you admit everybody on the payroll wants changes made,' he began. 'Mitch has got to give somewhere. These suggestions should help both of us—and that's what we all want, right?'

Without comment, Batchelder took the folder and began reading. After some minutes, he looked up: 'You've gone way too far,' he said flatly.

Whetmore shrugged. 'Try thinking of it as a starting point for discussion,' he advised.

Batchelder scowled in thought. 'Have you shown this to Phoebe Fournier, or Cleveland? Or anybody else, for that matter?' he finally demanded.

'Hell no!' said Whetmore, shaking his head. 'I'm not letting anybody screw this one up. We've got to keep our eye on the big picture.'

Ironically, Batchelder riffled the closely typed pages. 'The big picture?' he said. 'It seems to have picked up a lot of detail.'

Whetmore's demands included employee power at every level. He had outlined so many committees, subcommittees, reviews, and votes that they almost obscured his purpose.

'Mitch will blow a gasket when he sees this,' Batchelder warned.

21

'Oh, come on,' said Whetmore with assurance. 'You give a little to get a little. Sure, we'll yield on some things, then you'll yield on other things.' He paused for effect. 'The trick, Clay, is for us to pick the right things.'

Batchelder remained impassive. 'Well, I hope you're ready for a rough ride. You're going to have them all climbing the wall.'

'They chose me,' said Whetmore, 'they can live with me.'

He watched Batchelder drum his fingers and, when the silence protracted itself, added: 'I don't see why you're making such a big deal out of this, Clay. There was going to be a fight anyway. I've just changed its direction a little.'

'Sure,' said Batchelder, barely able to say even that. 'We'll just have to wait and see how the meeting tomorrow goes.'

Whetmore was willing to call it a day. 'Exactly,' he said. 'But I wanted to give you and Mitch the broad outlines. That way we avoid shocks and surprises. In the end, you'll find that we can all work together real smoothly. We'll manage a few big changes, and that will take care of the little problems. That's how I see it.'

Torn between contempt and apprehension, Batchelder watched him withdraw.

'Phoebe, baby,' he said to himself. 'You picked a real winner.'

By that afternoon, she was beginning to think so too. All her plans to coach Alan Whetmore had foundered.

'You're never here,' she said, when she finally ran him to earth. Beside her, Joe Cleveland scowled

22

supportively.

'They pay me to go places,' said Whetmore, without breaking stride.

Phoebe knew he had been avoiding her, but she stuck to the main issue. 'We've got to sit down together,' she said, trotting to keep pace with him. 'I've got a lot of material that you aren't familiar with.'

'Not now,' he said dismissively. 'I'm in a hurry.'

'Look, we're meeting with Mitch and Clay tomorrow,' she snapped.

Finally, he halted. 'The meeting's at noon, isn't it? Okay, I'll give you an hour before that. If you have anything useful, I can incorporate it in my presentation.'

Then, turning smartly, he marched off.

Dumbfounded, Phoebe stared after him. 'Who the hell does he think he is?'

Joe tactfully raised another problem. 'What do you suppose he means when he talks about his presentation?'

'God knows,' she said tartly. 'But whatever it is, we'll have to let him get it out of his system before we can show Mitch and Clay the really important figures.'

Cheering up, Cleveland said: 'Important is right—if you're talking about the petition. Almost everybody signed.'

Although she appreciated the effort, she had to set him straight. 'Actually those weren't the figures I meant, Joe. I'm talking about Sparrow's debt burden for Mitch's new toys.'

'Peace,' he said, begging for mercy. 'Stuff like that makes my head spin. Do you honestly think you could make Whetmore understand it?'

'I could,' she said balefully, 'if he'd give me the chance!'

But Alan Whetmore really was in a hurry. When he left Phoebe, he trotted to the bulletin board outside the cafeteria. After five minutes' scrutiny, he grunted with satisfaction and went to the nearest in-house phone.

'Mavis, this is Alan Whetmore. You say you need a pilot for Flight 723 tomorrow morning. I'll take it.'

'*You'll* take it? This is really Alan Whetmore volunteering?' Mavis asked sarcastically.

'Himself.'

'Why break with history now?'

His patience wore thin. 'Will you can the funny talk and just put me down? But one thing first. That flight gets me back here at eleven fifty-five, right?'

'Right.'

Whetmore was smiling as he cradled the phone.

At six o'clock, when Joe Cleveland thought the end of the workday was in sight, a harried young man came bursting into the service bay.

'Can you lend me a wrench? My car's just died on me!'

Cleveland had a good memory for faces. 'I've seen you in the locker room, haven't I? You're new.'

Norman Pitts blushed with pleasure, introduced himself, then said: 'And I've got the date of a lifetime tonight.'

Joe sprang to his feet. Here was a brand-new employee—and one who could have been

24

overlooked. 'Why don't I just come along and see what the trouble is?' he suggested.

On the way to the parking lot, Norman learned a great deal about employee activism at Sparrow. His car required less of Joe's attention. Within ten minutes, there was a sustained healthy throbbing.

'That should do it,' Cleveland announced, tossing the wrench to Pitts. 'Just put the filter back on, and tighten the nut. I have to split now. I want to get out of here myself.'

'Thanks a lot, and I'm sorry I held you up,' Pitts said gratefully. 'Do you have a date, too?'

Joe, a much married man for six months, flashed white teeth. 'You could call it that,' he said, strolling off.

A good deed should be its own reward, but in one of his pockets there was a copy of Phoebe's petition, duly signed by Norman Pitts.

CHAPTER FOUR

CROAKING NOISES

John Thatcher set forth for Logan Airport on Thursday at a psychologically satisfying moment. Rupert Vernon and associates had just departed, en masse, for their gunfight with the city fathers.

Even Thatcher's cabby was a happy omen. He not only spoke English, he had something pertinent to contribute. As they sped through the Callahan Tunnel to East Boston, he congratulated his fare on the unparalleled smoothness of their trip. Delays, bottlenecks and, too often, claustrophobic

25

passengers were nearer the norm.

'Then how do people ever catch planes?' Thatcher inquired.

'The smart ones take the MBTA,' the cabby retorted, with fine disregard of his own interests.

These were not idle words, Thatcher soon realized. They crept past the main terminal and proceeded to a recycled freight facility some distance from its glossier brethren. The buses that collected passengers from the subway stop were unloading beneath the Sparrow sign. Across the road, similar buses were waiting to ferry arriving passengers back to public transport.

Could this be the secret of Mitch Scovil's success? Sparrow's pitch was aimed at the subway crowd. If they were the only ones who could get to the airport, Scovil had a real edge over the competition.

Inside the Spartan terminal, Thatcher encountered the famous no-frills efficiency. Two-way traffic was kept moving briskly by cheerful personnel wearing the mouse-brown jackets that echoed Sparrow's brown-and-gray color scheme. Behind the scenes, however, management did not measure up. Following directions, Thatcher rounded a corner to come upon Mitchell Scovil at odds with his partners.

'Dammit, Eleanor, it's not my fault that Whetmore's been held up in Buffalo. And you know that the Sloan is a helluva lot more important than this garbage.'

Mrs. Gough stood her ground. 'Don't talk that way,' she said uncompromisingly. 'You promised to attend, and now you have to show up.'

'But the only reason I have to be there is to

explain the situation,' Scovil argued back. 'You can do that better than I can. Anyway, Eleanor—oh, hello, Thatcher. I didn't see you.'

Thatcher had drawn the obvious conclusion. 'I gather your meeting is late.'

'It hasn't even started,' said Scovil with a grimace, going on to introduce his partners.

Mrs. Gough was courteous but adamant. 'Late or not, I'm afraid that Mitch absolutely has to sit in,' she told Thatcher.

'Now wait a—' Scovil began, only to be overridden by Clay Batchelder.

'Eleanor's right, Mitch,' he said heavily.

Thatcher's appointment at Sparrow had paid its way as soon as Rupert Vernon's crowded taxi left without him. Now he was more than willing to retire gracefully. When he said as much, Mrs. Gough and Batchelder indicated gratitude. Scovil, however, was still reluctant.

'God knows how long we'll have to wait,' he began. 'I suppose I could give—'

Just then a door opened, and a small whirlwind burst into the corridor.

'Our wandering boy is finally back,' she announced unceremoniously. 'Let's get this show on the road, Mitch.'

Scovil had to capitulate. 'All right, Phoebe. I'll be along in a minute.' Then he had a happier thought. 'Thatcher, let me introduce Phoebe Fournier. She's what Sparrow is all about. Phoebe's been with us from day one and you wouldn't believe all the things she's done. Right now, she's heading the employee group that wants me to explain why Sparrow has to expand.'

Her correction was perfectly friendly. 'We're

27

going to do more than listen, Mitch. We've got some facts of our own to present.'

'Since when has anyone been able to shut you up, Phoebe?' he rejoined. 'By the way, this is John Thatcher, from the Sloan.'

She was thrilled. 'The Sloan Guaranty Trust? Is that the one in New York?' Without waiting for confirmation, she continued in a rush: 'Then your timing couldn't be better. You'll want to hear this, too. After all, the Sloan owns twenty percent of Sparrow. If we're worried about our thirty percent, then you—'

'I beg your pardon?' Thatcher broke in.

Phoebe heard his doubt and produced the clincher. 'I just checked it out on the computer.'

Thatcher had heard that one before. 'Perhaps,' he said noncommittally.

Phoebe was not letting him off that easily. 'It belonged to Jim Vandervoort,' she persisted.

Good God! The Vandervoort Trust was the repository of one of America's great dynastic fortunes. In those vast holdings, there could be almost anything.

'It must have been part of his estate,' Thatcher muttered to himself.

The distinction was lost on her. 'Whatever!' she said robustly.

Just moments earlier, Thatcher had felt superior about the confusion prevailing at Sparrow. Now the shoe was on the other foot. It seemed all too possible that Kyle Yetter, on the third floor of the Sloan, was making decisions in total ignorance of what the sixth floor was doing.

Normally Thatcher did not rage against the Sloan's labyrinthine complexity, for the excellent

28

reason that he was in charge of it. But he was human, too. Clamping down hard, he said: 'Perhaps I should join this meeting of yours, Scovil. That is, unless you have any objection?'

Mitchell Scovil was somewhat rueful. 'None at all,' he said. 'It's not what I had in mind when I offered you an inside view. On the whole, we like to introduce people gradually to our way of doing things. But if you're strong enough to take the plunge—it's fine by me.'

Opening the door, he waved a spacious invitation. But as they trailed into the conference room, it was Clay Batchelder who, under the bustle of providing extra seating, introduced Joe Cleveland and Alan Whetmore.

'. . . and this is John Thatcher from the Sloan. He came up here a couple of days ago—and we're giving him a chance to see how things really work around here.'

Alan Whetmore did not echo management geniality, perhaps because the names meant nothing to him. Thatcher decided this must be the case when the pilot said waspishly:

'I don't think we want just anybody watching us while we try to negotiate.'

Far from being offended, Thatcher was amused. But Mrs. Gough, he saw, had been embarrassed.

'The Sloan may be paying for our new air fleet, Alan,' she said snubbingly. 'We're all very happy to show Mr. Thatcher anything he wants to see.'

Instead of replying, Whetmore shrugged the rebuke aside. 'All right, then let's get started,' he said.

He rose, and produced a sheaf of papers. 'Now Clay and Mitch have already read this, but the rest

29

of you will need copies to follow along while we discuss the points I've drawn up.'

Scovil glanced across the table, then turned to Batchelder. As papers were shuffled around, Thatcher heard him whisper.

'What's all this, Clay? I thought they were going to parade their numbers about California, then I was going to straighten them out.'

'For God's sake, Mitch,' Batchelder hissed back. 'I told you to look at the damned thing, didn't I?'

'Keep your shirt on. I'll read it now.'

Meanwhile Whetmore was already in full flight. '... the work force is tired of this breakdown in communication. To keep it from happening again, I've tackled the root problem. You'll find that...'

Thatcher, who never listened to introductory remarks, was skimming the first page. It prepared him for Scovil's initial reaction.

'This must be some kind of joke.'

Whetmore was reproachful. 'No it isn't, Mitch. As I explained to Clay, it may seem radical at first, but it sets us on the right path for the future. Just look at the organization table on page five—'

But that was not really necessary. Beneath the verbiage, Whetmore's aim was unmistakable—at least to Thatcher. This plan called for the total reorganization of Sparrow Flyways. With some curiosity, he flicked forward to see what further atrocities lurked.

Mitch Scovil, on the other hand, had already seen enough. 'I came here to tell you why Sparrow is taking on California,' he said evenly. 'If any of you would like to hear—I'm willing to go on.'

'That's only one part of the problem,' Whetmore told him. 'We've got to restructure the whole

Sparrow philosophy—'

'This damn thing proves you don't know the first thing about Sparrow,' said Scovil, flinging Whetmore's production across the table. 'Somebody should have told you that I wouldn't come here to give away management control.'

'We're not talking about control, Mitch,' Whetmore said earnestly. 'We're talking about employee feed-in.'

'With veto power over capital expenditures? Who are you trying to kid?'

Thanks to the usual breakdown in distribution, Eleanor Gough was only now receiving her copy. Without glancing at it, she said: 'You must be out of your mind, Alan. Everybody knows you can fly a plane, but that's it. You can't even read our annual report.'

Thatcher was growing more and more puzzled by Alan Whetmore, who had already demonstrated abysmal ignorance of banks and bankers. If Mrs. Gough was right, the man was also a business primitive. Why, then, was this uniformed nonentity so much more prominent than the much-touted Miss Fournier?

Whatever the reason, Whetmore occupied center stage. His brow furrowed with effort, he was still concentrating on Scovil.

'Look, this is a first approach. If there's anything you want to modify, we'll be reasonable. And we'll understand if you want to offer counterproposals.'

'There's only one thing I'm going to do with this bunch of crap,' said Scovil dismissively.

Whetmore's face set in mulish lines. 'Why are you being so damned stubborn,' he complained, 'when I'm willing to compromise?'

'What you mean,' Scovil translated, 'is that, instead of stealing the whole store, you'll settle for three-quarters. You're crazy.'

Clay Batchelder, sitting next to Thatcher, semaphored an appeal for intervention to Mrs. Gough.

Lifting her eyes momentarily, she said halfheartedly: 'We don't want Mr. Thatcher to get the wrong idea. Sparrow will always listen to reasonable proposals.'

If nothing else, she reminded Scovil that he had partners. 'Jesus, Clay,' he demanded, 'why didn't you warn me we had a nutboy on our hands? I've got better ways to pass the time than listening to this kind of bullshit.'

Scovil's casual contempt made Alan Whetmore forget his lines. 'You'll have to listen,' he almost stuttered. 'I represent ninety percent of the employees, and you can't run Sparrow without us.'

'I ran Sparrow before you came along, sonny boy,' said Scovil, losing his control, too. 'I can go on doing it.'

Throughout the hostilities, Phoebe Fournier had been reading steadily. When she finished the final page, she was white-faced.

'How come there were advance copies for Mitch and Clay?' she said quietly. 'While Joe and I walk into this mine field without warning?'

Her unnatural calm misled Mrs. Gough. 'What difference does that make?'

'It makes plenty of difference,' said Phoebe stonily. 'It looks to me as if this is some kind of end play. Now Mitch thinks he can go roaring ahead—without even hearing the real employee objections.'

'If anybody put Alan up to something, it wasn't us,' Mrs. Gough shot back. 'You're the ones who named him to the committee. We didn't.'

Thatcher saw that additional skirmishes were the last thing Batchelder wanted.

'Would both of you just calm down?' Batchelder pleaded almost desperately. 'This mess isn't your fault. And getting mad at each other isn't going to help.'

Mrs. Gough turned on him. 'What do you mean, it's not her fault? Alan Whetmore didn't just turn up here by accident. They must have had something in mind.'

Bristling, Phoebe defended herself. 'How could we know he'd try to pull something like this? But you know damn well, Eleanor, if you'd shown me that list yesterday, he wouldn't be here today.'

'How could I show you something I'd never seen?' Eleanor replied nastily.

Phoebe's disbelief was obvious, but before she could put it into words, Batchelder tried once again.

'That's my fault,' he said hurriedly. 'You weren't there when I gave the damn thing to Mitch.'

While Thatcher's attention had been diverted to their sideshow, the main event had been going strong. By now Scovil was on his feet, his body canted over the table.

'. . . your career as troublemaker is about to end.'

'If you think this is trouble,' Whetmore lashed back, 'you haven't seen anything yet.'

The threat was still hanging in the air when a new voice sounded.

'We're making this too complicated,' said Joe Cleveland. 'This stuff about committees is a lot of

33

smoke. All Alan wants is the part about an employee rep who gets to be vice-president with a seat on the board. And that shows you how dumb he is. Because, even if we really wanted that, it would be Phoebe—not him.'

His taunt made Whetmore swivel. 'What are you talking about? I'm the employees' official spokesman.'

With a menacing smile, Cleveland said: 'Not anymore. You've just been canned.'

Whetmore was already swinging back to Scovil. 'Forget these two,' he directed. 'You're talking to a grown-up now. And I'm the one who gets the seat on the board.'

'How dare you!' Eleanor Gough exploded.

'Damn the seat on the board!' Phoebe Fournier yelled. 'We want to talk about California.'

Scovil's contribution was even noisier. 'Nobody's going to be a director!' he thundered. 'Nobody gets a damn thing. This meeting is over, finito! And, Whetmore, if you ever try this again, I personally will wring your neck!'

Slamming the door to underline his threat, he stormed out of the room.

This abrupt departure confounded Alan Whetmore.

'He can't just walk out like that,' he sputtered foolishly.

Batchelder was unhappy too. 'Dammit, why didn't Mitch just read the stuff when I told him to?' he lamented. 'We could have avoided all this.'

Unbelievably, Whetmore took this for encouragement.

'You're right,' he said quickly. 'And once Mitch gets over the first reaction, he'll be willing to take a different tack.'

With a glint in her eye, Eleanor Gough said: 'Don't bet on it.'

But Clay Batchelder was belatedly recalling that they were not alone. 'We're forgetting Thatcher came here to take a look at Sparrow. Why don't you give him the grand tour, Eleanor? That way you can prove that we really know how to run an airline. We don't spend all our time at each other's throats.'

Mrs. Gough saw the wisdom of this. She was rising, when Phoebe Fournier interjected herself: 'Oh no you don't. That way, Mr. Thatcher will never hear our views at all. Why don't I just come along with you?'

Thatcher could see the abyss yawning before him. 'I appreciate your offers,' he said with great presence of mind. 'Unfortunately I have to get back downtown.'

Then, allowing no argument, he held the door for both ladies. As they preceded him, he observed Alan Whetmore and Joe Cleveland, still seated, glaring at each other.

Batchelder did not like the combination either.

'Okay, Joe, fun's over,' he said. 'We've gotten this far without trading punches. Let's call it quits and go back to work.'

Thatcher honored the effort, heavy-handed as it was. From what he had seen, Sparrow Flyways needed all the peacemakers it could find.

CHAPTER FIVE

LABORED FLAPPING

As Mitch Scovil stalked past, the executive receptionist flagged him down.

'Mr. Islington's here,' she announced, conscientiously adding: 'He's down at the water cooler. And people could hear you shouting the length of the corridor.'

'Oh hell,' he groaned, abruptly deflated. He could walk out on Alan Whetmore, but not the problem.

Five short minutes at the water cooler constituted a crash course in Sparrow gossip. With Don Islington, this could spell disaster. He was selling the aircraft that Scovil was determined to buy. What Islington learned about Sparrow had to be rigorously sanitized.

As a result, Scovil was radiating self-confidence by the time Sally ushered in Islington.

'Great to see you, Don,' he said. 'Hey, Sally, how about getting us some coffee? To tell you the truth, Don, if it wasn't for the house rules, I'd order something stronger. We've just had a meeting that had to be seen to be believed.'

Islington's long, narrow face was pendulous with chronic disappointment. 'I heard,' he said briefly. 'Does that mean it's no-go for California?'

'Are you kidding?' Scovil replied with a laugh. 'I run Sparrow—not some bunch of kooks.'

Islington wanted to believe him. As a customer, Sparrow Flyways might not rank with the

Department of Defense or United Airlines, but global budget-cutting made any sale look good.

'They said your people are ready to fight any expansion,' he pointed out.

'Window dressing!' Scovil snorted. 'Highway robbery is what this bunch was after. Here, take a look at this if you want a good laugh.'

He tossed Whetmore's manifesto across the desk. 'This is the brainchild of one of our pilots. Have you ever seen anything like it?'

He waited until Islington was obediently reading, then threw in a casual afterthought. 'And to make matters worse, we had the Sloan right there, drinking it all in.'

'The Sloan?' Islington said eagerly. 'I know you've been talking to Yetter in New York. You mean you've gotten far enough for him to come up?'

Financing was always the sound barrier in deals like this.

'Oh, we've moved past Yetter,' said Scovil airily. 'These days we're talking with John Thatcher.'

Islington began to hope. 'Then you'll want to show him these payback plans we've come up with. We're extending the time period by a generous margin. But before we get to that, what about this pilot? Is he serious about pulling the rug out? And if he is, what are you going to do?'

'I've been thinking about that,' Scovil acknowledged. 'And you know what? I know exactly how to handle Alan Whetmore.'

Phoebe Fournier's well-developed instinct for smelling a rat led her to Mavis Tassone in scheduling before the hour was out.

37

'That bastard,' she spat, when she heard the details. 'He set me up from the beginning.'

'I thought it was fishy,' said Mavis sympathetically. 'Whetmore volunteering is Whetmore up to something.'

'Then why didn't you warn me?' said Phoebe, itching for a whipping boy. 'Don't you realize how much Alan has cost us?'

But Mavis was not a born cheek-turner. 'Don't blame me. I thought he was trading shifts for his latest girlfriend. If you feel like criticizing, look at what you've done. It was your bright idea to put him on the committee.'

'Oh, don't,' moaned Phoebe, who already felt like kicking herself. 'There are thousands of us. And our stock and our jobs could both go down the drain because of Alan Whetmore. With him around, nobody's going to listen to us—not Mitch and not the Sloan. Oh, damn, damn, damn!'

She was arching her fingers back, then curling them forward, like a cat flexing and retracting its claws.

'I've never seen you like this before,' said Mavis uneasily.

'I'll kill him,' said Phoebe, still talking to herself. 'So help me God, when I find him, I'll kill him!'

Joe Cleveland was getting even less sympathy. Sparrow's senior mechanic listened to the obscenity-laden description of Alan Whetmore's behavior, then produced his one all-purpose response:

'What do you expect when you get mixed up with pilots?'

Cleveland wanted a spark, any spark, to burn off

38

his anger.

'... and Clay didn't help, either. Telling me to butt out—as if taking care of Whetmore wouldn't be a public service.'

His chief, mounting a ladder, did not bother to look down. 'What do you expect when you tangle with the brass?'

Eleanor Gough, putting her accumulated spleen to good use, went straight to the water cooler.

'Well, I hope you're satisfied,' she said to the gathering. 'I work like a dog to set up this meeting and what do you do?'

Her audience was not visibly cowed. 'We've got a right to make Mitch listen to us,' said one of them spiritedly.

'He goes along with that,' she said. 'That's why Mitch was there. But, instead of a reasonable discussion, we got Alan Whetmore demanding to be vice-president of Sparrow.'

As she had gambled, this was news to them.

'Alan?' gasped a programmer. 'That's plain silly. The one you should talk to is Phoebe—'

'Phoebe's the one who dragged in Alan—and that little list of his,' Eleanor cut in. 'And I've got to tell you, I don't think there's going to be much listening around here for a long time. Mitch is boiling mad. And for that matter, so am I!'

By outstaying Joe Cleveland in the conference room, Clay Batchelder lost his chance to rehash the situation with Scovil.

'Mitch has got Mr. Islington with him,' said Sally a little avidly. 'Do you want to join them?'

She was reaching for the intercom, but

39

Batchelder shook his head. 'Skip it,' he said, disappointingly normal. 'I'm not in the mood. I'll catch him later.'

Whatever his feelings, Batchelder always found work the best form of release. He spent the next hour and a half revising all the equipment procedures he could find. When he returned, Scovil's empty cubbyhole told its own story. The coat was gone, the desk was bare. Sally, reappearing a few minutes later, confirmed the obvious.

'Mitch decided to call it quits after Mr. Islington left. Naturally, everybody has been looking for him ever since.'

'I'm glad he got away early,' said Batchelder. 'It's been a long day, and the sooner it's over, the better.'

But Sally had some good news for him. 'Mitch's day isn't over, Clay. He went home, but he's having dinner tonight with Mr. Thatcher.'

'Well, I'll be damned,' Batchelder exclaimed, pleased and surprised. 'That old son-of-a-gun pulled if off despite everything!'

The old son-of-a-gun had not pulled it off. It was John Thatcher himself who had taken the initiative. This was the direct consequence of the telephone call he made as soon as he cleared Logan.

'Yes, Mr. Thatcher,' said Miss Corsa, sounding poised for action despite the miles between them.

In his haste, Thatcher began barking commands. He came to his senses soon enough.

'You're not the one I should be shouting at,' he said, making amends. He then glossed this apology with an appeal to her loyalty. 'But I don't like

40

having the Sloan's affairs explained to me by a girl who isn't old enough to be my daughter.'

Miss Corsa liked it even less.

'I'll have our Sparrow holdings checked immediately,' she assured him.

'Of course, she could be making a mistake,' Thatcher interjected hopefully.

Miss Corsa was ready for all contingencies. 'If she is, I'll call back to tell you. But if this Miss Fournier is correct, I'll ask Mr. Nielsen to talk to you.'

Half an hour later Homer Nielsen's cranky accents greeted Thatcher. 'John? Miss Corsa seems to think there's some problem with our Sparrow stock.'

'There certainly is,' said Thatcher. 'Can you explain how twenty percent of a company like that got into the Vandervoort Trust—and why we've let it stay there?'

'Because there's not a damned thing we can do about it,' Nielsen said thumpingly. 'This isn't part of the general trust. It's one of those rinky-dink deals to celebrate paternity. You know what they're like.'

Thatcher did indeed. In spite of the family's boundless wealth, all male Vandervoorts insisted on creating nest eggs for children who were millionaires at birth. It was a gesture they enjoyed mightily.

'And a damned nuisance for us,' said Thatcher, completing his thought aloud.

Nielsen produced the honk which served him for laughter. 'And this one's worse than usual. We have no power to dispose of the stock. All we can do is invest the dividends.'

'I suppose that was only to be expected,' said Thatcher, who knew that Nielsen had a taste for horrors.

'You see, Jimmy originally owned ten percent of Sparrow,' Nielsen said merrily. 'That only cost him three dollars a share. But two weeks before his death, he picked up another ten percent—just when the stock was hitting its all-time high. That cost him an arm and a leg. But no matter how much Sparrow falls, we're stuck with it. We've got eighteen years to go until Jimmy's son comes of age.'

Thatcher contemplated a time dimension that would appall any prudent man. 'Obviously, we're going to have to make our presence felt up here before that.'

After Nielsen hung up, Thatcher continued to ponder the situation. Miss Fournier had been quite right about the Sloan's twenty percent of Sparrow's stock. Could she have been just as accurate in her fleeting reference to *our* thirty percent? If so, Sparrow was a disaster in the making. The Sloan could not sit idly on the sidelines—not for eighteen long years.

So, for openers, Thatcher decided to invite Mitch Scovil to dinner.

CHAPTER SIX

CHIEFLY NOCTURNAL

Rupert Vernon, either with his shield or on it, was due back at the hotel at any minute. Bearing this in mind, Thatcher set off to meet Mitchell Scovil with far too much time to spare. He stilled the pangs of conscience with a lesson culled from experience. Going directly from one demon entrepreneur to another was counterproductive. By inserting space between Scovil and Vernon, he was exercising banking acumen. Today this involved wandering through Historic Boston, instead of redesigning it.

Fortunately, the New England Aquarium crossed his path. Thatcher seized the opportunity to enjoy a brief and refreshing interlude. When closing time came, he proceeded through light rain to Quincy Market, drawing invidious comparisons between man and fish as he went. It was after seven o'clock before he returned to duty.

He was already ensconced in the bar when Mitch Scovil rushed in a few minutes later, appearing at the head of a short flight of stairs. After a worried look around, the younger man located Thatcher. Smiling broadly he shrugged off his raincoat, stopped for a word with the hostess, then hurried down the stairs.

'Our table's ready,' he announced when he reached Thatcher. 'Why don't you bring your drink along?'

Scovil began by playing the host, with suggestions from the menu and consultations about the wine list. But, as soon as the waiter departed, he confronted Thatcher squarely. 'Well, I asked you out to Sparrow, and you got a real eyeful, didn't you!'

Thatcher could see that he had been cast as audience, with Scovil choosing the subject matter. To set things straight, he said: 'And an earful, too. I find that Miss Fournier was absolutely correct.

The Sloan does have control of a full twenty percent of Sparrow's stock. Tell me how Jim Vandervoort became so deeply involved in the company.'

If Scovil was taken aback, he managed to hide it. 'Oh, Jim was one of our miracles,' he said. 'When deregulation came along, a bunch of us working at Bayou Airline could see it was the chance of a lifetime. The trouble was, we had to come up with five hundred thousand dollars as seed money—and that was a bare minimum.'

'Not much,' said Thatcher, playing his part. 'I mean, in view of the size of the undertaking you had in mind.'

'That's what all the bankers said,' Scovil replied. 'It may not have seemed like much to them, but it was damned near impossible for us. But then things began to happen. Fritz Diehl's father died and left him something. Then he ran into his old college roommate, who just happened to be Jim Vandervoort. And Jim—God bless him!—said that, if we could each ante up one hundred thousand, he would too. Naturally, Clay was raring to go, but I was still the problem child. Then guess what? The next week I bought a winning ticket in the lottery. How's that for timing!'

'Excellent, if somewhat unorthodox,' said Thatcher, considerably entertained. 'However, that still adds up to four hundred thousand dollars, doesn't it?'

His simple arithmetic came as a surprise to Scovil.

'Oh, and Eleanor, too,' Scovil said, as if everybody knew. 'But Jim's real contribution came when we went grubbing for venture capital. He and Fritz would waltz in together. Between the Ivy

44

League touch, and the Vandervoort name, lenders started falling all over themselves. In those days, Clay and I stayed in the background.'

His voice was tinged with indulgence—or was it derision? Either way, the romantic touch was a mistake. Thatcher always grew suspicious when a simple question flushed Technicolor answers.

'Remarkable,' he said politely. 'Now that explains the ten percent Vandervoort acquired at three dollars. What about the second ten percent—which is what makes the Sloan your largest stockholder?'

Scovil was leaning back casually, one arm draped over the adjacent chair. 'That belonged to Fritz Diehl.' Unconsciously he clenched his fist. 'Fritz decided he could do better for himself.'

'It often happens,' said Thatcher blandly. 'Young men who can work together building the ship and launching it, often part company afterward.'

'I suppose so,' said Scovil, reaching for a bread roll. Breaking it into pieces seemed to occupy his attention as he continued. 'Anyway, Fritz decided to sell out. And that put us in a ticklish situation. We didn't want him to dump his shares on the market—even if we were doing pretty well. Sparrow's never had a really big following. Selling ten percent—all at once—could spell trouble. But that's when Jim saved our bacon. He had done so well with his original Sparrow that he was willing to buy Fritz's. And, of course, he could afford to. But it didn't make any difference. Jim never took an active part in management.'

'Did Fritz Diehl?' Thatcher asked bluntly.

After some hesitation, Scovil said tonelessly: 'Sure.'

Thatcher noted the constraint, but delivered his own message anyway. 'The end result, of course, is that the shares of both men have ended up at the Sloan,' he said. 'As you must realize, this materially changes the circumstances surrounding your application for financing. Kyle Yetter will no longer make his decision as a simple lender. Since we are substantial owners, we are interested in Sparrow's long-term vitality—quite beyond the firm's capacity to repay any debt due to us.'

Scovil quirked his eyebrows. 'And you didn't like what you saw this afternoon,' he said. 'There's no excuse for what happened. Believe me, it honestly was a glitch. Whetmore should never have been there, and I shouldn't have lost my temper. God, I just got suckered into going after a curve ball.'

'I'll accept that,' said Thatcher, holding up a hand. 'But it was my impression that Miss Fournier is strongly opposed to the expansion plan which is central to your current thinking about Sparrow. And she represents not only the majority of your employees, but thirty percent of your stock as well. Surely that's more than a glitch or a curve ball.'

'You're dead right. But that's because I never got the chance to explain,' said Scovil, who had come to give precisely this speech. 'Phoebe and her people don't understand that if it's risky for Sparrow to expand, it'll be riskier for us to stand still. We've had a long run of good luck under optimum conditions. In the current environment, if Sparrow doesn't grow, it'll be out of business in two years. Every day some airline folds, and the shakeout will go on until there are only a few lines left. It's the only way to go—the economics, the demographics prove it.'

46

'Have you considered the alternative?' Thatcher asked him. 'I mean acquiring other regional carriers?'

Already shaking his head, Scovil said: 'Not on your life! You can't mix the Sparrow system with a regular union shop. Look what happened to People Express. They went that route, and now they're dead. It could happen to us, too.'

The last remark was so unexpected that Thatcher wondered if it were a cue. 'So you're worried about being targeted for a takeover. Are there any raiders in sight?'

'Not yet,' said Scovil, choosing his words with care. 'But I know damn well they'll be nosing around if the stock sinks another ten points. That's why—'

'Any candidates?' Thatcher interrupted.

Scovil shrugged. 'I suppose any one of the takeover artists is possible, but my best bet would be a major carrier. And that's why Sparrow has to become too big to swallow.'

'You think your only protection is to become a major carrier yourself,' Thatcher suggested.

'Exactly!' said Scovil. 'And I can persuade the employees too. If not—well, they'll just have to lump it.'

'And what about Sparrow's famous participatory management?' Thatcher inquired.

'Look, I'm not knocking it,' said Scovil, leaning forward earnestly. 'The system was a winner in the past—and not just because it kept the unions out. But I've never made it into a religion, the way some people have. That's because I always knew it could only work for so long. When things get tough, the decisions get tough too—and someone has to make them. You can't take a round-table vote. Sooner or later, the system has to go. Right now, Sparrow is facing its first real turning point. Let me explain. . .'

By the time they were waiting for the check, Thatcher found himself considering the things that had not been said. For all Scovil's talk about a first turning point, he was ignoring an earlier one. Before Fritz Diehl's departure, everything had worked like a charm. Afterward, the erosion began. Even allowing for changing market forces, that could have been more than sheer coincidence.

This was suggestive enough to shed new light on Sparrow's current difficulties. If Scovil's sense of authority was already strained, any threat could be serious.

With his imagination outstripping the facts at hand, Thatcher made his farewells. Scovil's reply included a final assurance.

'I'm as confident as I've ever been.'

'Yes,' said Thathcer, keeping his thoughts to himself. 'I can see that you are.'

'And I've got damned good reasons, too,' said Mitchell Scovil.

The rain that had spangled coats early in the evening had turned into a penetrating clammy drizzle. Along the shoreline, where Logan Airport thrust into the sea, the fog was settling in.

At eleven o'clock, when most passenger flights were over, the murk blanketed runways and parking lots. By midnight, the terminal was a tomb with shuttered coffee shops and gated newsstands. Outside, visibility was measured in yards. Sound was muffled and distorted while, above the harbor, the foghorns bayed moutnfully.

48

Two security guards, driving the outer perimeter of the field, picked their way cautiously along the line of reflecting posts. A turn taken too sharply skewed their headlight beams across the fringe of scummy water.

'What's that?'

The driver, a veteran of many years, backed the jeep carefully and looked again toward the shapeless heap.

'A present from up the coast,' he predicted, clambering out and wading toward a human body face down in the rushes.

His companion was a rookie. Wordlessly, he followed, then picked up the legs and helped haul the corpse from the water. Swallowing hard, he stared at the invisible sea.

'Damned tide,' he muttered. 'Carries everything in here and dumps it.'

The driver was bent over, studying the sodden uniform.

'Not this one. He's a pilot from Sparrow,' he announced, straightening up. 'And the back of his head has been bashed in.'

CHAPTER SEVEN

DIFFICULT TO FLUSH

At seven o'clock the next morning a hand-picked officer from the Massachusetts State Police was midway through the Callahan Tunnel, waiting for a breakdown to be cleared away. He had been summoned from the other side of the state and, until ten minutes ago, had been making good time.

Now, instead of chafing, Captain Gregory Lemoine was studying a large-scale map of the area. Logan Airport was a virtual island, approximately one and a half by three miles. To the south, directly across from downtown Boston, lay the shipping lanes to the city's piers, a channel to the locks on the Charles River and, underneath all that water, one subway and two automobile tunnels.

Captain Lemoine did not worry about other exits. Indeed, from the eastern end, one could look out over Boston Harbor, Massachusetts Bay, and ultimately the Atlantic Ocean. The first solid object, apart from a remote island housing a correctional facility, would be Spain.

When Lemoine finally left the tunnel, he drove directly to the spot where Alan Whetmore's body had been found. The area had been roped off and several troopers were squelching through the mud, while a biting east wind flattened the beach scrub. The tide had retreated and a noisome aroma was rising from the flats to greet a few gulls squawking desolately overhead.

'Christ!' said Lemoine, a landsman to the core.

He did not leave his car for two reasons. Protocol required that he meet with the head of the permanent force at the airport, fortunately an old acquaintance. More important, there was no visibility. An unenthusiastic sunrise had begun just before he entered the tunnel, but it would be hours before the fog burned off.

Five minutes later he walked into a small out-of-the-way office to find Lieutenant Crawley hard at work. The whine of jets speeding early morning commuters down the Eastern Corridor was

50

clearly audible.

'You're not going to like this one,' Crawley warned him.

'I already·don't,' Lemoine grunted. 'Ed, suppose you start by telling me the real reason they yanked me out of bed and took me off a case?'

'There's some kind of labor trouble at Sparrow. Everybody is afraid it may be a company murder.'

Lemoine groaned. Politicians always take a fatherly interest in major employers.

'What makes them so edgy? On the way in, I drove past the scene. It's not exactly company headquarters. Maybe the guy was fooling around with someone's wife.'

Ed shook his head sadly. 'We found the weapon in the mud. It's a wrench marked: PROPERTY OF SPARROW FLYWAYS.'

'So? Maybe hubby works at Sparrow, too.'

'Nobody thinks so. They had a meeting yesterday where the president threatened to break Whetmore's neck. Then, some lady vice-president came out telling the world that Whetmore was ruining everything. And—wait until you get this one—some girl from the labor side said they had to get rid of him before he did any more damage.'

Lemoine bowed to reality. The victim's co-workers would know exactly what waves he had been making.

'Whetmore sounds like everybody's favorite. What have we got on the killing itself?'

Ed rummaged through the papers before him. 'Just a minute, the autopsy report is here somewhere.'

'Already?'

This was unprecedented speed in Lemoine's

51

experience.

'I warned you there was a lot of pressure on this one, Greg. Here it is. Whetmore's skull was fractured by one blow from the wrench, delivered from behind, and he crumpled over the guardrail there. It's only two and a half feet high, and we found shreds from his uniform in the cable. After that, it's anybody's guess. Whetmore could have slid into the water on his own, or the killer dumped him in.'

'Or even a combination,' Lemoine suggested. 'He slid in, and the murderer rolled him over face down. I suppose we're not going to get any footprints on that surface.'

Crawley shook his head. 'Not a chance. However it was done, Whetmore's death is technically due to drowning although he would have died anyway. Did I mention that the wrench was clean?'

'You didn't have to,' Lemoine said equably. 'Okay, do we know anything about Whetmore, yet?'

'Aged fifty-two, unmarried, a commercial pilot for over twenty years. So far, that's it. The people at Sparrow are stonewalling, claiming they don't know much about him—or anything.'

Lemoine looked up. 'If the help isn't talking, how come you know so much about the meeting?'

'They're not talking to us. But, boy, are they talking to each other.' Ed beamed. 'The first shift come on at five o'clock and they want coffee. I've had a man sitting in their cafeteria since it opened. A lot of them were blabbing about the meeting even before they heard of the murder.'

'Okay. Now what about Whetmore's movements? Do we know why he was down by that godforsaken bog?'

Ed had no idea. 'The early shift wouldn't know,' he explained. 'The people who might won't show up for hours.'

'Well, we've got a hell of a lot to do. We'd better start by getting organized.'

The result of their efforts was a list of assignments, divided between the two forces. The Logan regulars would circulate throughout the airport searching for witnesses who had seen Whetmore, with or without companions. The homicide specialists would devote themselves to the coroner's report, the laboratory examination of the wrench, and Whetmore's apartment. Captain Lemoine reserved for himself interviews with the principals.

In short order, he discovered two things about Sparrow. The staff arrived early and unanimously regarded his investigation as an intrusion.

At eight o'clock, Eleanor Gough was the first to sound a note which he would hear again. 'I don't have much time. Can we do this quickly?' she said, pausing in mid-stride.

'This is a murder case.' he retorted.

Her impatient grimace said it all. The murder of Alan Whetmore was a tragic crime of violence, but it had nothing to do with Sparrow Flyways.

'Then you shouldn't mind talking to me about that meeting of yours,' said Lemoine ironically.

To his surprise, she did not. Where he saw motive, she saw unlucky coincidence.

'... and,' she concluded a few minutes later, 'all this is going to make a bad situation worse. I do wish Mitch hadn't flown off the handle yesterday.'

'You said some pretty strong things yourself.'

'I was furious,' she agreed absently. 'First with Phoebe, then with Alan. The whole meeting was so stupid. This is a critical time for Sparrow and the last thing Mitch needs is to be distracted.'

Even a request for her movements did not puncture her absorption. 'Let's see. Oh yes, I was in my office until about four-thirty, then I went over to accounting and I stopped by procurement. Then about six, Clay was ready to leave and we went out to dinner together.'

She refused to take yesterday's fireworks seriously, she denied having seen Whetmore after the meeting, and she wanted Lemoine to finish so that she could find a replacement pilot.

Clay Batchelder was just as bad.

'I've got to hand it to Whetmore,' he said. 'Getting himself murdered was probably the only way he could cause even more trouble.'

Asked about his movements, Clay was willing but vague.

'I was all over the lot. Oh yes, I wanted to catch Mitch after he was through with Don Islington, but I let it go too late. When I asked Sally—she's our receptionist—she said he'd already gone home. So I must have been with her around five. And I remember I went out to the maintenance manager after that. I caught Eleanor for dinner about six or six-fifteen. Somewhere around then, anyway. Are you through with me? I've got a hell of a lot to do.'

Insofar as possible, Sally confirmed these statements. 'Everybody was in and out all the time,' she said cheerfully. 'That's the way it always is.'

'Doesn't anybody tell you where they're going to be?' Lemoine demanded.

'Not unless they're taking off downtown or

something. They usually check back with me about messages and things every now and then.'

It sounded like a criminal's paradise to a policeman.

'And Scovil had left by the time Batchelder was looking for him at five?'

'Oh yes. Mitch must have been gone for a quarter of an hour by then. I remember Mr. Diehl was looking for him around ten minutes earlier.'

Other than that, Sally could only say that both Batchelder and Eleanor Gough had been out of the office for some time before making their dinner plans.

Labor matched management in insouciance.

'Oh, I could have strangled Alan,' Phoebe Fournier admitted freely.

'I thought it was Mrs. Gough you tangled with,' Lemoine reminded her.

'Only because I was surprised. But Eleanor's too smart to pull something that raw. Alan was the dumb one, and it had to be his own clever idea. That includes lying to me about his morning schedule so I couldn't squash him before the meeting.'

After Phoebe, came Mavis Tassone.

'Yes, Alan Whetmore piloted the morning flight from Buffalo, but he wasn't on duty for it,' she reported. 'He called me and volunteered to cover for that specific flight. I knew there was something funny about it. Alan never put in an extra hour in his life.'

Joe Cleveland, tracked down in the cafeteria, even admitted to a threat that had not yet made its way to the police.

'Sure I was burned up after the meeting. I said

55

I'd deck Whetmore if I ran into him, but I didn't. He thought he was going to use the rest of us, and it was time somebody straightened him out.'

'Or got rid of him?' Lemoine suggested.

Joe never batted an eye. 'All we had to do was bounce him.'

By nine-thirty Captain Lemoine had a mass of unhelpful detail and one missing person.

'Isn't Scovil in yet?' he asked.

'No, but we know where he is,' Ed Crawley reported. 'He called to say he was having a late breakfast at the Marriott. They expect him here at eleven.'

Lemoine frowned at this first break in the pattern. 'You know, all these people are pretending this meeting yesterday was just your usual office row, but one thing they couldn't hide,' he said slowly. 'There was an outsider there, some banker called Thatcher. You want to bet that he's being primed, right now? Maybe I should join this breakfast.'

But when Lemoine was ushered to Mitch Scovil's table at the Marriott, the man with the receding hairline was introduced as Fritz Diehl.

'Fritz is a vice-president at A&P these days, but he used to be with Sparrow,' Scovil explained.

'Sorry to interrupt your breakfast, Mr. Scovil, but I expected you to come to the office when you heard about Whetmore.'

Scovil's answer was pat. On a normal morning he would have been at his desk by nine, but today he had gone to the Boston Athletic Club for a workout. When he encountered Diehl in the weight room, they had decided to breakfast together. News of

Whetmore's death reached him only when he called his office. From that brief account he assumed the pilot was another mugging victim.

Lemoine ignored this justification. 'You go to this club regularly, Mr. Scovil?'

'Not as regularly as I should, but I manage to get in once a week or so.'

Fritz Diehl seemed amused. 'I've been telling Mitch for years that you've got to do it every day, but he's too lazy.'

'And the two of you met by accident?'

They both nodded.

On the face of it, their account was plausible. These days executives did meet at the Nautilus.

Lemoine tried another tack. 'You see, we're trying to get a fix on Whetmore's movements,' he said. 'We know he was at your meeting after he came in from Buffalo but, after that, it seems to be a blank.'

Scovil now exhibited the curiosity that should have surfaced earlier.

'Didn't Sally tell me the murder was around midnight? Whetmore could have been doing anything by then.'

'The body was discovered at midnight. But he was killed a lot earlier. Probably between four and seven.'

Scovil pursed his lips in a silent whistle. 'That makes a big difference,' he conceded. 'Someone should have seen him around. But I'm no help to you. I went home early.'

'And when would that have been?'

If Scovil noticed that the subject had shifted from Whetmore's movements to his own, he gave no indication.

57

'It must have been a little before five.'

'You say that's early,' Lemoine pressed. 'Any particular reason?'

Scovil smiled. 'There sure was. I was having dinner with my banker and I wanted to review my facts in peace and quiet. When the Sloan is financing a multimillion-deal expansion, they're happier if you know what you're talking about. Wouldn't you agree, Fritz?'

'I sure would,' Diehl said urbanely.

During this exchange Lemoine finally identified the tickle that had been bothering him.

'I understand you were out at Sparrow yesterday yourself, Mr. Diehl?'

'That's right. When I visit A&P's regional office here, I have dinner with Eleanor Gough if there's time. I tried to catch her, but she wasn't in her office. Then I asked for Mitch, but he wasn't around either.' Diehl paused before adding softly: 'Mitch is always my second choice.'

Scovil chuckled. 'Fritz and Eleanor are friends from way back.'

Lemoine's gaze remained fixed on Diehl. 'Then you didn't actually see Mr. Scovil?'

'Nope. Didn't get Eleanor either. I ended up eating alone.'

'It's a shame we didn't make contact, Fritz,' Scovil commented. 'You could have had dinner with Thatcher and me.'

Diehl's glance slid sideways. 'That would have been a real pleasure, Mitch,' he murmured.

Lemoine's professional instincts were flashing a warning. These two men were sparring with each other, and that meant he should separate them.

Without undue concern for etiquette he

58

announced his decision.

'I've got some more questions, Mr. Scovil. But as they're about internal affairs at Sparrow, we'd better be private.'

Fritz Diehl remained relaxed to the end.

'That suits me,' he declared. 'See you around, Mitch.'

'Sure thing, Fritz.'

Within two minutes Lemoine was congratulating himself. At least he was getting his witness's undivided attention.

'I'm not denying I got hot under the collar yesterday,' Scovil said almost boastfully. 'I've got a pretty short fuse and Whetmore was completely unreasonable.'

'You sure you want to go on record that way, Mr. Scovil?'

'You mean because he was murdered?' Scovil was no more impressed by this fact that anybody else at Sparrow. 'You're not listening to me, Captain. When I say unreasonable, I mean off-the-wall . . . flaky . . . out of sight. Nobody was going to take that stuff seriously.'

'Apparently Whetmore did.'

Scovil snorted. 'We don't know what he was really aiming at, but it wasn't what he put down on paper, believe me.'

Lemoine was at his most phlegmatic. 'I don't know much about this sort of thing.'

'You don't have to. Just read that list.'

'So what are you saying? That Whetmore was around the bend?'

'No.' The flat negative was bitten off as if there was more to follow. Scovil's gaze flickered over the captain, then away. It took a moment for him to

59

recapture his fluency. 'I'm just saying that list wasn't a threat, that's all. If you don't believe me, then ask anyone. Ask Clay, ask Eleanor, for God's sake, ask Phoebe.'

Lemoine had a better idea.

'No, I think I'll ask John Thatcher instead.'

CHAPTER EIGHT

LANGUID WARBLING

Within forty-five minutes, Thatcher found himself assisting the Massachusetts State Police in their inquiries. Not that he had any choice in the matter. Captain Gregory Lemoine had appeared out of the blue and extorted an hour from Thatcher's already tight schedule. Then, treating the hotel like his squad room, he invited Thatcher to begin at the beginning.

'Well, I met Scovil for the first time last week in New York,' Thatcher said. With more care than usual, he outlined Scovil's overtures to the Sloan Guaranty Trust.

Lemoine patiently encouraged him to get to the point. 'I see. And that's how you happened to be sitting in on this Sparrow meeting yesterday afternoon?'

'I'm afraid so,' said Thatcher with real regret.

Discussing the financial intricacies unfolding at Sparrow was at least congenial. Unfortunately, Lemoine was more interested in raised voices, slammed doors, and threats of personal violence. Thatcher did his best, but he was happy to have his recital end.

'. . . and that is the full extent of my recollection,' he said, finally. 'I may have missed some of the minor exchanges, but I think I've told you everything of substance.'

Lemoine was quicker than he looked. 'Well, I'm grateful for all the facts I can get,' he said ambiguously. 'But I'm looking for someone who cracked Alan Whetmore's skull. So the important thing is how mad these people really were.'

Thatcher did not hesitate to rebuff this none-too-subtle invitation to editorialize.

'I am the last man who can tell you that,' he said, stating a policy position. 'Remember, these people are almost strangers to me. For all I know, Scovil may lose his temper every other day, then forget about it instantly. I could tell you that neither Mrs. Gough nor Miss Fournier struck me as capable of homicidal mania—but I do not know either of them. Batchelder and young Cleveland are unknown quantities—and so, for that matter, was Whetmore himself.'

'Okay, you don't know these particular people,' said Lemoine, still angling. 'But you do admit that all this fighting is way out of the ordinary, don't you?'

Thatcher had to agree that it was somewhat unusual.

'How unusual?' said Lemoine, pushing his advantage. 'Is it the kind of thing that would happen at your bank, just to take an example?'

'I certainly hope not,' said Thatcher, tempted to claim that the Sloan operated on unadulterated sweetness and light.

But since they were talking about murder, he was

61

more realistic. 'What struck me at Sparrow was not the dissension. That can, and does, occur anywhere. It was the fact that everybody was caught by surprise, and by an unpleasant surprise at that. Nobody came prepared for what took place—and that, to put it charitably, shows extremely poor organization on both sides of the dispute.'

Driving the point home, he managed to get in a few good words for his own team. 'Yes, we at the Sloan can have meetings where people pound the table. But at least those people have done their homework.'

'Even when you're negotiating with the union?' Lemoine interjected quickly.

'Especially when we're negotiating with the union,' said Thatcher emphatically. 'They present written proposals, we present written proposals. Then everybody goes away and vents emotions in private. The negotiations themselves are dull as dishwater, and that is the way we intend to keep them.'

Lemoine grinned. 'I'll remember that when I talk to the boys down at the PBA,' he said. 'Now, after the meeting, what did you do, Mr. Thatcher?'

For several intoxicating moments Thatcher wondered if he figured on the suspect list. Then common sense and Lemoine brought him back to earth.

'You say you had to wait for Scovil at the restaurant?' the captain said, ignoring the aquarium altogether.

'Perhaps five minutes,' Thatcher replied. Simple humanity, as well as other considerations, made him hope that he was not tightening a noose.

Lemoine pondered, then veered unexpectedly.

'It must have been raining by the time you got there.'

Thatcher agreed that it had been drizzling and tried to guess what Lemoine was after.

'How wet was Scovil when he came in?'

Dutifully Thatcher flipped through his mental photographs. 'His coat may have been damp, but it was not sodden. That is all that I can remember.'

'No umbrella?'

'Not that I saw,' said Thatcher.

Lemoine retreated into private cogitation. When he emerged, it was to make preparations for departure.

'Thanks again for helping out, Mr. Thatcher,' he said, lumbering to his feet. 'I've got a feeling you may have pointed us in the right direction.'

From Thatcher's point of view, Captain Lemoine's departure came moments too late. Rupert Vernon was just bustling in, a new roll of blueprints under his arm.

'For the benefit of the Back Bay Association,' he began without preamble. 'They have some bee in their bonnet about sidewalk usage, so I've given them enough umbrella tables for the South of France. I can't imagine what they think will happen from November to May. You do have snow here, don't you?'

'Frequently,' Thatcher agreed.

'So I thought. Have you ever noticed how adamantly summer-minded all these civic bodies are? They want bright airy clothes, people strolling of an evening, children with ice-cream cones. If I had lambs roasting on spits in the forecourt, they'd

63

rally to my support without question.'

Thatcher proffered what comfort he could. 'Most community groups are only advisory, Rupert,' he said. 'And this is not an election year. You should get your permits and clearances before any candidate starts campaigning against you.'

'The financing comes first,' Vernon remarked, his eyes gleaming.

'I see no insuperable difficulty.'

'Aha!' Reassured, Vernon now turned his attention elsewhere. 'I could not help noticing that chap who just left. Not the customary uniform, was it?'

Briefly Thatcher explained the Boston Metropolitan Police, the Massachusetts State Police, and the tangled jurisdiction at Logan Airport. He was resigned to explaining more than that. After all, he had canceled out with the British contingent, and they all knew why.

'I met the murder victim yesterday afternoon,' he concluded his short tale, 'and the police had a few questions.'

Artlessly, Vernon recounted the latest television bulletins. 'They claim there was bad feeling between the victim and the company president. Now that's the fellow you dashed off to meet yesterday evening, isn't it?'

'The police had a few questions about my dinner as well,' Thatcher admitted.

Vernon was smug. 'Let this be a lesson to you, John,' he said. 'I don't claim that Wilson and poor MacTavish are the most scintillating companions I could provide, but at least my dinners do not attract police visitations.'

Yesterday Thatcher had reminded Mitch Scovil of the Sloan's double-edged interest in Sparrow. But what if Scovil himself was about to be plucked from the scene? Rumors alone were enough to galvanize the market.

Without delay, Thatcher dialed the Sloan and asked for Everett Gabler.

'Everett,' he said, 'what's happening to Sparrow?'

'Down over two points.'

Of course Gabler knew. Many complained of his rigidity; nobody ever denied his capacity for detail.

Briskly Thatcher described the situation at Sparrow. A pending loan, a tricky expansion, employee disaffection, and now a possible murder charge against the president—together they created a picture that almost outstripped Gabler's capacity for prophesying disaster.

But not quite.

'There is one further element that you may not be aware of, John,' he said, characteristically complicating an already complex situation.

'Yes?'

'Walter Bowman has just been in,' Gabler said. 'There's talk on the Street that, when the stock hits twenty-five, there will be a takeover move.'

After Scovil's analysis last night, Thatcher took that talk seriously.

'We're going to have to send somebody in to look at the books,' he decided. 'Scovil is synonymous with Sparrow. If he goes to jail, God knows what we'll have to do.'

There was no more militant defender of the Sloan's privileges than Everett Gabler, but the habit of playing devil's advocate was too strong to be suppressed.

'I don't know, John,' he said dubiously. 'There is, after all, no question of reorganization. And the market may rebound if nothing happens to Scovil. They could object.'

'If they want our cooperation, they're going to have to give us theirs. Who can you spare for the job, Everett?'

For once Gabler was not ready with an instant response. There was silence for several seconds, then: 'If I can have a day or two to put things in order, I could be available.'

'Nothing better,' said Thatcher sincerely. Everett's skills in ferreting out falsehood was unparalleled. No paperwork of any sort could defeat him. But there were other considerations. 'If you are willing to undertake what may be a demanding chore. Sparrow isn't run like IBM, you now. They believe in the casual approach.'

But lack of a recognizable hierarchy, like accounting chicanery and deliberate obscurantism, was grist to Gabler's mill.

'So I gather,' he said with muted relish.

'Fine,' said Thatcher, eager to close with the offer. 'Then I'll start twisting a few arms at Sparrow.'

CHAPTER NINE

RANGES SOUTH

By the time John Thatcher had mobilized his troops, Captain Lemoine was closeted with the next

66

witness.

'Yes, I saw Mitch yesterday afternoon,' said Don Islington. 'I had to wait for him to finish his meeting.'

'Did you know what it was about?'

Islington pursed his lips. 'There was a lot of excitement around the water cooler. But I only paid attention to the parts about California expansion. After all, I'm selling Sparrow the planes.'

'What were they saying about Whetmore then?'

Thanks to Crawley's man in the cafeteria, Lemoine knew how they felt now. He wanted to learn if there had been any significant change.

'I never heard him mentioned. They were all gabbing about some girl named Phoebe.'

Despite the universal tendency to dismiss Alan Whetmore, Lemoine had proof positive that somebody had taken him seriously enough to murder him.

Lemoine was still pondering this anomaly when Islington added: 'Mitch was the one that told me about Whetmore.'

'What did he say?' Lemoine pounced.

'Oh, he was caught off base by that list, and I could understand why. But it was no threat to California, so that was okay.'

'About Whetmore,' Lemoine prodded.

'What's to say? We both agreed that he was poison, but Mitch said he knew how to handle him.'

When these unfortunate words evoked an appreciative silence, Islington tried to explain them away.

'Come on, Captain. Mitch had calmed down by then. He just meant there was nothing for me to

67

worry about.'

'Sure,' said Lemoine flatly.

The material awaiting Captain Lemoine when he returned to Logan increased his general dissatisfaction. First came the report on traffic conditions in the tunnel.

'It was a bad one last night,' Lieutenant Crawley summarized. 'Stop and go, mostly stop, from four thirty-five until six o'clock, with cars backed up to Airport Road.'

'Scovil's playing games,' Lemoine rumbled. 'According to him, he whipped through the tunnel and went straight home. Later on, he walked five blocks to the restaurant. The whole story stinks. Nobody was whipping through that tunnel last night and Scovil should have been soaked when he showed up to meet Thatcher.'

Ed Crawley was systematically checking off points. 'His condo won't do us much good. The tenants have plastic keys for the underground garage and there's always a mob at that hour.'

'You can bet that's what Scovil was relying on.'

'So you think he's lying.'

'He was doing something else from five to seven all right.' Lemoine took a deep breath and said prosaically, 'I just hope he wasn't killing Whetmore.'

Ed, thinking of all those politicians at the State House, agreed. 'Are you going to lean on him?'

'Not until I have to. Anything come up on Whetmore's movements, yet?'

'Yeah. It may not mean much, but it does narrow the murder time,' said Ed. 'Whetmore went from the meeting to the scheduling office and arranged his next shift. Then he must have picked up his car, because he showed up at a little Italian place a couple of miles away. At four forty-five he had a couple of beers and some cannelloni. Then he looked at his watch and made noises about wanting his tab in a hurry.'

'The time?'

Crawley shook his head sadly. 'The waitress didn't notice. Somewhere between five-thirty and six is as close as she'd come. The only other thing I've got for you is Whetmore's car. It was spotted at the far end of the lot at Whalen's Freight. They're a quarter of a mile from the murder spot.'

'Let me guess,' Lemoine said resignedly. 'Nobody noticed him parking.'

'Have a heart, Greg. It was misting and foggy. Besides, it was after regular hours so there was only one line of cars at the building. They couldn't have seen Whetmore if they'd looked straight at him.'

Lemoine's next words were a half apology. 'I think what burns me up is this business-as-usual attitude at Sparrow. They're too damned cheerful.'

'Then I've got just the witness for you.'

'I should have taken the wrench back, first thing,' Norman Pitts said miserably.

By now the murder weapon had been traced from Joe Cleveland's tool box to Norman Pitts's car.

'Well, what did you do with it?' Lemoine asked again.

'The thing is, I was late to work yesterday morning.' For some unaccountable reason, Pitts reddened. 'And the other guys notice that kind of thing here. So I rushed into the locker room to put on my jacket and decided to leave the wrench until

69

the coffee break. I was going down to the hangar then.'

Lemoine had already figured out what was coming.

'And where was the wrench in the meantime?'

'I just dumped it on the bench there. When it was gone at ten, I figured somebody had taken it back for me.'

The next piece of information that Lemoine elicited was even less helpful.

'They're so damn democratic here, they don't have a separate place for the executives,' he complained to Ed. 'Everybody uses the locker room.'

'Not everybody. Mrs. Gough and Phoebe Fournier are in the other one,' Ed pointed out. 'And by the way, they're still buzzing in the cafeteria...'

After Crawley's briefing, Lemoine decided to pay Mrs. Gough a second visit.

'Would you like to revise what you told me about the meeting yesterday?' he began.

'Not at all. This was just a bad time—'

'Baloney!' Lemoine said deliberately. 'I've had a man in your cafeteria all day. Half your work force wants to walk out because Scovil knocked off their boy. The other half thinks the same way, but they want to give him a medal.'

Mrs. Gough bristled. 'They're young and they're dramatizing the situation. But remember, Captain, I was at that meeting, and they were not.'

He had her where he wanted her.

'Exactly,' he shot back. 'But what set them off? You rushed out and told them Scovil was boiling

70

mad. Or weren't the kids there for that one either?'

Eleanor Gough was openly dismayed. 'Yes, I did say that, but you have to realize I had a reason,' she explained. 'They all heard Mitch slam out of the meeting. I didn't want them thinking he'd refused to listen. Whetmore's list could have been designed to produce that very impression, and I'm still not sure it wasn't. I had to get management's side out right away, and make it clear that Alan had pulled a fast one on us. That's why I exaggerated how angry we all were.'

Now that he had her in the palm of his hand, Lemoine hoped to get more from Mrs. Gough. 'I've read your personnel file on Whetmore,' he said, indicating a manila folder. 'But I'm looking for something more personal. Who were his friends at work? Who did he socialize with?'

'I don't think there is anybody.' She leaned forward earnestly. 'Most of our pilots have been laid off by other airlines. And when companies cut back, it's usually the younger pilots. Alan was almost twenty years older than the others. They just didn't have much in common.'

This was the first insight that had been offered to the police about the victim.

'So he was a kind of odd man out?' he said encouragingly.

'Yes, and it's one of the reasons Alan exasperated me. At his age, he wasn't finding it easy to get jobs, and he should have been grateful to Sparrow instead of causing trouble.'

Lemoine tapped the folder. 'He sure bounced around a lot. I suppose that's why he never got seniority anywhere.'

'Yes, he's worked for five different companies

71

just since Bayou Air. And there was nothing wrong with his technical ability. He simply didn't get along with people. That's why he was always having a fight and flouncing off.'

Lemoine thought he had missed something. 'What's special about Bayou Air?'

She was surprised he had to ask. 'That's where we all worked before we started Sparrow. The story's been written up dozens of times.'

'I don't get a chance to read that sort of thing. Suppose you tell me about it,' Lemoine directed.

'Mitch will have to get another PR man,' she said, before complying. 'Fritz Diehl and Mitch and I were all working at Bayou. When deregulation looked as if it was going to be a golden opportunity, they started scratching for money and a lot of other things. Clay was just a consultant at Bayou, but he knew all about the secondhand market, so they roped him in. They needed me because I could deal with the FAA. I sold my house to join them, and that's all there is to tell.'

Lemoine stared at her in disbelief.

'Then you all knew Whetmore before and you've been hiding it,' he charged.

'Don't be absurd!' It was the original Eleanor Gough. 'For heaven's sake, we barely saw him at Bayou. He was only there a couple of months before we left. By that time, Bayou was really seedy. Every now and then a pilot would get picked up for running drugs and a new one would be hired. They were always coming and going.'

One word more than any other rivets police attention.

'Drugs?' Lemoine repeated, with a sudden new perspective on the desolate meeting place where

72

Alan Whetmore had been murdered. 'You think that's what he was into?'

She was aghast. 'Not in a million years! He never would have been hired if there'd been the slightest suggestion of that. We're careful at Sparrow.'

'I'll bet you are.'

'You can be damn sure of it,' she replied angrily. 'Check with his other employers if you don't believe me.'

Lemoine had every intention of doing so. Before he could reply, a uniformed officer put his head in the door.

'Listen, Cap, they're calling you from the office. Something new has come up.'

While Captain Lemoine was interviewing Eleanor Gough, the magic hour struck when many shifts at Logan Airport changed. The troopers who had been questioning personnel at foreign exchange booths, at magazine stands, at coffee shops, squared their shoulders and began anew with the replacements.

In the main terminal one trooper plodded down an endless corridor to a small bar overlooking several departure gates.

'We're trying to trace the movements of this man yesterday afternoon,' he said, flourishing a photograph of Alan Whetmore. 'Did you see him?'

The new bartender, busy polishing a glass, cast a lackluster glance at the exhibit. 'Nope.'

'He looks a lot different without the cap. You want to take a gander at this one?'

The studio portrait showed Whtmore in full uniform. The snapshot caught him on the dance floor.

73

'It's not that different,' the barman corrected. 'And the answer's the same. Never saw him before.'

'Are you sure?'

'Of course I'm sure. That's a Sparrow uniform, and their terminal is half a mile from here. When they show up, we notice them.'

The trooper was already turning away when the barman was inspired to produce additional evidence.

'Hell, when Mitch Scovil walked in here, I told myself I hadn't seen anybody from his outift for at least six months.'

Taking a deep breath to steady himself, the trooper said: 'Are we still talking about yesterday?'

It sounded too good to be true.

'If you almost never see anybody from Sparrow, are you sure you can recognize Scovil?'

'Are you kidding? He's Kate McDermott's husband.'

The trooper had detected the note of a genuine enthusiast.

'You mean you watch her?'

'Every day,' the bartender said proudly. 'That Scovil is one lucky guy.'

Personally the trooper preferred homebodies. But this was no time to alienate his witness.

'He sure is,' he agreed sycophantically. 'But she's the one on the screen. How come you know what he looks like?'

'They're big news. They get their pictures taken all the time. Wait a minute, I'll show you.'

It soon became apparent how the bartender passed his spare time. From a shelf beneath the counter he produced a sheaf of reading material. There were tabloids and local magazines and

74

national magazines.

'See, *People* did an article on Sparrow, and there's a picture of them coming back from their honeymoon. And look, here in *Boston*, you can see them at a fundraiser last month. And, I remember, there was one someplace else...'

While the bartender was rummaging, the trooper organized his questions. One stood out as all-important.

'Was Scovil alone yesterday, or with someone?'

'He was alone, but I think he was expecting someone. He kept looking at the door and checking his watch. And everytime a batch of people came in, he gave them the once-over.'

'Are you sure he didn't meet anyone, even for a minute? If people kept coming in, you must have been busy.'

The barman shook his head stubbornly. 'I kept an eye on him. You see, I thought maybe he was waiting for Kate and I'd get her autograph. But whoever it was, he got stood up. Because he was still alone when he took off.'

'And when was that?'

This required tremendous concentration and an audible rundown of departing flights, before the triumphant conclusion. 'Must have been a couple of minutes after six. The gang for the Denver flight had to rush.'

Lemoine congratulated himself.

'I knew he was covering something. It can't be an accident, Scovil sitting in Logan and checking his watch until he gets up to leave, and Whetmore doing the same thing a couple of miles away.' Then, with a sudden attack of anxiety: 'He's sure about the identification, this barkeep of yours?'

The trooper was confident. 'One of those pictures was a big, slick job, clear as a bell. And, if you ask me, that guy moons over those pictures a lot. He's got a real case on Kate McDermott.'

'Scovil will have to come clean now,' Crawley predicted. 'Of course you can read this bar business either way, even if he did have a meeting with Whetmore up his sleeve.'

'Oh, sure,' Lemoine agreed readily. 'Whetmore was supposed to show up at the bar. Maybe he didn't make it because he was being murdered by someone else. On the other hand, maybe Scovil got tired of waiting and went looking.'

'If I were Scovil, I'd pick the first reading.'

Mitch Scovil picked neither.

'So I had a drink before going home. Big deal!'

'Were you waiting for Whetmore?'

'No way. I was through talking with him.'

'Then who were you waiting for?'

Scovil set his jaw. 'Nobody. I was having a drink, that's all.'

'The barman says you kept looking at the door and checking your watch.'

'I was waiting for the tunnel to clear. It's usually better after six.'

Lemoine was openly sarcastic. 'And that's why you kept an eye on the door?'

'What else is there to look at in that bar?'

They had reached a new plateau. Scovil was lying and he knew that the police knew he was lying.

'Mr. Scovil, I want you to think about your situation. We've placed you at Logan at the time of the murder. You left that bar at six and you joined

76

Thatcher at seven-thirty. You don't have any alibi. Isn't it time you came clean?'

'I wasn't killing Alan Whetmore, and that's all that concerns you.'

For the next ten minutes Scovil defended this position stubbornly enough to convince Lemoine that they were at a temporary standstill.

A story could be shaken; an unyielding silence presented no obvious point of attack. Lemoine had no choice but to withdraw, knowing he needed more ammunition.

Surprisingly, when it came, it had nothing to do with alibis.

'This is Jason Tiedeman. He was doing steward duty on the Washington run today,' Ed Crawley explained. 'That's why we didn't get to him before.'

Jason had been in the locker room at nine-thirty the previous morning. He had seen the wrench on entering.

'People always leave company property lying around that way,' he said priggishly. 'I was going to take it back.'

On the whole Captain Lemoine decided he preferred Norman Pitts.

'And why didn't you?'

With no diminution of righteousness, Jason explained that he had visited the men's room first. Then he had greeted Mitch Scovil who was washing his hands. When Jason reemerged, both the wrench and Scovil were gone.

'Let's get this straight. Was anybody else around there?'

'Not at the time.'

'And when you exit from the men's room you

have to go through the locker room?'

'That's right. So I assumed Mitch had taken the wrench. But of course anybody could have ducked into the locker room. I was gone about three or four minutes.'

Lemoine smiled. 'I guess that means another little interview with Mr. Scovil.'

Inevitably the pressures on Mitch Scovil were beginning to take their toll.

'No!' he snarled, shouldering his way past Phoebe. 'I've got too much on my plate to waste time now.'

'You're just trying to stall us until it's too late,' she retorted.

'Look, Phoebe, in case you haven't noticed, we're in the middle of a murder investigation. And thanks to that little meeting you rigged up, I'm a number one suspect.'

She snorted. 'You mean thanks to keeping us in the dark about Alan Whetmore's fun and games.'

'Call it what you want! The most important thing for Sparrow right now is keeping me out of jail.'

'Don't give me that. They're asking everybody questions. And I say the most important thing is keeping Sparrow from losing a bundle.'

The last shred of employee democracy wilted.

'Then say it someplace else,' Scovil ordered. 'I don't want to hear it.'

CHAPTER TEN

FLOCKING TOGETHER

John Thatcher was not forced to use strong-arm tactics with Sparrow.

'Sure, send your man along whenever he gets here,' said Mitchell Scovil when he finally returned the call. 'I probably won't be around to talk to him. If I'm not wasting my time with the cops, I'm tied up with my lawyers, and they're nearly as bad.'

'How true,' said Thatcher encouragingly. When this did not flush more confidences, he added: 'But Gabler will really want to see your accounting people.'

'Okay,' said Scovil indifferently. 'I'll alert somebody to give him whatever he wants.'

Somebody was willing to do more than that. When Everett Gabler, loose ends tidily wound up, finally arrived at Sparrow, the welcoming committee consisted of Miss Phoebe Fournier.

'Morning, Mr. Thatcher,' she said brightly. 'I volunteered to show Mr. Gabler the ropes.'

'Very nice of you,' he replied, straight-faced.

But Phoebe was not sailing under false colors. 'I wanted another chance to talk to you,' she admitted. 'Come along and I'll show you the work station I've set up.'

When she was not facing the public, Phoebe exchanged her uniform jacket for a Sparrow sweatshirt. Everett Gabler, assimilating the jogging shoes, inhaled sharply.

'Perhaps I should inform Mr. Scovil of my

arrival,' he said, hoping for better things.

'Not a chance,' she said over her shoulder. 'Good old Mitch has gone into hiding. He's trying to duck all the problems here. You'd think he's the only one who's had to talk to the police.'

Everett's initial reaction to the Sparrow style was not favorable, but he held his tongue.

'I put you next to one of the girls at the computer,' said Pheobe. 'That way, your data's right there. And here are the extension numbers of almost anybody you might need—although you can always stick your head out and yell.'

Shuddering, Gabler honored the efforts on his behalf. 'I'm sure it will do very well,' he said nobly.

When he busied himself at the desk, Phoebe turned her attention to Thatcher. 'Now let me tell you the real facts about California,' she said.

First, Scovil had tried to go over Kyle Yetter's head. Now, here was Phoebe playing the same game with Gabler.

"Fine,' said Thatcher, standing fast. 'We'll both be happy to listen.'

She not only accepted his ruling, but improved on it. 'Actually I should wait until Mr. Gabler finishes. Then he'd be on our side.'

Gabler preferred to have his support solicited, not assumed.

'Before I hazard any judgment, I shall have to study Sparrow's assets and liabilities, your relative costs—'

Excitedly she broke in: 'You can forget about that. We taught the industry about cost-cutting and, believe me, they learned. Nowadays, the only advantages we have left are our debt ratio and our image.'

80

Everett had always been death on intangibles.

'Image?' he repeated sternly.

'You bet,' Phoebe insisted. 'Sparrow offers good service at a fair price, but what we really market is the package—plain New England frugality and hard work. We're like those stores that sell salvage goods in old warehouses—that is, if you know the ones I mean.'

Thatcher realized that Miss Fournier, like so many people, wondered if Wall Street bankers knew the facts of consumer life. Fortunately, Everett Gabler was here to set her straight.

'I have read about them,' he said austerely.

'Well, some of the people you see there are real comparison shoppers,' Phoebe said. 'But most of them just assume the stuff is cheap.'

Thatcher thought she deserved some support, so he weighed in 'Wallenstein, Ev, Wallenstein.'

For her benefit he went on to describe one of the Sloan's larger customers, who had made a pile by hanging garments on rusty pipes and selling them at list.

'You see?' she said gratefully. 'As soon as Sparrow builds flashy passenger lounges, we lose our appeal. Unless we scrap this pie-in-the-sky California scheme, every one of us is going to see our money go down the drain!'

Gabler had not taken her full measure. 'Ah yes,' he said with misplaced kindliness. 'Sparrow has a stock-purchase program, doesn't it? That means that you all have something at stake.'

'Ten thousand shares,' she said promptly. 'That's what I've got at stake.'

Then she spilled it all out. 'Eighteen months ago, it was worth four hundred and twenty thousand.

81

Last week, it was three hundred and fifty. Today? Well, maybe we can blame that on Alan's murder, but I'm worrying about tomorrow. I'd like to see my stock go up—and if Mitch tries to turn himself into United Airlines, it won't happen.'

With numbers like this, Gabler tended to thaw.

'Well, Miss Fournier, you may have a legitimate quarrel with management. At least you will have strong stockholder support at your annual meeting.'

'Aha! But how much?' she riposted. 'That depends on the Sloan.'

Everett would not have it any other way. 'Therefore, the most useful thing I can do from your point of view is to complete my evaluation. It's going to take at least a week.'

'A week?' she said blankly. 'You haven't forgotten that next Thursday is Thanksgiving, have you?'

Gabler, rummaging through his briefcase, replied too absently to suit her.

'Wednesday will be a real madhouse. You won't get a thing done,' she said.

'Then I am sure that Mr. Gabler will not add to your difficulties on Wednesday,' said Thatcher.

'Certainly not,' Everett chimed in.

Rapport having been established, Thatcher thought he might get back to poor Rupert Vernon. Before he left, he decided that a cautious word of encouragement might not be amiss.

'I realize that you and your colleagues are impatient, Miss Fournier, but Gabler's time will be well spent. At the moment, there is nothing effective you can do to advance your cause with Scovil, anyway.'

He did not add that if Mitchell Scovil were

82

arrested for murder, her cause would take on new dimensions.

His restraint was unnecessary. If Phoebe was listening, it was to some inner voice.

'Then, I'll leave you two,' Thatcher said, more loudly.

'Fine,' said Gabler, champing at the bit.

Between them, they roused Phoebe Fournier from her trance.

'Nothing we can do?' she murmured, testing each word. 'Is that what you just said?'

Without waiting for an answer, she jumped to her feet and marched to the door, pausing only for one buoyant exclamation.

'You've just given me the greatest idea ever!'

Everett was the first to break the silence. 'And what precisely do you suppose that meant?'

Thatcher did not have the faintest idea. 'But, from the little I have seen of her, I expect we will find out soon enough.'

Joe Cleveland was aghast when Phoebe outlined her latest brainstorm.

'Shut down all Pittsburgh flights on Wednesday afternoon? Have you lost your marbles?'

Phoebe was pleased at this response.

'I knew you'd say that at first,' she purred. 'Because you're surprised. But think for a minute, and then tell me what's wrong with it.'

Joe cast around. 'For one thing, it's got to be against the law. Isn't that what they call an illegal work stoppage?'

'How can it be? It's standard operating procedure at Sparrow.' Phoebe smiled broadly. 'One of us is always pulling the plug on a scheduled flight. If it isn't equipment failure, it's lack of personnel. There was even that foul-up in Albany with fuel.'

'But those were all legitimate,' Cleveland protested.

'We're expected to use our best judgment for the good of the company. That's what participatory management is all about. Isn't that what Mitch says at every orientation?'

Joe was familiar with the quotation. 'That's not the same as asking people to dynamite our own operation just before Thanksgiving.'

'Maybe not. But our best judgment is that Pittsburgh should be closed down, and now we've decided to test it. Besides, half the roster there won't know what's going on. They'll just follow orders in good faith. I know this wouldn't work at most airports. But Tom Reardon is the world's biggest incompetent, and we're dead in the water in Pittsburgh, anyway. Come on, Joe, the meeting is in ten minutes and I know that, between us, we can persuade them.'

Joe struggled to express his misgivings. 'Oh, they'll probably love the idea. In fact, that's what gripes me. Half of them are already dying for action. But that's because they honestly think Mitch killed Alan Whetmore. They're going to get the wrong idea about why we should do this.'

'What difference does that make?'

'It makes a lot,' he said stubbornly. 'We've always managed to hash things out. I don't say it doesn't take time and effort, particularly with some of the dodoes we've got. But that's the way it's been done—out in the open, with everybody knowing what's going on. And that's the way we should be acting now.'

Phoebe was trying to show she understood.

'Joe, nobody would like that better than me,' she said earnestly. 'But we're not the ones who've changed the rules. Look what happened last time. We never had a chance because of Alan Whetmore.'

'And whose fault was that?'

Phoebe flushed. 'How could I guess he was going to pull that stunt?'

'We knew what he was like.'

'The more I think about it, the more I'm convinced it wasn't Alan's idea,' she replied. 'Somebody sold him that stuff about capital vetoes, counting on his eye for the main chance. If that's the kind of thing they're doing, we've got to loosen up ourselves.'

'Okay, so we get tougher. That doesn't mean we have to con our own people.'

Phoebe moved from defense to offense.

'Do you admit we have to get to Mitch before it's too late?'

'Yes,' he said unwillingly.

'All right, then,' she challenged. 'Name one other way we can do it.'

When he was silent, she continued her argument. 'We're still after the same thing, Joe. Remember the old story about how you can't convince somebody unless you get their attention first. That's all we're doing, we're slapping Mitch with a fly swatter to get his attention.'

Within moments a dozen Sparrow employees had become co-conspirators. Their surroundings provided the necessary atmosphere.

For security reasons, the gathering was taking place in an enormous hangar currently housing

85

grounded aircraft. The group was huddled in a shadowy corner, its members perched on rough crates and low dollies. Every word or footfall stirred up ghostly resonances under the lofty roof.

As Joe had feared, everyone's imagination was fired by Phoebe's inspiration. The enthusiasm, however, mirrored widely differing aims.

There was the subgroup demanding retribution against Mitch Scovil, murderer.

A fledgling pilot made those feelings absolutely clear.

'Look, I know Alan was no big loss. But we've got to take a stand. That's what solidarity is all about, isn't it?'

The romantic in the crowd was convinced that delay was not only cowardly, it was dangerous.

'It's like I said, all along. We should have walked the minute we heard about Whetmore. For all we know, Phoebe and Joe could be next. I say we put guards on them.'

Singlemindedly, Phoebe ignored side issues.

'Then you agree about Wednesday?'

'The sooner, the better,' the romantic replied truculently.

Then there were those who felt Mitch Scovil's intransigence justified all-out war.

A supply clerk removed a slice of pizza from his mouth to formulate a battle cry. 'Mitch wants to throw his weight around, we'll show him who's got the real clout,' he said, his ferocity impeded by strings of cheese. 'We'll tear his company apart.'

'Not his company, our company,' Joe growled.

'Joe's right,' Phoebe said hastily. 'We're not tearing anything apart. This is going to be a neat, restricted operation. We stop flights in and out of

86

Pittsburgh from two o'clock to six o'clock. That's all. Remember, we're just rapping Mitch across the knuckles to remind him we could do worse.'

'I'll see that the orders go out to Pittsburgh, all right,' said a young woman, making notes. 'The shift should leave, but to make sure, we ought to send somebody out there.'

'That's no problem. I'll volunteer for a flight to Pittsburgh,' said Phoebe, as if wild horses could have kept her away.

'Someone may smell a rat,' the romantic said darkly.

There was a chorus of hoots. The extra flight at Thanksgiving always required volunteers, and Phoebe's record was exemplary.

'What about headquarters on Wednesday?' asked a health-food enthusiast, unwrapping his bean sprouts. 'Does anybody know how the brass are splitting it up?'

The Sparrow partners rotated duties every Thanksgiving.

There was moment's silence and a forest of wrinkled brows. 'Wait a minute! I've almost got it,' pleaded a young man whose memory was about to erupt to the surface. 'Mitch handled Wednesday last year, so it will be Eleanor or Clay.'

'It doesn't matter,' Phoebe declared. 'That's the beauty of it all. If Rita can get the orders transmitted, Pittsburgh will be a fouled-up mess before anyone hears what's going on.'

The girl with the notepad was confident. 'Trust me for that.'

'Attagirl, Rita!'

As every obstacle crumbled, the exuberance was growing. Then a precisionist interrupted the cheers.

'Shouldn't we have somebody in charge at this end? What about you, Joe?'

'I'm off on Wednesday and Thursday,' Joe said expresionlessly. 'And Betty would kill me if I tried to change now.'

Joe's family obligations were too well established for his refusal to cause comment.

'Barney, you can handle it, can't you?' Phoebe intervened, without missing a beat.

'Sure, sure.'

They were past the point of no return. Any group that becomes absorbed in technicalities has implicitly made the big decision. The romantic was already looking beyond Pittsburgh.

'What do we do when it's all over?'

'Then we tell Mitch where he gets off,' said someone, with immense satisfaction.

'Not just Mitch,' Phoebe announced. 'Don't you see? We're bound to get some publicity from this. It may not be much, but it does give us a chance to make a statement. And we're not throwing it away.'

As might have been expected, there were as many ideas about the contents of the statement as there were reasons for the work stoppage.

'We don't have time to do it now,' Phoebe said unblushingly. 'I'll draft a press release, and then you can all have a crack at it.'

By the time the session broke up, they were ready for anything.

'We'd better leave one by one,' the pilot intoned.

He walked to the door and peered to the right and left.

'All clear,' he whispered, before sauntering away with ostentatious nonchalance.

But the patch of blazing blue sky now visible

broke the spell. Without undue caution, his comrades returned to their normal activities.

'What? We don't synchronize our watches?' Joe asked sarcastically when he and Phoebe were alone.

'Of course they're excited,' Phoebe defended them. 'After all, they've been wanting to do something for days.'

'If you ask me, your fly swatter is turning into a bulldozer. And what's this statement going to say? It'll have to be a dilly if it's going to satisfy everyone.'

Phoebe was unruffled. 'It will have to be pretty general, but it will say what we want, trust me.'

Joe's silence was not reassuring.

'You're making too big a thing out of this, Joe. Pittsburgh's the only place that will be inconvenienced. The real impact at Sparrow will come later.'

'You mean after six o'clock? When the mess has to be straightened out?'

Phoebe meant more than that.

'I'm not talking about the work, I'm talking about the worry,' she said grandly. 'That's where we really score with Mitch. He'll be afraid we intend to hit again and again over the weekend. That's what will bring him to the table. He won't be able to think about anything else.'

Joe was much more receptive to badgering Mitch Scovil than to grounding Sparrow passengers. His heavy frown began to lift, and Phoebe continued the good work by laying a coaxing hand on his arm.

'Besides, what could possibly go wrong?'

CHAPTER ELEVEN

RUFFLED FEATHERS

The Wednesday before Thanksgiving proves that mass evacuation is really possible. Within hours, eighty percent of the population relocates to distant feeding grounds, in a migration with predictable characteristics. Airport parking lots are filled at dawn, highways are jammed by noon, and Amtrak, for one shining moment, actually turns away prospective passengers.

For Phoebe Fournier, the day began with a flourish. Bryan had sent her off in style with a lavish breakfast at the Parker House. They ordered bacon and eggs with the daredevil feeling that they were provisioning Phoebe to go over the top. Then, at ten o'clock they plunged into the subway, embraced passionately, and separated.

By the time Phoebe flew into Pittsburgh at one-twenty, the pace of the day was well established, and she savored the atmosphere like a connoisseur. The signs of pressure were everywhere. All baggage carousels were several flights behind, and the indicator board had lost any connection with reality. The whole overstrained apparatus could be toppled by one small push.

At five minutes to two she was back in Sparrow's quarters, beginning her countdown. Soon Rita's orders should be arriving from Boston. The first would cancel all flights into and out of Pittsburgh. The second would release the Pittsburgh afternoon shift from duty. Would those orders come through?

And, if they did, would they be obeyed?

Crossing her fingers, Phoebe stationed herself on the floor, in full view of the world. Waverers might be heartened by the sight of their leader. As she watched the minute hand on the clock, a young male clerk suddenly frowned at his monitor. Turning to consult a colleague, he caught sight of Phoebe. He raised a questioning eyebrow, and she gravely nodded. Instantly a grin broke over his face and then, without hesitation, he left his station. Seconds later, the girl to his right excused herself to a passenger and moved away.

With the awe of Dr. Frankenstein seeing his monster stir, Phoebe witnessed the complete evaporation of the Sparrow staff.

'It's so easy, it's unbelievable,' she whispered to herself as she hurried backstage. This was no time to encounter Tom Reardon. She had already chosen the women's locker room as her coign of vantage.

There the prospects looked good. Around her, girls were slipping out of uniform, snatching up purses, and dashing off.

An aide reported within ten minutes. 'You can relax, Phoebe. Charlie says three of the pilots have changed and are leaving right now. The computer staff walked in a body. Only one of the ticket clerks tried to make trouble.'

'What did he do?'

'Nothing. Charlie pointed out that, if he stayed, he'd have to handle the public alone. So he decided to take the orders at face value.'

Only then did Phoebe realize she had been holding her breath. The tide was now irreversible.

Still, Phoebe felt oddly unconvinced. Her aim had been to create chaos and, so far, all she had

91

seen was some people changing clothes. There had to be more to it than that. Even the Sparrow lobby, when she returned to it, was unsatisfying. Instead of havoc, there was empty space. True, the employees had disappeared, but so had most of the would-be passengers. The action, Phoebe discovered by trailing the last stragglers, was over at the main terminal.

There, the turmoil was all that she had anticipated. Bewildered travelers were charging the counters, trying to exchange nontransferable tickets for nonavailable space. Agents who had never before raised their voices to the public were openly snarling.

'Mister, I don't know what's going on over at Sparrow. This is Eastern! Would you get out of the way and let me take care of our customers!'

Nobody paid the slightest attention and the lengthening lines began to twist into knotted coils. Information booths were disappearing, engulfed by howling mobs. Mothers' voices were raised in desperation, fathers were urging calm.

Phoebe took in the panorama with guilty pleasure. It was not what she had foreseen.

'After all, nobody has to go away for Thanksgiving,' she had reasoned to herself and others. 'They'll simply go back home.'

But now, with the carnage spreading beyond Sparrow, her press release was surely becoming doubly important.

Five minutes later, she received a rude shock over the phone.

'What do you mean, you're not interested?' she demanded.

'We've already chosen our travel stories for the

92

day,' the voice replied inflexibly.

'I'm not talking about human interest, I'm talking about news!' she protested.

The voice explained that, on this day, chaos at an airport had no news value whatsoever.

After calling every television station in Pittsburgh, Phoebe had to accept the inevitable. Nobody cared about her lovingly drafted statement, nobody was interested in horizontal management. Abandoning her dreams of a press conference, she reminded herself that the walkout was designed to exert pressure on Mitch Scovil.

'And it's worked,' she declared. 'Publicity doesn't mean a thing.'

It is always a mistake to underestimate others. From the outset, Phoebe had assigned the roles in her drama. She was the heroine and Mitch Scovil was the outwitted opponent. Nobody else had a speaking part.

The three men who would insist on writing their own lines were sales engineers holding tickets on the four o'clock flight from Pittsburgh to New York. At noon, they had joined forces over a well-oiled luncheon. By the time they had been poured into the airport limousine, they were the merriest spirits aboard.

Like everybody else, when they found a tomblike void at Sparrow they marched to the main terminal. Unlike everybody else, they soon adjourned to a bar for consultation. During the first and second rounds they merely bewailed their predicament. It was, they agreed, one hell of a note when a man could not share Thanksgiving with his family. With the third round, a tiny seedling of originality emerged.

They were all middle-aged men, slow to baseless recrimination. As they watched the angry confrontations outside, they grew censorious.

'That's not right,' said the small, dark one, waxing more and more lugubrious. 'Those TWA clerks are just poor slobs doing their job. None of this is their fault.'

The one with the beefy build and the thick neck was angry, but just. 'No, Tony, it's not their fault. And the airport manager didn't do anything either.'

The chubby one had been confused even before leaving the lunch table. 'Manager?' he echoed, groggily rising. 'I'll tell him what a great sale I made.'

'No, no, Louis.' They hauled him back into his chair. 'The airport manager, the one who's pinned to the wall.'

With the next round, each continued down his own emotional path.

'I'll tell you what,' the ex-athlete declared truculently. 'That bunch at Sparrow has had its fun and, so far, we've been paying through the nose. I say it's time they did.'

Tony agreed in principle, but saw practical difficulties.

'There isn't anybody over at Sparrow, Frank. You saw how empty it was. They've all gone home to their families,' he reasoned dolefully.

'There's nobody out front,' Frank retorted. 'They're all in back, laughing while we sweat.'

'They shouldn't be allowed to get away with it,' Tony moaned.

Lou wanted action, not words.

'Lead the way!' he cried, heaving himself erect

with a blind wave that embraced three-fourths of the horizon.

The office on which they were descending was not, as they fondly imagined, a den of malevolent, snickering troublemakers. It contained only two occupants.

Tom Reardon, as Phoebe had anticipated, was making a bad situation worse by nonstop misdirected activity. He had delayed notifying headquarters of his plight as long as possible. Instead, he called his vanished employees at homes they would not reach for hours. Then he tried activating his six o'clock shift only to founder in a bog of baby-sitting and car-pooling arrangements.

In all these efforts he was supported by his assistant, Mrs. Virginia Kaltenbrun. Ginny was a true-blue loyalist. All attempts to enlist her in the ranks of the dissidents had failed, as her personal allegiance was to Tom Reardon, not Sparrow. In the face of outright aberration, the employees had given up.

When the three sales engineers rolled into the office area, spied the door marked MANAGER, and burst through it, she was around the corner at the copying machine.

Being a man of great consistency, Tom Reardon went straight for nonessentials.

'This is a restricted area,' he said fussily. 'You'll have to leave at once.'

'Restricted!' Frank bleated sarcastically. 'You mean it's where you're hiding.'

This was too close to the truth to be acceptable.

'It's my office. It's where I'm supposed to be.'

'Shame on you,' Tony cried.

95

Reardon realized he was dealing with passengers who had some ground for complaint.

'I'm sorry about the mess here today,' he said perfunctorily, 'but Thanksgiving is always a difficult time and we're doing everything that can be done.'

A confused babble about home, families, and the sacred obligations of contract failed to impress Reardon. He was still convinced that he was the chief victim of Phoebe's plot.

'You'll just have to be patient until I can sort things out,' he snapped.

This was far from satisfying to his guests.

'That may be quicker than you think,' Frank growled.

'What's that supposed to mean?'

'I've got news for you, little man. If we can't go home, then neither can you. How's that for an incentive?'

With these words, Frank planted his broad shoulders across the door, leaned back, and projected a bleary challenge.

Reardon had no intention of engaging in a shoving match.

'Nonsense,' he said, sounding like a schoolmaster. 'Get away from that door instantly or—'

'Or what? Who's going to make me?'

'Or I'll call the police,' Reardon said severely.

'Wanna bet?'

Startled, Reardon swiveled to check on the activities of Frank's accomplices. Tony was no problem. In the corner of the room he was quietly weeping and telling over the names of his loved ones as if they were so many beads. 'Won't see

96

Helen ... won't see the twins ... won't see Uncle Mario.'

But, on the other side of the desk, Lou had quietly carried off the telephone. Collapsed into a distant chair, he was playing with the dial. As his hands momentarily separated, so did the phone. He cocked his head, listening to the dial tone with innocent expectancy.

Reardon had been more exasperated than alarmed by the invasion. When Frank barred the exit, he remained composed. When Tony began sobbing, he grew disgusted. But, with the desecration of his telephone, something snapped. Let these three spend the night in the drunk tank, he decided vengefully. They richly deserved it.

And, once again, Tom Reardon did the wrong thing.

'Ginny! Call security!' he bellowed without warning. 'They've got me in here, and they won't let me go.'

On the other side of the door, Mrs. Kaltenbrun never doubted who *they* were. Already convinced that the Sparrow insurgents were capable of any atrocity, she wasted no time responding to this call for help.

'They've broken into Sparrow headquarters,' she gasped to the airport switchboard. 'And they're holding Mr. Reardon hostage.'

She could not have chosen a more unfortunate word. At Pittsburgh, as at every other airport in the world, the staff had been drilled and redrilled. To avoid panic during crisis, they had been turned into automatons who reflexively pushed the right button.

First, additional civilians must be prevented from

entering the danger area, so all approach roads were sealed off. Then, all potential victims must be removed, so the guards cleared the terminal. Finally, the danger must be contained, so fire doors were slammed and barred to isolate the Sparrow facility from the rest of the world. As these steps were taken at the airport, a convoy of rescue vehicles set forth from downtown, and the FBI announced that sharp-shooters were on the way.

To Phoebe Fournier, who was munching a broccoli croissant at the operative moment, ensuing events were a nightmare. A guard rushed into the coffee shop and ordered everybody out because of terrorists. Phoebe was preparing to obey orders when she heard that Tom Reardon's office was the eye of the storm. Flinging prudence to the winds, she ducked down a side corridor and raced toward Sparrow, only to be brought up short by a barrier of steel. She then made the mistake of deliberately seeking out a guard.

'Don't worry. We'll get your friends out safely,' he said, hustling her through the deserted lobby.

Unbelievingly, Phoebe gazed around. Everywhere there were signs of disorderly flight. Counters were covered with half-finished tickets. Luggage lay abandoned in the check-in stalls. One newsstand had several dollar bills lying next to the cash register.

'You're making a terrible mistake,' she insisted. 'You've got to let me go over there.'

The guard had been dealing with hysterical women for a quarter of an hour.

'Through this door,' he said, opening it for her.

Outside there were thousands of evacuees, waiting in long bedraggled lines. The lucky ones had their coats with them. But waitresses from the coffee shop shivered in thin uniforms while adults stripped off jackets to wrap around infants. From every direction there were the laments of people separated from their companions.

Compelling as the scene was, Phoebe was more shaken by the silence overhead. She knew at once that the airport had been closed to traffic. Her mind leaped to the inevitable convulsions at other airports. In New York and Washington, there would be Pittsburgh-bound flights cluttering the runways. Philadelphia and Baltimore would have to clear space for diverted flights. Every little ripple would be reducing the day's finely tuned schedules to a shambles.

With one small push, she had triggered an avalanche.

'My God,' she gasped. 'I've closed down the whole East Coast.'

CHAPTER TWELVE

HELPLESS ON LAND

Ever since his winning lottery ticket, Mitch Scovil knew he had been born under a lucky star. The sequence of events that Wednesday seemed to prove he was right.

While Phoebe was watching the clock in Pittsburgh, Scovil was picking up his wife at Channel Three. Thanks to traffic leaving the city and bottlenecks along the turnpike, the drive to Hartford took twice as long as usual. Kate and

Mitch occupied the time discussing the changes in her family during the last year. This was part of Kate's master plan. She was determined that, for at least twenty-four hours Mitch was going to forget all about Captain Lemoine.

When they finally pulled up to the McDermott home, they moved from one hermetically sealed capsule to another. Everybody and everything was circling the swaddled six-week-old packet named Joshua McDermott Haviland. While his proud parents beamed, the grandfather was cooing and gurgling, and Kate's brother was dangling a strange feathered object.

Mrs. McDermott forgot herself so far as to greet the Scovils with a radiant face and her first uncensored remark since their marriage.

'I'd almost given up hope of a baby,' she cried. 'I knew it was useless to expect anything from you.'

Mitch was somewhat taken aback. Until today he had been under the impression that his mother-in-law regarded him as flawless. Kate, of course, was not surprised, but anything was better than Sparrow Flyways and its unsolved murder.

An hour passed before Mr. McDermott tardily recalled his duties as a host and served drinks. Mrs. McDermott, with a squawk of dismay, remembered there were appetizers to be heated and fled to the kitchen with her daughters. The men, left to themselves, shifted position. Joshua's father stretched his long frame in an easy chair and turned his mind to new matters.

'It's a good thing we weren't coming here by plane,' he said, lofting his glass in congratulation. 'We'd never have made it.'

Idly, Mr. McDermott asked: 'What's wrong with

the planes? The weather's all right.'

'Don't you know about the hostage stand-off in Pittsburgh?' his son-in-law asked incredulously. 'It's thrown off air schedules in half the country.'

'WHAT?'

Scovil had reared upright, followed by a wail from the crib. 'I've got to call my office. I may have to leave right away.'

Kate, coming in with a tray of steaming cheese puffs, almost dropped it. 'Oh no!' she cried despairingly.

She should have had more faith in Eleanor Gough.

Nobody had ever been tempted to claim that Eleanor Gough was born under a lucky star. She had married early and watched a young husband die of a wasting disease. Driven to the marketplace to support two children, she had been overworked and underpaid. For twenty years, she had cleaned up other people's messes. It was a bad thing for her that she was on duty Wednesday afternoon, and a damned good thing for Sparrow.

By two-twenty she was receiving phone calls from station managers in New York and Philadelphia, querying the cancellation of service to Pittsburgh.

'Why the hell didn't you call me at once?' she stormed when she finally got through to Reardon.

Virtuously he outlined his attempts to secure a staff.

'You should have asked for emergency crews from Philadelphia while there was still time,' she raged, before setting to work herself.

When she tried to communicate her results to Pittsburgh, she was defeated by the familiar busy signal. She was still simmering when an excited clerk rushed in to announce that TV was reporting a hostage crisis in Pittsburgh. By four-thirty Eleanor Gough knew what was going on and exactly how much damage she had to contain.

At five-thirty Mitch Scovil's voice was simply another distraction.

'That's all right, Mitch,' she said, after explaining to him how Phoebe Fournier's walkout had mushroomed into a national crisis. 'I can handle it.'

'I could start right away,' he offered.

Mrs. Gough gritted her teeth. 'That's nice of you, Mitch, but it would take you hours to get here. That's what I told Clay when he called.'

'I hate to have this all land on you,' Scovil persisted.

The last thing she wanted was another cook at this particular stove.

'Don't give it a thought. The worst is almost over,' she lied shamelessly.

Mitch might be persuaded to stay put, but he insisted on talking.

'How could Phoebe do this to me?' he complained.

'I wouldn't worry about it,' she said tersely, not mentioning his many rebuffs to Phoebe.

'Not worry?' he repeated. 'What about the publicity Sparrow will be getting?'

Mrs. Gough had wasted as much time as she could afford. 'The FAA is coming through on another line, Mitch. I have to go,' she said, before adding hastily: 'And don't bother too much about the publicity. I have a feeling we're going to be luckier than we deserve.'

She hung up before he could reply.

The FAA was not on the line at that moment, but it was for the rest of the evening. Sparrow—and every other airline—had to retrieve its passengers. Even with clearances for a revised schedule stretching into the wee hours of the morning, monumental housekeeping chores remained. Mrs. Gough spent hours on the intricacies of connecting flights and vouchers for everything from hotels to taxi transfers.

Unfortunately her decisions had to be effected in Pittsburgh by Tom Reardon. Since his release from captivity, he had adopted a posture of open hostility to all passengers.

'A honeymoon couple?' she gasped, after interrogating him at midnight. 'And you just gave them a voucher for dinner? Not on your life.'

'This is already costing us a fortune. We don't owe these people an arm and a leg.'

Eleanor was adamant. 'Now, if ever, is the time for a gesture!'

Mrs. Gough's instincts were right on the money. As she had hoped, the media were not interested in Sparrow—not when they had sharpshooters and police cordons. And, when the Pittsburgh Massacre dissolved into three boozed-up engineers, the cameras left.

On Thursday morning her gesture paid off. Thanksgiving is a slow day for news and the networks are grateful for what they can get. They all decided to tell the world about the honeymoon couple. Who could resist them? They had come to the airport from the wedding reception, planning to spend the weekend at Niagara Falls.

103

'And you missed your wedding night?' a reporter throbbed.

'We did better,' the groom said practically. 'Sparrow is sending us to Hawaii for ten whole days.'

'Hawaii,' the bride repeated, glowing. 'And we're staying right on Waikiki beach.'

'With Sparrow picking up the tab,' the groom marveled. 'Isn't that wonderful?'

Most of America thought it was.

Before the sun rose on Thanksgiving morning, airlines on the East Coast had put the whole tawdry episode behind them. Clay Batchelder could not.

Stifling a yawn, he stood and watched the honeymooners extol Sparrow until his wife thrust a mug of coffee at him.

'You have to leave in five minutes,' she announced.

Their only daughter was coming home from college. She had been due yesterday afternoon, yesterday evening and, most recently, at the crack of dawn today. As a result, Clay, unlike everybody else at Sparrow, had suffered through long hours of airport turmoil as a member of the general public. He had asked hopeless questions, instead of giving misleading answers. He had paced the floor, checked his watch, and called home until far too late.

And now he was going to do it all over again.

'I still don't see why Jill has to come in to Providence,' he grumbled. 'At least if it was Logan, I could have helped Eleanor last night.'

Criticism of her children was not allowed under Mrs. Batchelder's roof.

'Eleanor didn't need you,' she said unflatteringly. 'Jill did.'

'Sure, honey,' he said, despite a novel thought. Why did Jill, world-traveler since junior high school, have to be hand-carried from Providence to Duxbury?

He managed one sip of coffee before his wife started again.

'If you don't leave now, you're going to be late.'

'Okay, okay,' he said, abandoning the mug.

But he was still thinking like a civilian. 'It would have been easier to pick her up at Ithaca in the first place.'

'And whose fault is that?' she demanded rhetorically. 'The whole mess began with your precious Sparrow.'

As usual, it was ten minutes before Clay found the right reply.

'Sparrow didn't cause the mess. Phoebe Fournier did,' he said to himself. 'And I hope she's happy.'

Far from it. On Wednesday night Phoebe had returned home so pale and drawn that Bryan barely recognized her.

Thursday was hard on her, too. They were spending the holiday with Bryan's married brother, his wife, and the television set. It was one defeat after another. First, the wrong football team won. Then, opinion-makers began telling the nation what to think about Pittsburgh and never mentioned Sparrow. Instead, the pundits focused on themes worthy of them. What was wrong, they asked, with a country that could overreact so disastrously? Was our transport system hostage to our own fears?

'Oh for God's sake!' Phoebe exploded. 'They've

got it all wrong. It was our work stoppage that sparked everything.'

Julie Kiley brought to the festive board her own peculiar sympathies.

'I think they're being much too hard on those engineers,' she declared, her spoon poised over the stuffing that she was adding to each serving of turkey. 'They looked like nice men to me. They just didn't expect people to push the panic button.'

A sober and repentant threesome had been interviewed more than once.

'Come on, Julie,' Douglas Kiley protested. 'They caused a lot of inconvenience to other people.'

'Oh, they shouldn't have done it. But you know how maddening it is when you have a serious complaint and the people in charge don't seem to give a damn,' Julie persisted. 'These men decided the man at the top was going to listen, whether he wanted to or not.'

'So they took him prisoner?' her husband asked ironically.

'They were simply trying to get his attention,' she said with gentle mulishness as she passed heaped plates.

Both brothers accepted every syllable as more of Julie's muzzy benignity. Phoebe, however, was turned to stone. It was, she told herself, sheer accident that Julie was reproducing, almost word for word, her own justification to Joe Cleveland.

Bryan had another bone to pick.

'They were plastered,' he said, from the virtuous heights of one glass of Vouvray. 'Even if they'd gotten their plane, they would have been a menace. You know what Phoebe always says about drunks on board.'

106

Before Phoebe could weigh in with an appropriate anecdote, Julie had an even more unfortunate insight.

'I realize that. But this was a childish temper tantrum.' She paused to smile affectionately at the high chair containing her own tantrum-thrower. 'I've seen little Bryan try to wreck the room because I'm too busy to pay attention to him.'

Phoebe gulped. She knew that nobody was equating the Sparrow walkout with kicking and screaming on the floor. Nonetheless, she did not care to risk more of Julie's wide-ranging charity.

'This sweet potato casserole is wonderful, Julie,' she said enticingly. 'I know about putting marshmallows into it, but there's something else, isn't there?'

Julie forgot all about human waywardness.

'I grated fresh ginger in,' she said proudly. 'I've always wanted to try it, but the roots were hard to get until recently.'

'What a great idea!' said Phoebe, submerging the fact that she had eaten an identical casserole at her mother's Thanksgiving table for twenty-two years.

John Thatcher had worked late on Wednesday and risen early the next morning. By ten o'clock he had driven to his daughter's house in Connecticut. His weekend was going to be spent with his grandchildren and his son-in-law's parents.

Sad to say, his only response to the television bulletins about Pittsburgh was unashamedly self-centered.

'I was right to drive. In fact, it's a mistake to get anywhere near a common carrier at Thanksgiving.'

Normally this statement, like almost any other,

would have encouraged an outpouring from his fellow father-in-law. After a lifetime teaching classics at Columbia, Cardwell Carlson lectured automatically. But he barely opened his mouth before he was interrupted by a shriek from his wife.

'He's circling,' she cried. 'Get him into the yard.'

The Carlson home, like the McDermotts', contained a new arrival. But, after four children, Laura and Ben Carlson were settling for an eight-week-old Newfoundland puppy. He was not, as the breeder had guaranteed, house-broken.

Between the puppy and the grandchildren, Thatcher did not read the *New York Times* until well after dinner. Page one featured the usual photographs of airport drama. Page twenty-three, however, contained a small paragraph identifying an employee walkout at Sparrow as the primary cause of the subsequent upheaval.

'Phoebe Fournier!' Thatcher snorted, but that was the beginning and end of his reaction.

He had put his professional instincts to rest for a full four days. There were others, he knew, more sternly dedicated to duty. Everett Gabler, for instance, proposed an early return to Sparrow on Friday. But Everett, thank God, had all the old-fashioned virtues. He would not lightly intrude on John Thatcher in the bosom of his family.

Unless, of course, Sparrow had further bombshells to explode.

CHAPTER THIRTEEN

CLOSE TO EXTINCTION

Along with Gabler, Mitch Scovil was returning to work on Friday. Travel on the day after Thanksgiving was always so light that he had even scheduled some nonroutine activities.

Weeks before Alan Whetmore's murder, Channel Three had planned to showcase Scovil on a forthcoming weekend magazine show. Today they were taping at Sparrow.

'... and it will make a nice change from the publicity we've been getting,' he yodeled from the bathroom.

It was seven-thirty in the morning, and Kate was nervous as a cat.

'No black or white clothes!' she yipped suddenly, remembering another last-minute caution.

'I'm not exactly a beginner, honey. And I don't usually wear a black suit to work, anyway,' he said, emerging for inspection.

She grinned at the rebuke, but could not help running an eye over him. He was irreproachable in a light green shirt and dark brown suit.

'Why don't you ever look this good just for me?' she teased.

He had drifted over to his mirror and spoke with his back turned.

'By the way, don't you think we ought to send a present to the baby? After all, we are his aunt and uncle.'

Proud of her domestic staff work, Kate replied

too quickly. 'We sent a silver porringer a month ago.'

Her husband was not interested in mere gestures. 'I was thinking of something personal,' he said, reproachfully. 'Something that Josh would enjoy.'

Kate still felt that any extracurricular distraction should be encouraged.

'I think I know what you mean,' she said. A life-sized giant panda would be a sure-fire success with her husband, if not with Josh's parents. 'I've got the day off. I could stop by F. A. O. Schwarz this afternoon.'

'Good,' he replied instantly. 'I'll meet you for lunch and we'll go together.'

By the time he talked himself to the door, he sounded like a man without a care in the world. He rushed off, leaving his wife to ponder the vagaries of men and the unnecessary alarms experienced by their womenfolk.

Captain Gregory Lemoine was also back at work, and he was not satisfied with the progress of his investigation.

'Try and get this through your head, Doyle. One way or another, Scovil is the key to this thing. I've already got him on opportunity and motive. All I need is the means. Let me put that wrench into his hands, and I can crack him like an eggshell. You hear what I'm saying?'

Doyle shifted restively but retained his wooden expression.

'I hear you, Captain. Loud and clear.' He then made the mistake of trying to justify himself. 'But my team has questioned every single solitary employee who went into that locker room. I didn't

110

stop with the men who were on duty here. I went after the ones who were on stopovers in Boston or the ones who were filling in for somebody. Hell, I even chased down a guy who's on vacation. Not one of them admits to seeing that damned wrench.'

His efforts backfired with a vengeance.

'What did you say?' Lemoine asked savagely. 'You questioned all the men? Why the hell haven't you been after the women?'

Doyle stared at him as if he were insane.

'Women don't use the men's locker room,' he said warily.

'So what?' snarled Lemoine. 'The wrench left the locker room in the morning. It wasn't used on Whetmore until five or so. It was someplace else in between. When a thing goes missing, you don't just try and trace it forward. You try backward, too!'

Under this hail of censure, Doyle stiffened, but he was not convinced.

'Anybody who took that wrench as a murder weapon wasn't flashing it around,' he protested.

'It was that meeting of theirs that got them going. Maybe there wasn't any intention of killing before then.' The captain's heavily patient voice suddenly cracked like a whip. 'Now get out of here and question those women!'

Doyle was only too happy to go, particularly as Lemoine was already baying for his next victim.

'Where the hell is Paretti? I told him to have that court order for Whetmore's safe deposit box first thing this morning.'

Sally, the receptionist, was typing dementedly and flinging harried glances at the clock when Doyle entered. He paid no attention to her obvious race

111

against a deadline and began fishing for information. His first two casts produced only blank incomprehension. At the third trial, enlightenment dawned.

'You're not talking about the wrench Mitch brought here from the locker room, are you?' she asked incredulously. 'Why in heaven's name didn't you say so?'

He ignored her question in favor of several of his own. When had this taken place? At what time had the wrench come in, at what time had it left?

'Let's see. Mitch must have dumped it on the coffee table just before I went for my break,' she said, only to be reminded of a long-standing grievance of her own. 'I don't know how they expect me to keep this area tidy. The three of them cart in everything but the kitchen sink. You should have seen how Eleanor left the place on Wednesday night. When I came in, it looked like a war zone.'

Doyle was not interested in her housekeeping problems. He was recalling, with new respect, Lemoine's theory about spontaneous combustion.

'What about *after* the meeting? Did you see it then?' he pressed.

This required far more thought. 'I don't know about after the meeting,' she finally decided. 'But it was there when Mr. Islington arrived. I remember because I straightened the pile of magazines, and I put the wrench on top as a paperweight.'

Thereafter she had no recollection of ever seeing the wrench again.

And Sally was more exasperated than impressed when Doyle accused her of concealing information. Since she knew exactly what Norman Pitts and Jason Tiedeman had told the police, she failed to

112

see why Doyle was making such heavy weather of her testimony.

'Norman left the wrench in the locker room, Jason was there when Mitch took it, so you should have figured out he brought it here. This is where all the junk ends up. Although,' she added fair-mindedly, 'Eleanor and Clay are a lot worse than Mitch.'

Lemoine's rebuke to his subordinate rankled even more now that it was proving to be well-founded.

'That's a lot of hot air. You know damned well you should have told us about this,' Doyle said suspiciously. 'And I want to know why you didn't.'

'Because nobody had the sense to ask me,' she snapped, immediately producing a fusillade of flying typewriter keys to signal the end of the conversation.

Eleanor Gough came strolling into headquarters in a leisurely manner at eleven o'clock. Her only reason for appearing was to sample public opinion at Sparrow. A preliminary reconnaissance told her that employees everywhere were responding to the Pittsburgh shutdown.

The hard-liners, still identifying Mitch as Alan Whetmore's murderer, were the loudest.

'I said all along the shutdown wasn't enough. And look what happened,' one of them demanded. 'We should've all walked, the way I said. At least people would have known what we were protesting.'

Today the water cooler was the nerve center of the moderates.

'Come on, admit it! It was a hare-brained scheme
113

all along,' said an excitable programmer.

'You sure aren't going to bring Mitch to the bargaining table by calling out SWAT teams,' somebody else agreed.

Down in the cafeteria, they were complaining about lack of prior consultation.

'They want solidarity, they better tell us what they're planning,' a stewardess said as she thumped her water glass angrily.

Even Norman Pitts was beginning to raise his voice among his peers.

'I signed the petition, and I'm glad that I did. But I haven't forgotten we're trying to run an airline. You shut down the country's air traffic and you simply encourage people to use their cars instead.'

It was better than she had hoped for, Mrs. Gough decided as she finished her circuit. Let splinter groups flourish if they gave Mitch time to mend his ways with the work force.

She was mentally composing the speech that would convert him when she entered the executive suite.

'Oh, Eleanor,' Sally called, 'there's a visitor in there.'

Mrs. Gough paused with her hand on the doorknob and a frown on her face. The calendar, she knew, was clear.

Respectfully, Sally stilled her keyboard. 'It's Alan Whetmore's brother,' she intoned. 'Representing the family.'

'Good heavens! I suppose I'll have to take care of him.'

Within ten minutes Mrs. Gough realized that she was not dealing with another Alan. Vincent

Whetmore was a dried-up little man who set the record straight at once.

'My mother wants me to bring the body back,' he said glumly. 'She's eighty-three, and she gets upset.'

Nobody had to tell Eleanor what horrors this statement encapsulated. Under her sympathetic guidance, a picture of the Whetmore family in Ohio began to emerge. Alan had disappeared into the Air Force long ago. His annual Christmas card was the chief communication between widely spaced visits.

'We weren't at all alike,' Vincent conceded. 'Alan was the ambitious one. I just stayed in the same old job, while he was always going on to something better.'

Who was Mrs. Gough to dispel this illusion by explaining that Alan's career had been largely downhill? As nearly as she could fathom, Alan had spent those short visits flourishing snapshots of himself and his current companion enjoying Caribbean beaches or world-renowned ski resorts.

While Alan had been chasing the good life, Vincent had married, raised a family, seen his father through a final illness, sheltered his widowed mother, and was now picking up the tab for the nursing home.

Mrs. Gough said something meaningless about different choices.

'Sure, Alan had a right to live it up,' said Vincent, honing in on the purpose of his visit. 'But he was making big money. The price of just one of his fancy weekends would have been a real help.'

Ostensibly, Vincent was here to seek guidance in the air transport of a body. He was naturally hoping for something more and Mrs. Gough obliged.

115

'You're not to concern yourself with the costs,' she said firmly. 'Of course the coffin will go by Sparrow. And we'll handle the local arrangements in Boston, too.'

Eleanor Gough was a generous woman, and she had been touched by Vincent's plight. She could have gone whole hog and extended Sparrow's largess to the funeral itself. But she had taken the measure of Mrs. Whetmore, Senior, who clearly intended to enshrine the younger brother at the expense of the son who had borne the brunt. That, of course, was life, and Eleanor was too old to fight it. But Alan's mother was not going to stage an extravaganza—not with Sparrow's money.

Resolutely she turned to technical detail. 'There's a considerable amount of documentation that you'll need, particularly as we'll have to transship the coffin in Buffalo,' she began. 'Now, in theory, the undertaker will supply everything. But you'll be safer if I have Sally type up a master list for you to check against.'

It was not the first time that Sparrow had been involved in long-distance obsequies, and Mrs. Gough had the regulations at her fingertips. When she left the room, she expected to be back within five minutes.

But Vincent Whetmore sat patiently waiting for over an hour.

The Channel Three crew had arrived at Sparrow at nine o'clock. By late that morning, Mitch Scovil had been filmed consulting an employee about the day's roster, peering into a computer monitor, and stripping off his jacket to lend a hand with luggage. Finally they had moved outdoors for the ultimate

116

sequence, to film Scovil striding across the compound.

Luckily, his thoughts were invisible. Kate, he decided, should have warned him about this three-ring circus. The men ahead, with video equipment on their shoulders, were not the major culprits. It was the audio expert who was wreaking havoc. Before each sequence it was necessary for him to perform strange rites with his supersensitive devices. He would then make one unreasonable demand after another, all in the name of quelling background noise.

Now he was again bringing the entire operation to a halt. But this time the director of the epic was showing fight. In a feature about an airline executive being shot at an airport, he refused to agree that the sound of aircraft was objectionable.

The audio zealot remained unyielding. 'Then you've got to scrap that business of him talking to the foreman outside,' he insisted. 'Nobody's going to understand what they're saying.'

The director's reply was lost in the din of two jets zooming overhead.

While Scovil waited for them to settle the dispute, he realized that they were obstructing traffic in the area. Personnel in greasy coveralls were making wide circles around the group that now included the cameramen, the director's gofer, and some flunky whose duties had never been clarified. Loaded dollies being pushed around the corner squealed in protest as they suddenly veered to avoid collision.

In the confusion Scovil failed to notice the police cruiser pulling up.

'Mr. Scovil? Mr. Mitchell Scovil?'

Scovil swung around and scowled at the familiar uniforms. 'Yeah, I'm Scovil. What is it now?' he asked unenthusiastically.

'Captain Lemoine wants you to come down to the station for questioning.'

To Scovil this was simply another unwelcome intrusion by the police.

'Are you crazy? Can't you see I'm busy? Whatever it is, it will have to wait.'

'It can't.' The trooper paused. 'Captain Lemoine thought you'd rather come down voluntarily than the other way.'

Scovil's eyes narrowed. 'What's that supposed to mean? The other way?'

'I have a warrant for your arrest, Mr. Scovil. We can *take* you downtown.'

There was no longer any room for incomprehension. Scovil stared back, the blood draining from his face. But his voice was steady.

'I've already told Lemoine I'm not answering any more questions without my lawyer,' he rasped defiantly.

The trooper could have been soothing a recalcitrant child. 'That's all right. Your lawyer's meeting us at the station. So we'd better get started.'

Scovil was dragging his feet when he caught sight of other activity.

'Oh for Christ's sake!'

The film unit had become a news team, aiming cameras at him like so many bazookas.

'Let's get the hell out of here,' he growled, diving for the cruiser.

CHAPTER FOURTEEN

CONCEALED NEST

Minutes later, when the troopers rushed Mitch
Scovil into Captain Lemoine's office, a skirmish was
already underway.

'. . . no cause to drag my client down here like
this,' Steven McAllister was declaiming. 'Oh, hello,
Mitch. I'm surprised they didn't clap you into
handcuffs while they were at it.'

Unmoved, Lemoine dismissed his men. As they
trudged out, Scovil said: 'Thanks for getting here
on such short notice, Steve.'

'It wasn't easy,' McAllister told him.

Their byplay glanced off the man behind the
desk.

'Sit down, Mr. Scovil,' said Lemoine with
exaggerated courtesy. 'Mr. McAllister has just been
telling me what a big shot you are.'

'Captain Lemoine, there is no need—'

'Dammit, who cares—'

With heavy irony, Lemoine flattened their
protests. 'But I already know that. Half the
politicians in town keep telling me how important
you are—and that includes the State House. So I
can't afford to horse around, even with a warrant.
That's why I got you down here so fast. Now's your
chance to convince me that you didn't murder Alan
Whetmore.'

Stubbornly, Scovil shook his head. 'I've already
told you everything I know,' he insisted.

McAllister, careful not to look in his direction,

119

leaned forward earnestly. 'Let's stop playing these cat-and-mouse games. I assume you think you've found incriminating evidence, Captain Lemoine. Suppose you go ahead and tell us what it is?'

He got more than he bargained for when Lemoine placed the murder weapon in Scovil's hands immediately before the meeting.

'. . . and so, in spite of the fact your client's been swearing he never even saw the wrench, he's the only one who knew where to find it. Anybody else just stumbled on it.'

Scovil, his lips tightly compressed, studied a late-season fly buzzing against the window pane. In the silence, Lemoine smiled and waited. Then McAllister chose his tactics.

'So you have witnesses of unknown credibility,' he said scornfully. 'Captain, after what happened in Pittsburgh the other day, we all know that there are Sparrow employees with grievances against Mitch Scovil. How can reliance be placed in anything they say?'

'You want lie-detector tests?' Lemoine challenged.

But even State Street lawyers know about polygraph machines. Automatically McAllister reeled off a denunciation of circumstantial evidence. He was just getting up to speed when his client cut him short.

'All right,' said Scovil. For the first time he was backing down from a confrontation with Lemoine. 'I picked up that damned wrench in the locker room. I suppose I must have dumped it on the coffee table without really thinking. But I don't know what happened to it after that. I didn't kill Alan Whetmore, and I don't know who did.'

Lemoine was almost kindly. 'There you are,' he said approvingly. 'We've just been here a few minutes, and we're already making progress. Who knows how much we'll dig up after a couple of hours.'

'Hours?' Scovil repeated blankly.

'Take it easy, Mitch,' McAllister interjected.

'Yeah, relax and make yourself comfortable, Scovil,' said Lemoine, dropping honorifics. 'We're going to be here for as long as it takes, even if that's the rest of the day. Unless you decide to cooperate. Suppose I tell you how you killed Alan Whetmore and when. If you want to speed things up, tell me why you did it.'

'Shut up, Mitch,' McAllister said briskly. 'Let me take care of this. Captain Lemoine, first I want to say—'

But Scovil barely listened. He was staggered by the implications of Lemoine's flat accusation. The comforting crowd of suspects had just vanished, leaving one man alone in the spotlight.

And Captain Lemoine was inches away from making an arrest.

'Is that you, Mitch?' Kate demanded after being called to the phone at the Magic Pan. 'Do you know how long I've been waiting?'

'It's me, Kate—Clay.'

Her heart constricted. 'What's wrong?' she gasped, visualizing every possible disaster.

'Mitch is all right,' Clay said hastily. 'That is . . . I mean . . . oh hell, the cops picked him up an hour ago. It's probably just for more of their questioning—but I wanted to get you as soon as I could, before all hell breaks loose. I wasn't there,

121

but apparently your people from Channel Three were right on the spot, taking it all in.'

'Oh no!' she murmured, stricken.

Sounding in need of consolation himself, he muttered: 'It was bad luck, but the news would have gotten out anyway.'

As far as Kate was concerned, he was wandering from the essentials. 'What station have they taken him to? Is his lawyer there? You don't mean the police have actually arrested him, do you?'

Her rapid-fire string of questions caught him short.

'Hell, I don't know, Kate,' he said. 'Everything here happened so damned fast.'

'Tell me,' she said, determined to extract every possible crumb of information.

'Why do you sound that way?' she demanded when he finished speaking. 'You don't think Mitch is guilty, do you?'

'You know better than that,' he replied gruffly. 'It's just that I'm pretty shook up. Having Lemoine pull a trick like this is the last thing I expected. And I still don't see what makes him think he can do it—'

Once again they were straying, and Kate cut in ruthlessly. 'Thanks for calling, Clay. Now I've got things to do.'

But two steps into the foyer demonstrated that she was already running late. Bona fide customers were swamped by reporters.

'There she is!'

'Kate, do you know your husband has been arrested?'

The death-beetle click of the cameras made her flinch. Assuming a brave smile, she earned the

122

undying gratitude of the Magic Pan by saying: 'Just let me get my coat and I'll make a statement outside. Not that there's much I can tell you...'

'... every expectation that Mr. Scovil will be resuming his duties shortly,' Eleanor Gough dictated grimly. 'In the meantime, Sparrow Flyways is maintaining normal operations.'

Sally was not sure whether this was a full stop or fatigue. 'Is that all?' she asked.

'That's it,' said Eleanor. 'No, tell anybody who calls that that's all Sparrow will have to say until sometime later.'

'Sure,' said Sally, making a note. 'But you know the employees will be dying to talk.'

'Oh, damn the employees,' said Mrs. Gough.

To keep Sparrow from lapsing into shock, she had been coaxing and bullying to the point of exhaustion. The press release represented her first step in a more meaningful direction. It came as an afterthought, the result of an urgent call from the business editor of the *Boston Globe*.

'I just hope that will keep everybody quiet,' she said in a rare moment of weakness, 'until Mitch can straighten everything out himself.'

But financial markets do not tarry. The bald fact that the CEO of Sparrow Flyways was being detained by the police hit the newswires early and promptly sped to trading desks around the world. If Sparrow had been one of the blue chips, there would have been convulsions from the Ginza to Leadenhall Street. As it was, most of the disquiet was confined to Wall Street, where it translated into a burst of activity rare on the day after

123

Thanksgiving. A wave of sell orders pounded the price of Sparrow stock down six points in as many minutes. In the lull that followed, a retraction—or news of Scovil's release—could have reversed the decline. When neither came, the tempo picked up again. With the downward spiral threatening to spin out of control, the market authorities stepped forward and halted trading in Sparrow stock.

To the general public, this was a footnote to the story. For Fidelity, Drexel Burnham—and the Sloan Guaranty Trust—it was the beginning of a long wait.

At lesser banks, other agitations were disturbing the Friday somnolence. In Boston, the decorum of the Copley Institute for Savings was being ruffled by Lieutenant Paretti and his court order. However, after Copley's pro forma reluctance, Alan Whetmore's safe deposit box was finally produced.

'Here you are,' said the assistant manager solemnly.

'Thanks,' said Paretti, raising the long, narrow lid.

Besides three paper clips, he discovered a package wrapped in brown paper. A flick of his wrist broke the Scotch tape and the contents spilled onto the desk.

One-hundred-dollar bills—and lots of them.

'Looks like more than petty cash, doesn't it?' he remarked prosaically. 'We'd better count it.'

Reverting to type, the assistant manager dealt and sorted the bills with poker player's hands.

'Fifty thousand dollars,' he summed up, 'in used bills. And I don't think they're marked, either.'

'Uh-huh,' said Paretti, who had access to experts

124

of his own on this subject. 'Now you told me that Whetmore just rented the box three weeks ago, didn't you?'

'I have the date right here,' said the assistant manager, consulting his file. Then curiosity got the better of him. 'Can you tell me what this is all about?'

But Paretti was on a short leash. 'I've got someone else to talk to first,' he said. 'Where's the nearest phone I can use?'

The Copley Institute for Savings was all cooperation. The resistance came from the police switchboard.

'. . . screw Mitch Scovil,' Paretti said heatedly. 'Lemoine told me he wanted this—or he'd have my hide. You'd better put me through, Foley.'

'Greg won't be happy about this,' said Foley, complying.

Before the day was out, however, others would be.

CHAPTER FIFTEEN

IMMATURE MALE

At first, Kate McDermott had been grateful when Clay Batchelder and Eleanor Gough arrived to share her ordeal. But, as the hours passed, Clay became less of a comfort and more of a threat to Kate's precarious self-control.

From the beginning he had been unable to sit still. He had made endless phone calls, he had insisted on helping Eleanor with the coffeepot and,

125

as the afternoon wore on, he had even tried to force drinks on everybody. Kate could forgive his restlessness; it was more difficult to excuse some of his unguarded remarks.

At one o'clock he had said: 'Lemoine's crazy—that's all.'

By two-thirty, self-interest had appeared.

'How could they do this to us?' he groaned.

And now, as he stood staring over the harbor, he was ready to lash out at anyone and anything.

'If Mitch had only gone home the way he said he did, he wouldn't be under arrest. Why the hell did he need to do his drinking at Logan?'

Kate, closing her eyes, wondered if a shrill scream would shut him up. It would certainly relieve her own feelings.

'Mitch hasn't been arrested,' Mrs. Gough corrected sharply. 'And none of this is his fault. How could he know Alan Whetmore was going to be murdered?'

Kate tried to smile. 'I know Clay didn't mean it that way.'

With a start, Batchelder remembered where he was. Flinging himself into a chair, he began a shamefaced apology. Then came the sound they had all been waiting for. A key was turning in the door.

Kate flew across the living room. Clay, already on his feet, hung back to give her a clear field while Eleanor Gough froze into immobility, her eyes glued to the archway.

For a moment they could hear only indistinct murmurings. Then Mitch Scovil appeared, his arm around Kate.

'That one was a lot closer than I like,' he said, tired but unmistakably triumphant.

Clay and Eleanor were bursting with questions, but Kate would not allow Mitch to say one word until he had showered and changed.

'Now, you can make the drinks, Clay!'

Fifteen minutes later Scovil rejoined them in jeans and a plaid shirt. The coffee table, with cheeses at one end and pâté at the other, was ready for a party. Kate, glowing with joy, would have extended her embargo against serious talk, but Mitch was burning to tell his story.

'Lemoine thought he really had me nailed,' he chortled. 'When he found out I was the one who'd had the wrench—'

Both his partners exploded and, when an explanation was forthcoming, they reacted differently. Eleanor was aghast at the tightrope that Mitch had been walking. Clay, relaxed and beaming, was inclined to be jocular.

'It used to be me and Eleanor always carting hardware around. You picked a great day to start, Mitch.'

Scovil acknowledged the shaft with a broad grin. 'It was touch and go for a while, there. Then, right in the nick of time, the cops found fifty thousand bucks that Whetmore had salted away in a safe deposit box. Talk about luck! Lemoine didn't know what the hell it meant, but I did.'

He looked around his audience, savoring the baffled expressions he encountered.

'You still don't get it?' he challenged. 'I figured that one out while I was with Don Islington after the meeting. C'mon, Eleanor, what was the first thing you did then?'

'I rushed out to circulate our side of the story to as many people as possible,' she answered, puzzled.

127

'And why did you do that?'

'If the employees thought we'd stamped out of a normal meeting, the situation at Sparrow would have gotten worse.' Eleanor was becoming testy at explaining the obvious. 'For all I knew, Alan's little ploy could have been designed to create that impression. So I—'

'Aha!' said Scovil gleefully. 'You were already halfway there, you just didn't go far enough. Of course somebody fed that garbage to Whetmore in order to create a ruckus at Sparrow. Whetmore didn't think of it himself, and he wasn't in the habit of doing favors for other people. It's plain as the nose on your face when you think about it. Somebody was buying himself some labor trouble at Sparrow.'

Mrs. Gough was shocked. 'You mean a competitor? It's hard to believe a major airline would resort to anything like that.'

Scovil leaned forward to press home his arguments. As he spoke he began waving a cracker like a conductor's baton.

'Consider your own reaction. You instinctively wondered whether we'd been deliberately suckered. And who else would shell out fifty thou for the privilege of upsetting our applecart?'

Kate had become interested in spite of herself. Wrinkling her nose in thought, she said: 'But you can't be sure the fifty thousand was a bribe. Whetmore could have saved it over time. Maybe he was trying to evade taxes.'

Far from being a problem to Scovil, this was an opening. 'I haven't told you the best part. Whetmore got the cash all at once three weeks ago.'

'That's hard to explain away,' Mrs. Gough

128

agreed. 'And I have to admit Alan would be the ideal candidate for a job like that.'

Batchelder had been pondering every word. 'You've got to admit more than that, Eleanor,' he said slowly. 'Mitch's idea covers damn near everything.'

'It hit me when I was describing the meeting to Islington,' Scovil preened himself. 'That list of demands was so phony it jumped off the paper. I knew we'd been set up.'

'Anyway, Lemoine must have bought it,' Clay answered. 'You did say the pressure went off you as soon as he found out about the safe deposit box.'

'Well, he sure as hell couldn't come up with a reason why I'd slip dirty money to one of my own pilots to wreck the joint.'

Eleanor could see broader grounds for Lemoine's action. 'Even if he wasn't completely convinced by your theory, he had to let you go. At the very least, the fifty thousand shows that Alan was into something so fishy it could easily have been the motive for his murder. You're right, Mitch, having the money pop up was a godsend for us.'

Scovil examined his drink, decided it required freshening, and moved to the bar. When he next spoke he was almost invisible, bending over his glass behind a barricade of ice buckets and mixers.

'Actually I was able to give Lemoine more than a theory. I finally gave him what I've been sitting on. You see, after Don Islington left, I went out to the parking lot, intending to go home. And guess what I saw!' He paused to let the suspense mount. 'Alan Whetmore was having a nice, cozy confab with Fritz Diehl.'

The climax fell flat.

'So?' Eleanor said impatiently. 'Sally already told us that Fritz came by that afternoon.'

Scovil's tone hardened. 'But she didn't tell us that Whetmore was reporting results to Fritz.'

'Mitch!'

This time Eleanor Gough was outraged. Before she could say anything intemperate, Batchelder asked the question that needed an answer.

'But why did that make you stay at Logan?'

'Seeing them together like that really floored me, Scovil admitted. 'I knew, if I followed Fritz in and tackled him right then, he'd have some fancy story up his sleeve. So I decided to bump into him casually when he didn't know how much I'd seen. Since there was only one plane to St. Louis after five, I hung around the gate. When he never showed, I figured I'd catch him the next morning at the gym.'

Mrs. Gough had been biding her time.

'Are you out of your mind, Mitch?' she asked stonily.

Scovil, having already extracted half agreements, pressed his advantage.

'Come off it, Eleanor. You realized within five minutes that Whetmore was making patsies out of us. You admit that getting his payoff three weeks ago ties it into our meeting. And you haven't come up with any alternative to a competitor. Now you act as if I'm throwing you something from left field.'

'Why don't *you* come off it?' she snapped angrily. 'You've been deliberately leaking hints about California for months. And the reason you've been doing it is precisely to needle all the transcontinentals. Well, you've had your fun, you've stirred up a lot of hornets' nests. Now maybe one of them did bribe Alan Whetmore. But you haven't proved a thing against Fritz.'

Kate, watching her welcome-home party turn into a pitched battle, tried to intervene.

'Couldn't we talk about this some other time?' she suggested. 'The important thing is that Mitch isn't under suspicion anymore.'

This remark drew a derisive snort from Mrs. Gough, but it was Kate's husband who ignored the plea for peace.

'Nobody's pulling a stunt like this simply to prevent our expansion. A minute ago you couldn't believe any of the majors would act this way and now suddenly they're all suspects. Fritz isn't piddling around with distraction. He wants to take over Sparrow. That's what he's been after all along.'

'And you told that story to the police?' Eleanor cried in horror.

'I could have told Lemoine about Fritz and Whetmore right off the bat,' Scovil said defiantly. 'But I sat on it, hoping the cops would settle things by themselves. Just how long do you expect me to cover for Fritz?'

Eleanor knew that Scovil had been protecting his own alibi, but she stayed with the main issue.

'Nobody expects you to cover anything,' she insisted. 'There's no reason you shouldn't tell them you saw Fritz. But spilling out accusations that have no foundation—'

'Like hell they don't. I heard Fritz when he walked out on us. You heard him, and so did Clay.'

Batchelder was not eager to leave the sidelines.

'I don't like it any better than you do, Eleanor,

131

but we've got to face facts,' he said, appealing to her sense of justice. 'Fritz did say he'd take over Sparrow.'

'If it comes to that, Mitch said a lot of things, too. They were both furious, but they were talking about normal competition.'

'I'm not so sure,' Clay continued unhappily. 'I learned something during Sparrow's first two years. Fritz plays to win.'

'And he's a smoothie,' Kate suddenly chimed in. 'I remember saying so.'

She and Fritz Diehl had barely overlapped in Scovil's life. Mrs. Gough could shrug off Kate, but not Batchelder.

'Do you realize you're accusing Fritz of being a cold-blooded killer?' she demanded, shifting brutally from bribery to murder.

Scovil was ready for her.

'It's a choice between him and me,' he retorted. 'Besides, we don't know it was all that cold-blooded. Maybe there was a fight about money. It would have been just like Whetmore to try for a second helping. So Fritz lost his cool and beat his brains in.'

The graphic description created another hurdle for Batchelder to clear. 'I suppose it could have happened that way,' he said, only partially convinced, 'but it doesn't sound like Fritz.'

Scovil, still intent on Mrs. Gough, dismissed Clay's difficulty.

'The trouble with you, Eleanor, is that you buy Fritz's nice-guy act. Just look what's happened to Sparrow in the past couple of weeks. We began at thirty-five, where at least we had a ten-point cushion against the sharks. Then Whetmore's death

132

pushed us down to thirty-three and today I get hauled off by the cops in front of TV cameras. I'm afraid to ask how much we lost this afternoon.'

'They suspended trading,' Mrs. Gough said briefly. 'We won't know what the damage is until the market opens on Monday.'

'And you still don't see that Fritz is behind this,' Scovil marveled. He shook his head silently at this denial of reality.

'We're going through a bad patch because of Alan's murder. But he wasn't necessarily killed for that reason,' Eleanor said, casting around for another interpretation. 'You might just as well say that Fritz was responsible for the slide to thirty-five.'

The words were out of her mouth before she realized how double-edged they were. It was unwritten law at Sparrow that the stock's slow retreat from its high was due to changing conditions, increased competition, or black clouds over the Persian Gulf. Never, under any circumstance, was it attributed to the loss of Fritz Diehl's managerial skills.

Appalled by her inadvertent clumsiness, Eleanor Gough knew that further discussion would only convince Mitch that she had blurted out a long-held opinion. Deciding that the least said, the soonest mended, she began to gather her belongings.

Kate McDermott, confused by her husband's lowering brow and Clay's open consternation, remained a lady to the bitter end.

'Oh, Eleanor, what a shame you have to run off so soon,' she said.

CHAPTER SIXTEEN

NOTE THE BULL NECK

Fritz Diehl was not content with simple success. To be satisfactory, his success must appear effortless. Over the years he had honed the image of a man born to control himself and everything that came into his orbit. This was the public Fritz Diehl. In private, he spent hours losing battle after battle with the forces of nature.

His neighbors in St. Louis were accustomed to the ghostly glow bathing his collection of African violets. Every amenity that money could buy had been lavished on those pots. Lighting, temperature and humidity were all ideal. Deadly chemicals were stockpiled to repel blight or mite.

But nothing worked. While humble enthusiasts with one growlight took prizes at the annual flower show, Diehl could not even mount a respectable entry. Without rhyme or reason his charges flourished, withered or, most cruelly of all, maintained a feeble status quo.

When the phone rang on Sunday, Diehl had just discovered that Little Miss Muffet was drooping. Still immersed in his pharmacopoeia, he lifted the receiver.

'Mr. Diehl, this is Captain Lemoine of the Massachusetts State Police,' a gruff voice announced. 'We met in Boston.'

When there was no response, the caller added impatiently: 'You remember, don't you?'

Diehl, feeling as if he had been caught in his

underwear, was busy transforming himself from one person into another.

'Of course I remember,' he managed to say. 'What can I do for you, Captain?'

A voice never tells the whole story. To the policeman sitting at Logan Airport, it sounded as if Diehl were being deliberately patronizing.

'For starters, you could tell me why you've been keeping quiet about your meeting with Whetmore the day he was murdered.'

But Diehl had prepared this answer over a week ago.

'I haven't been keeping quiet about it. It just wasn't important.'

Lemoine was stung, more by the tone of indifference than the actual words.

'Sure. I turn up at your breakfast table asking about Whetmore's movements, and it wasn't important.'

The sarcasm failed to ruffle Diehl. By this time he had hooked an ankle around a stool and dragged it to the potting bench. Unconsciously he was re-creating the atmospherics of his office at A&P. Seated at a desk with a phone to his ear, he became a vice-president again.

'You were asking about a murder at midnight,' he said reasonably. 'What does my seeing Whetmore in the middle of the afternoon have to do with that?'

'Scovil was the one who thought Whetmore was killed at midnight. Actually he was killed around six, and the body discovered at midnight.'

'Six o'clock!' Diehl whistled softly. 'I can see how that changes things. But you must have explained the timing after I left.'

135

Lemoine's brow creased. He recalled explaining the time discrepancy, he recalled dismissing Diehl from the breakfast table. But for the life of him, he could not pinpoint the order of these events.

'This has been public knowledge for over a week,' he said accusingly. 'Are you claiming this is the first you've heard of it?'

'A Boston murder doesn't get that much coverage here in St. Louis, and I came back a couple of hours after I saw you.'

Lemoine chuckled. 'Our little murder may not have gotten national attention before Thanksgiving, Mr. Diehl. But it's gotten plenty since. Or didn't you notice the TV clips of Mitch Scovil being hauled off in a squad car?'

'Oh, I saw them,' Diehl admitted readily. 'I even heard you released him. But Thanksgiving weekend in the airline business doesn't leave a lot of time for reading the fine print.'

Lemoine had no intention of being diverted.

'All right. For the sake of argument, let's say you haven't kept up with the story on Whetmore's killing. Suppose you tell me why you wanted to talk to him that afternoon.'

'He wanted to talk to me,' Diehl corrected mildly. 'I'd just parked when he came over and reminded me that we'd been at Bayou together. So we had the usual exchange. I asked him how he liked Sparrow, and he asked me how I liked St. Louis. And that was it.'

'Come on. You don't see the guy for years and suddenly he wants to pass the time of day. Didn't you think that was funny?'

Diehl was patience itself. 'It happens all the time with pilots. When they realize they can only fly for

136

another year or two, they start buddying up to every airline executive they can find. If you don't believe me, ask around.'

Captain Lemoine knew that Alan Whetmore had barely squeaked through his last physical, but there are two sides to every coin. If Diehl had been looking for somebody at Sparrow to corrupt, then Whetmore would have been a Grade A prospect.

Doggedly the captain plowed ahead. 'Where did Whetmore go when your talk broke up?'

'He headed into the parking lot and I assumed he was getting his car. But I went straight into the office and didn't see.'

'That's right, you said you were looking for Mrs. Gough.'

Diehl sounded bored. 'Yes, but she wasn't there. So I asked for Mitch, and the receptionist said he'd just left.'

Carefully, so as not to alarm his quarry, Lemoine maintained the same monotonous rhythm.

'You didn't bother asking for Batchelder?'

'I didn't have to. His door was open and I could see his empty office when I looked for Eleanor.'

Bingo! The only way Diehl could have seen through that doorway was by advancing into the conference room beyond the coffee table.

'Mr. Diehl, the wrench used to murder Alan Whetmore was lying on the coffee table in the conference room earlier that afternoon. Was it still there when you were in the room?'

The silence was so protracted it was painful.

'Mr. Diehl, I'm waiting for your answer.'

'I'm thinking,' Diehl said stubbornly.

Like policemen the world over, Captain Lemoine wanted the people he was interrogating to be

137

nervous, flustered, and speaking too quickly. But there was no hope of that with this clever bastard. He was too smooth and too careful.

On his part, Diehl realized that one word could suggest that the wrench had left the conference room with Mitch Scovil. It would also be a statement, admittedly self-serving, that he himself had not been near the weapon. He knew this, and he knew that Captain Lermoine knew it.

Neither man was surprised at the form of the answer.

'I'm sorry, Captain,' Diehl said perfunctorily. 'I've been trying to picture that table without any success. I have no idea what was on it.'

Lemoine had heard this evasion in many guises.

'How very convenient,' he observed.

Diehl's shrug was almost audible. 'Well, that's the way things are.'

'I'll want a signed statement from you. The boys in St. Louis can send a man over.'

'Unless you're in a hurry, that isn't necessary. I'll be on the East Coast this week, and I can stop by,' said Diehl, making it sound like any other business appointment.

This show of bravado was too much for Lemoine.

'See that you do!' he snarled.

★   ★   ★

In the world of corporate jostling the man who keeps his cool has won. But police investigators play a different game.

Fritz Diehl returned from lunch on Monday unaware that round two with Captain Lemoine had already begun.

'Mr. Merrick wanted to see you as soon as you got back,' his secretary said, causing Diehl's eyebrows to rise.

The president of Atlantic & Pacific knew that his days were numbered, but he did his best to forget that unpalatable fact. At policy meetings he had to face his would-be successors, but at all other times, he tried to ignore their existence. A tête-à-tête instigated by Wilfred Merrick was unheard of.

But curiosity was not enough to deflect Diehl from the rules of in-house fighting.

'I'll drop by his office after I've seen Ben,' he said casually, making it clear that he was not a flunky leaping to attention.

When he sauntered into the presidential suite half an hour later he expected to find irritation; instead he met uncharacteristic geniality.

'Have a seat,' Merrick invited with a flap of the hand. 'Glad you could make it.'

The unmistakable gleam of anticipation in those elderly blue eyes was enough to set off alarm bells. Outwardly composed, Fritz Diehl was all wariness as he sank into a chair.

'Something come up?' he inquired with minimal interest.

'We had an unexpected call from the police this morning. They want to go through some of our books.'

Merrick paused, relishing every word.

'Of course I could have made them go through a lot of red tape,' he continued. 'But why bother, I said. After all, if they've got good grounds, they can always get a subpoena.'

This was arrant nonsense. Standard procedure dictated that such a request be forwarded to the law department which, at the very least, demanded time-consuming compliance with every formality.

'But you just invited them right in,' said Diehl appreciatively.

'That's right,' said Merrick, enjoying himself. 'It's a shame you weren't around earlier. Did I mention that it's your disbursements that they're checking?'

Diehl nodded as if his approval had been solicited.

'I don't see how you could have done anything else, Will, not with that great Merrick tradition of cooperating with the law.'

Merrick winced. Two years ago, during a grand jury investigation, Merrick's nephew had abruptly left A&P to take up employment in Taiwan.

Nonetheless, Merrick was still convinced that he was going to witness Fritz Diehl's discomfiture.

'Of course this is all flow-back from that mess over at Sparrow. The police have found out that someone was bribing their people.' Merrick waggled his head solemnly. 'And that's not the kind of dirty play I'm prepared to condone.'

'If it's going to make the front page, who would?' Diehl asked, like a man miles removed from the storm center.

Fritz Diehl had been playing roles all his life. He was seething with suppressed fury at Merrick's futile vindictiveness. Didn't the old imbecile see he was no longer a contender? Diehl was still too young to realize that, after a certain age, a struggle doomed to defeat is preferable to no struggle at all. But not one sign of his rage was reflected in the polite, attentive expression he presented to the president of A&P.

140

Merrick, on the other hand, was incapable of sustaining any pretense. He had foolishly imagined his opponent would collapse after the first salvo was fired. As soon as a longer engagement threatened, he reverted to form.

'I'll be reporting this to the board,' he snapped. 'When the police are combing through our files, the directors have a right to know.'

'That'll be a big surprise for them.' Steepling his fingers beneath his chin, Diehl looked as if he were gently strolling down memory lane. 'Let's see, at the last board meeting you were sure Stevenson had inflated his profit reports. And two months ago Werner was supposed to be playing patty-cake with a supplier. So this time it has to be me or Duvalier. I'll bet the suspense is killing everybody.'

It was true that Merrick had been attacking his possible heirs at recent board meetings, but it infuriated him to hear a major felony equated to the misdemeanors of Stevenson and Werner.

With red spots mottling his corrugated cheeks, he shot back. 'We're not talking about penny-ante stuff anymore. We're talking about bribery and murder.'

Instantly, Merrick knew he had made a mistake. For months he had been trying to sell the picture of Fritz Diehl as an unscrupulous opportunist who wanted to go too far, too fast. Even a hint of shadowy payments in a deserted parking lot would flesh out that image. He should have stopped while he was ahead.

Fritz Diehl's affable smile emphasized the error. 'So that's your pitch, is it? That I'm the kind who runs around whipping out his six-shooter and going rooty-toot-toot? I think the board may want a little

141

more than your say-so on that.'

'You've been up to something,' Merrick insisted stubbornly. 'Otherwise the police wouldn't be rummaging through your books.'

'But they won't find anything. And you know what? The directors may not be crazy about your blind effort to land A&P with a stink.'

Merrick was beyond rational considerations.

'You wouldn't be so sure of yourself if you weren't safe here in St. Louis. I'll bet the Boston cops would pull you in just like Scovil.'

'Then they'll have their chance. I guess you've forgotten the bond dealers are meeting tomorrow.' Diehl had risen and was drifting toward the door when he added: 'You should try to stay on top of these things, Will, even if it is getting a little difficult for you.'

This solicitude for failing powers deprived Merrick of the last shred of restraint. His explosion of obscenity came, exactly as Diehl had intended, in time to be overheard by three witnesses in the reception room.

On the whole, Fritz Diehl had every right to be pleased with his own performance. He had not deviated by one hairbreadth from his normal behavior. But the encounters with Captain Lemoine and Wilfred Merrick had taken their toil.

At five o'clock, he paused to give his secretary last-minute instructions and to pick up tickets for the dinner flight to New York. Then, suitcase in hand, he was on his way when she hastily called him back.

Fritz Diehl, the man who never forgot anything, had left his briefcase on his desk.

142

CHAPTER SEVENTEEN

STORMY PETRELS

Monday was not a wonderful day at Sparrow, either. The CEO was back at the helm, trading had been resumed, and the usual flights were taking off. Unfortunately, too few people had noticed the colorless account of Mitch Scovil's release, Sparrow stock was stalled at a disappointing 29 7/8, and most of the work force was still reliving Pittsburgh.

For the first time since Sparrow's inception, Scovil flinched at the prospect of appearing in public.

'I'm scrubbing my trip to New York,' he announced. 'You'd better handle the bond dealers' meeting, Clay.'

Batchelder hesitated. He was uncomfortably aware that bond dealers were a long way from his usual responsibilities.

'Just your being there would prove the cops let you go,' he pointed out.

'And half of Wall Street would think I'm out on bail,' Scovil rejoined savagely, 'Look, it's just a couple of days, and you could knock off Islington, too. You wanted to see him about the new specs, anyway.'

'Hell, it's not the time, Mitch. But I'm no good at talking finances to the big-money men.'

Scovil's face cleared. 'Forget about that, Clay,' he urged. 'The important thing now is to make sure that everybody in New York knows that the police are finally moving in the right direction. And it's going to sound a lot more persuasive coming from you than from me.'

Batchelder was relieved at this change in emphasis.

'Now that I can do,' he promised.

Phoebe Fournier took one look at Joe Cleveland and braced herself.

'So nothing could possibly go wrong,' he greeted her.

She flushed, remembering her unequivocal assurances in the airplane hangar. 'All right, all right, things got out of hand.'

'That's one way of describing it.'

'It's not my fault if a couple of drunks went ape.'

'There are always drunks at Thanksgiving.'

'They don't always run around taking hostages.'

At this impasse, they both settled back on their heels and glared at each other. Joe, however, had barely begun his indictment.

'And what about the famous press release? I haven't heard anything about that.'

Here Phoebe felt she was on firmer ground. 'The release was never central,' she informed him. 'It was only an explanation for the public if they asked for one. But the main point of the exercise was to put pressure on Mitch. Now that he knows we can shut him down, he'll listen to reason.'

'You can forget that tune, Phoebe. Mitch has got bigger things to worry about.'

'Are you talking about the police goof on Friday? They let him go right away,' she countered. 'So that's all over.'

'Mitch came within an inch of being arrested for murder, and it could still happen. He has to concentrate on that,' said Joe. 'We've got to face facts. Pittsburgh was a washout.'

Phoebe was not ready to concede this point.

'I suppose you think you could manage things better,' she said.

'No, I wouldn't be any good at it. But we'd get a lot farther if you stopped trying to manipulate everybody.'

The word was a red flag.

'I am not manipulative!' she snapped.

'Oh yeah? You were going to use Alan Whetmore and he turned out to have ideas of his own. You were going to use Sparrow's passengers last Wednesday, and three of them broke ranks. You're always surprised when other people call their own shots. But worst of all is the way you keep trying to duck Alan Whetmore's murder. Has it occurred to you that if Mitch didn't kill him, someone else did?'

'Of course I realize that,' she said loftily. 'It's just not our problem.'

'Like hell it isn't. It means somebody around here has got an angle we don't even know about, and he's playing for keeps.'

While Phoebe searched for a rebuttal, Joe arrived at a conclusion.

'You know what your trouble is, Phoebe? You're great with numbers, but you're lousy with people.'

By the time they parted, Joe Cleveland had managed to unload a good deal of his dissatisfaction on Phoebe. There was no disputing some of his contentions. But she refused to admit that the biggest snarl in airline history had yielded no leverage whatsoever. She was still clinging to this comfort when an unkind fate brought Eleanor

145

Gough around the corner.

Mrs. Gough barely glanced at Phoebe. If any confirmation for Joe Cleveland's views were needed, here it was. Eleanor was the apostle of wholehearted devotion to Sparrow. Eleanor had borne the brunt of Wednesday's dislocation. By rights, she should have been foaming. Instead, she was going to pass without a glance.

It was unbelievable and, for Phoebe, intolerable.

'Eleanor!' she called out abruptly.

Mrs. Gough blinked in an effort to refocus her attention.

'Yes?'

Other concerns had not only taken priority over labor disaffection, they had apparently obliterated all memory of it.

'I suppose you've got plenty to say about Pittsburgh,' Phoebe suggested defiantly.

She was wrong.

'Wasn't that disgraceful?' Mrs. Gough murmured.

The remark could have been directed toward Sparrow employees or drunken sales engineers or an airport staff that cried: *Wolf!*

'It's disgraceful that we have to resort to that kind of action to get Mitch's attention.'

'Oh, do stop being so childish, Phoebe.'

There was a weary patience about this plea that was more offensive than any accusation.

'And since when is worrying about the future of Sparrow childish?'

'If it will make you feel better, I admit that Mitch should have taken the time to explain his plans to you.'

By now Phoebe was itching for a real fight.

'Look, we're not miffed because Mitch hasn't personally explained his wonderful plans to us. We want him to scrap them.'

Mrs. Gough swept on as if there had been no interruption. 'But when I finally got Mitch to a meeting, what did you do? You sprang Alan Whetmore on us. Then the meeting blew up, Alan got murdered, and Mitch had a lot of other problems. You have nobody but yourself to blame.'

'Oh yeah? You're forgetting that I never saw Alan's precious list. Why didn't you and Clay make Mitch read it beforehand? Or you could have just come to me. You wanted the whole thing to explode in our faces.'

'We didn't choose Alan Whetmore. He was your responsibility.'

Phoebe did not see it that way. 'It's not my fault he got himself murdered. And it's certainly no reason for us to sit by and let Mitch go ahead with plans that spell disaster.'

'You've done pretty well out of Mitch's judgment so far,' Mrs. Gough said acidly.

'But times have changed, and he isn't changing with them. He acts as if deregulation started last week.'

'Don't be ridiculous.'

'Oh yeah? Then why have you been complaining about Pittsburgh and Tom Reardon until you're blue in the face?'

Nobody enjoys having his inconsistencies shown up. Mrs. Gough's lips tightened. 'I do not necessarily agree with Mitch on every single detail.'

'Then why are you pretending he's Mitch the Infallible? And expecting us to swallow it?'

'There's such a thing as loyalty.'

147

'Loyalty?' Phoebe laughed mockingly. 'Why don't you show a little loyalty to us?'

'Now what are you talking about?'

'You're the one who developed the employee policy around here. You're the one who preaches team spirit.'

'And what's wrong with that?'

'A lot, if you think you're some kind of Lady Bountiful. None of it was a gift. We've worked our tails off while you've dangled the carrot of co-ownership.'

Phoebe had the satisfaction of seeing Mrs. Gough's eyes narrow.

'Even on a team somebody has to have the final say. Haven't you learned anything in the field, Phoebe?'

But now that Phoebe had found a crack in the facade, she was determined to split it wide open.

'Crap! That's just an excuse. You've made your pile, and you're not interested anymore.'

'That is simply absurd!' Mrs. Gough retorted.

'Do you think we don't notice what's going on? I was here from the start, remember? You and Fritz Diehl came up with a bunch of ideas. What's more, you were ready to fight it out with Mitch if it took months. That's how we got the profit-sharing plan and stock bonuses.'

Eleanor Gough was openly snarling. 'Is there supposed to be some point to what you're saying?'

'It proves I'm right,' said Phoebe, smashing away against her opponent. 'When was the last time you were interested enough to fight for anything? Hell, half the time you don't bother to sit in with Mitch and Clay. It doesn't matter to you if Sparrow goes under and takes thousands of us along. Why should

148

it? You know damn well you won't lose out.'

'How dare you? You're sitting on a lot of stock yourself.'

Now that she had drawn blood, Phoebe was zeroing in for the kill. 'But I still care about the others. That's where we're different. For five years you've been conning us into splitting a gut, and now you're opting out.'

'You miserable little brat. You have about as much idea of the real world as a baby. Why don't you stick to what you're good at and leave the grown-up decisions to—'

'To Mitch the Pope?' Phoebe cut in. 'Forget it, Eleanor. At least I try, which is more than can be said for you.'

'Sure you try,' raged Eleanor. 'While you were trying to wreck Sparrow last Wednesday, I was the one who pulled us through.'

'Housekeeping work!' Phoebe instantly riposted. 'That's how you put in your time while you're thinking about something else. You're willing to assign new recruits and, if there's an emergency, you'll fool around with refunds and new schedules. But when it comes to the gut decisions, you can't be bothered. I suppose you get your fill of that, building up your estate.'

Mrs. Gough had moved so close that she was almost spitting in Phoebe's face. 'It beats putting in time by making trouble.'

The more furious Eleanor became, the better Phoebe felt.

'You're the one who's been causing trouble. In fact, it's all your fault. Mitch has gotten used to handing down his edicts and having you lap them up. Now he expects the rest of us to roll over and

149

play dead. Well, it isn't going to work. We've got too much at stake.'

'Stop sounding like a soap opera! Mitch has more at stake than anyone. Sparrow means more than money to some of us.'

Phoebe smiled nastily.

'Sure, Mitch gets his kicks out of being the hotshot who walked all over the majors,' she admitted. 'That's why he's so rattled now. The going gets a little rough and—'

'You don't know what rough is,' Mrs. Gough scoffed. 'Until now you've been on to a sure thing. You may have given a lot. You got a lot, too. And in spite of your smoke screen about responsibility, that's what you're worried about. Your stock has been dropping and you're hysterical with fear. You don't have the stomach for a real risk.'

The counterattack threw Phoebe on the defensive.

'At least I'm reacting to cold hard facts. I'm not falling to pieces because of some fantasy about People Express and a takeover by A&P.'

'Takeovers happen in the real world.'

'They sure do, and sometimes they happen from inside,' said Phoebe, trying to regain the initiative. 'Maybe Mitch should stop worrying about Fritz Diehl. There are other ways he can lose Sparrow.'

But Mrs. Gough had recovered her composure. Stepping back a pace, she examined Phoebe dispassionately.

'Yes, but you couldn't even begin to count them, Phoebe,' she said, abandoning an exchange that no longer mattered to her.

CHAPTER EIGHTEEN

EXTREMELY LONG BILL

It was only natural that every airline in the country should be represented at the meeting of the National Association of Bond Dealers. Municipal bonds mean bigger and better airports, as well as improved water supplies and sewage systems. But before the money can be spent, it must be raised—which explained the attendance of another group.

'Today?' John Thatcher asked in pained surprise.

Miss Corsa was adamant. 'You're appearing on a discussion panel at two o'clock.'

Children are not the only ones who hope the day of reckoning will never come.

'I thought that wasn't for months,' grumbled Thatcher. 'At least I'm not spending two whole days listening to every mayor in the country. Who have we got covering the meetings?'

In spite of the best efforts of the program committee, those attending did not expect to gain much from the scheduled events. They came to make deals, broaden contacts, and exchange rumors.

'Mr. Bowman and Mr. Yetter are both already at the Hilton,' Miss Corsa said encouragingly.

And, indeed, the first person Thatcher saw when he emerged from the elevator was the Sloan's chief of research. Acquiring information was the breath of life to Bowman, a past master at sifting fact from fiction.

'Hello, John,' he called, 'I was just congratulating Diehl here on the last quarter's earnings. A&P is back in the black.'

Diehl's teeth gleamed. 'Glad you noticed,' he smiled. 'If you think that's good, just wait until next quarter. Most of the fat's been trimmed. *Finally*.'

His emphasis on the last word was unnecessary. The fat at A&P had been notorious for years.

As Bowman performed belated introductions, Thatcher studied Mitch Scovil's *bête noire* with interest. On the surface he looked like a thousand other executives. If he had ever been an exemplar of the youth culture at Sparrow, he had wisely shed that image.

Recalling Everett Gabler's assignment in Boston, Bowman nudged the conversation in a helpful direction. 'Now that Sparrow's stock is so weak, I suppose all the majors are taking a look at it.'

'Not us,' said Diehl pleasantly. 'We're doing too much reorganization to think about acquisitions.'

'Well, I'll bet somebody is. How often do you get the president of a hot prospect in the slammer?' Bowman asked with his usual gusto.

Diehl corrected him. 'They let Mitch go right away. It was probably some kind of mistake.'

The use of the first name had jogged Bowman's compendious memory. 'I forgot. You were with that bunch for a while.'

'That's right,' Diehl agreed.

Thatcher decided not to waste Bowman's efforts.

'But what you may not know, Walter, is that Diehl sold his stock to Jim Vandervoort.'

Fritz Diehl lifted an inquiring eyebrow.

'The Sloan handles the Vandervoort Trust,'

152

Thatcher explained.

'Oh, I see,' said Diehl. 'Of course I knew that Jim's estate went to his son. Then you probably know more about Sparrow these days than I do. I haven't had time to keep up.'

Walter Bowman nodded approval. What was past was past in his book.

'You've had your hands full in St. Louis,' he said.

But Thatcher decided to make one more cast. 'That stock has not been an unmixed blessing,' he observed.

'You couldn't expect Sparrow's early rate of growth to continue,' Diehl said reasonably.

Thatcher wanted more than generalities.

'No, but we didn't expect their employees to shut down the East Coast, either.'

Diehl guffawed. 'That's Phoebe for you. Never a dull moment when she's around.'

Smiling politely, Thatcher let Walter Bowman return to his real interest, the projected earnings at A&P.

Fritz Diehl was either genuinely indifferent to Sparrow or putting on a very good show. Naturally he was not volunteering the information that he had been on Sparrow premises the day of Alan Whetmore's murder. Thatcher could scarcely blame him for that. Anyone could see that Fritz Diehl was a very prudent young executive.

For the next hour and a half the corridors of the Hilton rang with the professional chitchat so dear to Walter Bowman. John Thatcher might just as well have been in another county. Immured in a small auditorium, he traded bromides with three other

153

men on the subject of Making America Competitive Again. This endeavor was not particularly taxing because Thatcher knew that by tomorrow nobody, including himself, would remember a single commonplace. The sole purpose of the exercise was to generate expensive transcripts which the bond dealers could sell to institutional libraries for dead storage.

With duty done, Thatcher sallied forth to freedom, ran smack into Clay Batchelder, and unwittingly created a social problem.

'God, that's right,' said Batchelder after two members of the crowd pouring into the corridor congratulated Thatcher on his performance. 'You were on some kind of symposium, weren't you? I meant to take it in.'

'I doubt if it would have interested you,' said Thatcher truthfully. 'It was mostly about the manufacturing sector. And of course Pulford got off his usual shots about agriculture.'

Batchelder did not pretend to be an habitué of these circles.

'Actually this sort of shindig isn't my bag,' he confessed. 'I'm just here to tell everybody that Mitch is out. But, with Gabler on the spot, you must already know.'

'Oh yes, Everett called me on Friday.'

'It was such lousy luck,' Batchelder lamented. 'An hour would have made all the difference.'

Thatcher thought he knew what they were talking about.

'The presence of the television crew was certainly unfortunate,' he said, suppressing Gabler's opinion about the insensate thirst for publicity.

'That's not what I mean. By an hour later, the
154

cops were finally on the right track. If poor Mitch had just been out of the way on Friday morning, the whole thing would have been cleared up by the time he got to the office.'

'Perhaps he should take up golf.'

Batchelder was in no mood for jokes. 'You know that they found fifty thousand bucks in Whetmore's secret safe deposit box?'

'I hadn't heard,' said Thatcher, instinctively scanning a host of possibilities.

'Someone was bribing him to cause trouble,' Batchelder continued. 'Whetmore deliberately staged it so that Mitch would refuse to budge and all hell would break loose.'

'That is certainly one interpretation,' said Thatcher, reserving judgment. 'But if Whetmore did take a bribe, then it will be important to find out who paid him.'

They had reached the limits of Batchelder's frankness.

'The cops aren't saying,' he muttered, looking elsewhere.

'. . . well, the talk around here is that it was Fritz Diehl,' reported Kyle Yetter.

Yetter and Walter Bowman were comparing notes when Thatcher ran into them.

'And I suppose Diehl's goal was to drive the stock down for a takeover?' he suggested.

'Actually there are two theories,' Bowman expanded. 'The first one is the takeover bit. But the other crowd says that it was to block Sparrow's expansion. They claim that A&P would go back in the red, at least temporarily, if a price war broke out. And profits are the only thing that will make

Diehl their next president.'

Thatcher frowned. 'Somehow this all sounds too convenient for Mitch Scovil. I wonder what the police think of this theory.'

It was a point of honor with Walter to mine some nuggets that had been overlooked by his colleagues.

'They're buying some of it,' he announced with a triumphant smile. 'Steve Werner from A&P tells me that the cops are going through Diehl's disbursements back in St. Louis. Of course, Steve's been trying to sink a knife into Diehl ever since he came aboard.'

Thatcher dismissed in-house rivalry. 'Tell me,' he asked, 'is everybody assuming that Diehl murdered Whetmore?'

'Well, they're all executives themselves and they don't often bash in brains for the good of the company,' said Walter with some contempt. 'Most of them would like to think the labor people up at Sparrow executed a traitor. Then there's the gang that really believes Mitch Scovil's PR. They say he goes with his emotions. He just saw red and began swinging. A few of them are sticking with Diehl, to keep things simple. But everybody agrees that the murder was an attempt to cover up the mess.'

Yetter was outraged. 'What a bunch!' he exploded.

'At least you aren't contemplating a credit accommodation for A&P,' said Thatcher, looking on the bright side.

'I wouldn't lend a penny to either one of them,' Yetter said roundly. 'Not until this is settled once and for all.'

Thatcher agreed that credit extensions were out of the question. 'Unfortunately that still leaves the

156

Trust Division with the baby.'

'How much of this junk are they stuck with?' Walter Bowman asked.

'Twenty percent of Sparrow,' Thatcher said crisply, 'and they can't get rid of it.'

Bowman produced the only consolation available. 'Well, the market's cooled off since Scovil's release. Sparrow didn't go anywhere today.'

Grateful for a staff that kept up with the market wherever they were, Thatcher wished his subordinates good hunting and made his way to the elevators. Down in the lobby, where tourists and traveling salesmen replaced bond dealers and municipal authorities, he spotted one familiar face. Fritz Diehl was also shaking the dust of the Hilton from his feet.

Thatcher raised a hand in greeting, but the gesture was not acknowledged. Diehl, his face set in lines of stone, straight-armed the revolving doors that led to the street. As he disappeared from sight, Thatcher realized he was not witnessing a departure.

It was a flight.

Fritz Diehl marched ten blocks at a furious pace, still bewildered by his experience at the Hilton. Shortly after leaving Bowman and Thatcher, he had begun to notice that conversations faltered and ranks closed whenever he appeared. An encounter with Clay Batchelder ten minutes before had been the final straw. Clay, visibly embarrassed, had uttered a few disjointed remarks, then remembered another appointment.

Steve Werner! The sudden idea made Diehl slow down and think. Werner had traveled east, too.

157

Had the S.O.B. done a real job on him? And if he had, how many people in New York thought Fritz Diehl had blood on his hands?

There was only one way to find out.

'Taxi!'

By nine o'clock that night Fritz Diehl was in his hotel room with a bottle. His tour of Wall Street had been a disaster. At two brokerage houses he had been told that the men he wished to see were out. At a third, a stranger had announced that A&P was being removed from the Buy List. At two investment banks he had been informed that now was not the time to make a move on Sparrow. When he disclaimed any such intention, his advisers simply smiled.

Fritz Diehl had taken too much punishment to risk more. He would have faced a firing squad sooner than enter one of the Hilton's bars after dinner at a crosstown hotel.

But solitary drinking affects different people in different ways. Some experience a warm glow and renewed confidence. Others plunge into self-pity and despair. For Fritz Diehl, three straight shots did nothing but leave a bad taste. Emptying his glass down the drain, he decided he had to know what he was up against.

Fortunately there was a way to find out, provided that Eleanor Gough was not working late. He wanted to talk to her in the privacy of her home.

She answered on the third ring.

'Eleanor? This is Fritz. For God's sake, what the hell is going on?'

He made no attempt to hide the strain he was under and she too skipped the niceties.

'Hello, Fritz,' she said slowly. 'I suppose I should have expected to hear from you.'

'Considering that I've had the police on my neck in St. Louis and everybody in New York thinks I'm a killer, you might expect me to be a little curious, yeah. Particularly when it's all coming out of the blue.'

The release of his frustration was providing all the warmth that alcohol had failed to achieve.

'Oh, Fritz, I'm so sorry. I thought by now you'd know.'

'Suppose you tell me,' he grated.

The length of the pause indicated that she was choosing her words with care.

'It was Alan Whetmore's safe deposit box. The police discovered that somebody paid him fifty thousand dollars two weeks before he was killed.'

'Go on,' he said grimly.

'Naturally that led them back to Alan's recent behavior at Sparrow. They seem to suspect he'd been paid to make trouble. So they've started to look at our competition. That must be why they've landed on you.'

As her voice trailed off, Diehl gave a bark of humorless laughter.

'Come on, Eleanor, who do you think you're kidding? I'm not your only competition, but the police aren't ransacking files at TWA and United.'

'I suppose it's because you know the setup at Sparrow,' she said with an effort.

Diehl sounded desperate. 'Eleanor, do you know what this is doing to me? We're not talking about my future at A&P. I'm a murder suspect. Don't I have a right to know why?'

Suddenly she capitulated. 'Mitch saw you,' she

said in a burst.

'Saw me doing what, for Christ's sake?' Diehl yelled.

'He saw you with Alan Whetmore in the parking lot. It looked as if you were getting a report from him.'

Diehl had always been afraid it would come down to this. 'Just tell me one thing,' he said dully. 'When did Mitch get this bright idea?'

'He said he got it right away and tried to contact you that night.'

Diehl began to see the outlines. 'Forget about what he says. When did Mitch take the world into his confidence?'

Mrs. Gough sighed. 'Last Friday. When the police picked him up.'

'I knew it was something like that! The minute the heat went on, Mitch looked for someone to throw to the wolves. You're lucky I was available, Eleanor. Otherwise it could have been you.'

'He only found out about the fifty thousand at the station. He couldn't be sure there was a payoff until then.'

'He thought he was wriggling out before,' Diehl countered. 'But he found out the police had built a strong case against him.'

Evasively she said: 'That kind of bribe would make anybody furious.'

'Furious? He was probably counting his blessings. Mitch screwed things up at Sparrow, then lost his head and bashed Whetmore. He was one damned lucky S.O.B. to have that money come to light.'

'Stop it! Stop it at once, Fritz!'

'You mean I shouldn't criticize my old friend

160

Mitch when he's trying to railroad me for something he did.'

Mrs. Gough was tired of being backed into corners.

'I mean I'm sick to death of both of you,' she decided. 'First, Mitch tried to make me agree that you're a murderer. Now you want me to say that *he* is.'

Diehl saw only an admission. 'Oh, great, he not only snows the police, he's going after you, too.'

'That's what you're trying to do, and I've had enough. I don't happen to think Mitch is a murderer, and I don't think you are, either. If you don't like it, you'll just have to lump it.'

Diehl was taken aback. 'But we're friends—' he began.

'It's been a one-way street long enough, buster! You and Mitch and Phoebe all go hell-bent after what you want. Then you expect me to tag along. Well, forget it. I'm tired of being pulled in all directions by the pack of you.'

'Now, wait a minute, Eleanor. Mitch is shafting me and I've got a right to be mad.'

'And that's where your rights end. Don't tell me what to do and think and feel. In a way, Phoebe's right. I've been ducking my responsibility. From now on, *I'm* going to decide what I want. Let's see how you all like that!'

Nonplussed, Diehl could only say: 'What does Phoebe have to do with this?'

'Oh, I've been a big disappointment to her, too,' Mrs. Gough said bitterly.

Fritz Diehl brushed this aside. 'Look, Eleanor, I don't know what the hell is the matter up there, but I'm not going to be a whipping boy for Mitch or

161

Phoebe. I've got enough on my plate already. I'll give you a call when I'm in Boston in a couple of days. Maybe you'll have simmered down by then.'

'Don't count on it!'

CHAPTER NINETEEN

READILY IDENTIFIED

In a bar at the Hilton, people were offering bets on Fritz Diehl's guilt. But, in the police cubbyhole at Logan Airport, Captain Lemoine was still studying the field.

'This was no dirt-simple killing,' he reasoned to the ceiling as he tilted back in his chair. 'Scovil didn't just blow his stack and swing on Whetmore the first chance he got. There's more to it than that.'

Ed Crawley liked the alternative. 'According to Scovil, it's Diehl who blew his stack.'

'Could be,' agreed Lemoine. 'But the boys in St. Louis haven't found a whisper of a fifty-thousand-dollar payoff in the A&P files. What's more, Diehl's basic story checks out. He does drop by regularly when he's in Boston to chat with the old-timers and take Mrs. Gough out to dinner.'

'So? That means he probably knew all about Sparrow's labor trouble.'

Lemoine scowled ferociously. 'That's not the point. Scovil was used to seeing Diehl shoot the breeze with someone around Sparrow. Suddenly it's so important he scrubs his schedule and starts

162

play-acting over at the main terminal. Why?'

'Scovil claims he wanted to pump Diehl.'

'Then how come he never got down to it? By the time I showed up at breakfast, the two of them had finished in the gym and were through eating. They'd been together for almost three hours. That whole rigmarole in the morning could have been a cover-up for what Scovil really did at Logan.'

Crawley never abandoned the obvious until he was forced to—which might have explained why he was now outranked by his old friend.

'You can't get away from the fifty thousand in the safe deposit box,' he argued.

'Oh yeah? That money was paid before Whetmore was named to the employee committee. How come he was worth so much then? And, even if Diehl was pulling a fast one, why should he kill Whetmore? It would make more sense if Scovil saw red after figuring out what was going on.'

'Unless Whetmore was trying to up the ante,' Ed pointed out. 'He could have threatened to blow the whistle unless he got a sweetener.'

This theory did not go far enough for Lemoine. 'Whetmore was in no position to go public about Diehl,' he said, then continued, 'but Whetmore could have been playing both ends against the middle. That's why I sent an accountant over to Whetmore's apartment.'

'Did he come up with anything?'

'Belliers says I can forget it. Whetmore didn't have anything out of the ordinary at all.'

Lemoine crushed his coffee cup in exasperation. 'No matter how you look at it, Whetmore was killed because of something going on in Sparrow. And we don't know that much about the company itself.

That's why we're stymied.'

'You could hand it over to the fraud section,' Crawley suggested.

'There may be a quicker way. The Sloan has had a guy living with the company books for over a week. I'll bet he knows plenty.'

The captain's subsequent instructions to Humphrey Belliers were brief and to the point.

'Look, if I go after Gabler, I'm a cop getting careful answers. But maybe you can cozy up to him as one accounting expert to another.'

Nature had blessed Belliers with a look of dewy-eyed innocence totally at variance with his character. 'Is that the dried-up little guy I saw with Phoebe Fournier?'

'That's right,' Lemoine said.

'Just lead me to him!'

The accidental encounter took place as soon as Everett arrived the following morning. Captain Lemoine withdrew, leaving his subordinate to pursue the acquaintance.

'They tell me you're going through the books,' Belliers began cleverly. 'I haven't done much corporate work, and I wouldn't know how to begin on a company that's as unusual as this one.'

Humphrey Belliers had known instinctively that there was no hope of expert-to-expert intimacy. But teacher-to-student was something else again.

Gabler took a happy breath and for ten minutes Belliers was instructed about Sparrow's peculiarities.

'And while the various stock programs have certain unusual features,' Gabler declaimed, 'I would have no hesitation in describing their

164

profit-sharing fund as the heart of their remuneration scheme. You know, of course, about their salary policy?'

'Tell me about it,' said Belliers encouragingly.

'There is a ban on wide differentials. Even the three partners take home relatively small salaries, with their real compensation coming from large slices of the profits. The philosophy is that everyone has a direct interest in the success of the company's operations.'

'Yes, I see that.'

Gabler frowned at the neophyte's too-ready concurrence. 'But this policy has built-in drawbacks when it comes to reinvestment. Scovil should have realized that major capital expenditures would alarm his employees. Ideally, he should have sold his proposal to them long before a crisis occurred.'

'That wouldn't have protected him against Whetmore's demands,' Belliers objected. 'They weren't about the California run.'

Gabler always had some nice distinction with which to prick his opponent's balloon.

'Only in one sense. Whetmore seized on the breakdown in communication to call for mandatory employee input. He never would have had that springboard if Scovil had displayed more foresight.'

So far Belliers had nothing to complain about. It never occurred to him there was any question of a quid pro quo. When Gabler interrupted his own lecture to ask about his companion's work, Belliers replied with vague generalities, little realizing that Gabler would require more.

'You say there is nothing in Whetmore's finances to raise questions?' Everett challenged.

'Well, nothing except the fifty K. And, if a
165

competitor slipped him one bribe, why should there be?'

Gabler's face tightened. 'That is mere speculation.'

'Supported by the evidence,' said Belliers, allowing himself to be drawn into specifics. 'Whetmore wasn't getting big sums from anywhere, and he was leading a pretty frugal life. Hell, I'm not talking about anything complicated like fancy tax shelters. He had one bank account. At the beginning of every month he deposited his pay check, and it was pretty near gone before the next one came along. Even his credit-card charges were almost nonexistent.'

Everett was still an instructor, but he was about to give a failing grade. 'I have now been working at Sparrow for over a week, and your picture of Alan Whetmore fails to accord with the view of his co-workers. They say he was a lavish spender with a flashy lifestyle.'

Belliers shrugged. 'He was probably just shooting a line,' he said, out of the depths of his experience.

By now Everett was itching to get his hands on the raw material.

'Then Whetmore was producing a remarkable amount of corroborative detail. In the face of this major discrepancy, surely you agree that further review is necessary. In fact,' he announced with magnificent effrontery, 'I would be extremely interested to see these records myself.'

The automatic refusal that sprang to the tip of Belliers's tongue was held in check by two considerations. First, it was his job to keep Gabler sweet.

Even more important, it would be a real pleasure to watch this old curmudgeon fall flat on his face.

An hour later Gabler was ensconced at Alan Whetmore's desk, surrounded by check stubs and bank statements. Humphrey Belliers was standing at the window, gazing down at the Back Bay and admiring the view. (In fact, he was looking above Gauthier College and, if Rupert Vernon prevailed, that view was doomed.)

The quiet had been undisturbed for fifteen minutes, and Belliers anticipated a confession of failure in short order.

'Aha!' Gabler exclaimed, his head still bent over his work.

Belliers swung around. 'What's that for?' he demanded irritably. 'There's nothing there.'

'Exactly. It's what isn't here that gives the game away.'

When Gabler finally looked up, Belliers gasped. He never would have believed that those faded blue eyes could sparkle so brightly.

'There are no checks drawn to cash,' Gabler intoned.

'Holy Christ!'

Humphrey Belliers was not as inexperienced as he had been pretending. He recognized the implications of Gabler's find immediately. Alan Whetmore's life had included a source of income that had never been funneled through his bank account.

'I've got to get back to headquarters right away. And I can't even give Greg Lemoine any order of magnitude,' he lamented. 'It will take weeks of legwork before we know whether we're talking

167

about five thousand or a hundred thousand.'

Gabler's mouth twitched, but his reply was as sedate as ever. 'I agree this should be reported immediately.'

Everett had found more than check stubs in Alan Whetmore's desk. He had also found the certificate of title for a car purchased from a Boston dealer. And there had been no car payments in Whetmore's modest array of monthly charges.

Other men might have walked away from temptation. Everett walked straight to Fine Foreign Cars, Ltd., on Commonwealth Avenue. Here they were not interested in the latest economy marvels from Yugoslavia or Korea. He had to stride past serried ranks of BMWs, Mercedes and Rolls-Royces to reach the office.

After asking for the manager, he flourished his credentials and burst into speech.

'I'm sure you've read about the death of Alan Whetmore and you will realize that his estate is in the process of being settled. I find that among the assets is an automobile purchased here in June, two years ago. It would be a great help if you could bring me up to date on the schedule of payments.'

'Certainly,' said Mr. Bronson, calling for a file.

As usual, every word that had fallen from Everett's lips was the naked truth. It was not his fault, he thought virtuously, if Mr. Bronson somehow concluded that the Sloan Guaranty Trust was handling Whetmore's estate.

When the file arrived, it triggered Bronson's memory.

'Oh yes, I remember this one. There aren't any payments on it. Mr. Whetmore paid for the Jaguar

168

with his previous car and twenty-five thousand dollars. He had recently moved to Boston, so his trade-in still had Nebraska plates. But everything was in order.'

'Splendid,' said Everett, unconcerned with motor-vehicle registration. 'I didn't realize that he'd written a check for the car.'

The manager cleared his throat. 'Actually he paid with cash. I'm not likely to forget.'

'Good Lord!'

'Well, it's still legal tender,' Bronson said apologetically.

As a banker, Everett was forced to agree. 'But that's a great deal to carry around. You must have been startled.'

'It was bigger than that. I think it's queer if they do anything but finance. A check, cash, what's the difference? Who plunks down twenty-five grand for a car?'

'What you say is very true. And I must thank you for your assistance. It's been a great help.'

Gabler thought they were through, but Bronson had different ideas.

'By the way, if the estate is selling the car, you might be pleasantly surprised at our offer. If anything, those Jags have appreciated. If you're looking for a sound investment, I always say you have to go a long way to beat...'

Like a good citizen, Everett stopped at the first public telephone booth to report to Captain Lemoine.

CHAPTER TWENTY

SEXES ALIKE

While Gabler waited for his call to go through, Mrs. Gough was nerving herself for an ordeal.

The decision to assert herself had, if anything, become firmer overnight. She could tolerate unreasonable appeals for sympathy, but Phoebe Fournier's accusation still rankled.

For two years, Eleanor Gough had been excluded from policy-making. Knowing how unsolicited suggestions would be received, she had deliberately refrained from a thoroughgoing analysis of Scovil's latest plan. But, the new Eleanor argued, expansion to California represented such a discontinuity in Sparrow's operations that Mitch ought to welcome as many critiques as he could get. Unlike her nagging about Pittsburgh's losses, this kind of opinion could be offered in the guise of admiration for the basic concept. And by the time they were done, she would have her foot in the door.

On this heartening note, Mrs. Gough polished off the day's chores and plunged into the files. By two-thirty, her face was drawn with shock, and she was no longer castigating herself or Mitch Scovil or even poor Clay. She was too intent on averting catastrophe.

But Mitch Scovil was nowhere to be found. When he finally appeared, an hour later, he was striding down the corridor as if he were in a race.

'Mitch,' she began, 'I've been looking for you. I want—'

He shook his head. 'It'll have to wait, Eleanor,' he said. 'I've got some important things to finish up.'

Before he could walk on, she planted herself in his path. She knew her adrenaline would never again be flowing at this rate.

'No, Mitch. Right now.'

Then she pivoted and marched into the executive quarters. After a brief hesitation he followed, frowning.

'Okay,' he said after closing the door. 'What's so bad that we can't talk outside? Don't tell me they've finally arrested Fritz?'

This was not an auspicious beginning, but Eleanor persevered. 'I've been going over our financials,' she said, rushing to put the first rocky moments behind them. 'The expansion, as proposed, could ruin us.'

His anxiety was dispelled at once.

'Is that all? My God, from the way you looked, I thought somebody had planted a bomb on one of our flights.'

Mrs. Gough had seated herself by Scovil's desk and was spreading out work sheets in a businesslike manner. 'This could be worse than a bomb,' she said tightly. 'I accepted the escalation in our debt burden, but I assumed that your final figures made provision for—'

'Why, Eleanor, you're scared,' he teased. 'I never figured you for one of our nervous Nellies.'

'Scared to death,' she admitted.

Scovil was still standing. He smiled down at her, and said: 'Let me give you a tip. No matter how scared you are, the big thing is not to let the troops see it.'

171

Doggedly she plowed ahead. 'We have to be realistic about the kind of competition we'll be facing. You're projecting a profitable run in the same period as Toronto. But we're not just filling a gap in service this time.'

'Damned right! We're leaving the minor leagues behind for good.' Perching on the corner of the desk, Scovil let the familiar phrases unroll. 'The thing is, Eleanor, we've got to expand or go under. A lot of people afraid to make the gut decisions don't realize that doing nothing is a decision, too.'

Grateful for any statement with which she could concur, Eleanor said: 'That's very true, Mitch. And I have no quarrel with the idea of expansion. It's how you go about it. For instance—'

'I knew I could count on you, Eleanor. Now, if ever, is the time to keep the faith.'

With a valedictory pat on her shoulder, Scovil rose as if they had ironed out their differences.

'We haven't even started, Mitch,' she said, without turning her head to follow his retreat. 'I said the trick in expansion is how you go about it.'

Reluctantly he came back several paces. 'You're not wondering why I haven't gone the acquisition route, are you?' he asked, heavily patient. 'I shouldn't have to explain to anyone in the business. Look what happened to People Express when they tried it. We'd end up mixing a union force with a nonunion force, and I'm too smart to make that mistake.'

'That wasn't the only mistake People made,' she said quickly. 'They didn't bother to consult their employees beforehand.'

This was too close to the bone for him.

'So what? The whole scheme was bound to fail.

172

Getting the employees to ratify it wouldn't have helped.'

'Perhaps,' she said, still determined to get them to numbers·instead of generalities. 'But the basic problem at People was overextension. For the past two years we've had enough cash reserves to cover any glitches. But once we lose that cushion, we could be overextended ourselves.'

'As if I didn't know that! California is going to need a lot of detail work, and that's where you come in. Remember, Eleanor, you're the one I always count on. And right now I need you to support me, not to start sniping at me.'

'But I *am* helping you. All I'm doing is warning you about some of the risks that you haven't insured against sufficiently. If you'll just look at my figures for the first six months' operation, you'll see that—'

Gently Scovil pushed back the proffered notes. 'I know all about the figures. It isn't as if I've got a lot of time to spare. I not only have to bring the Sloan up to scratch on the biggest deal Sparrow has ever made, I have to keep the police pointing away from all of us. C'mon, Eleanor, is it so much to ask you to stay off my back now?'

Instead of the pledge of allegiance he expected, he received an answer that confused him.

'That makes three times,' Eleanor said drearily.

'Three what, for Christ's sake?'

'I've asked you to talk numbers three times. And what have you done? You've told me to keep the faith, you've accused me of sniping, and you've used the police as an excuse. Mitch, are you afraid to talk numbers?'

'Now, wait a minute,' he flared. 'You know the

173

way we operate at Sparrow. Starting from scratch and getting where we are today was mostly a matter of faith. I wouldn't have gotten to first base if I stopped to analyze every little detail.'

Mrs. Gough's lips had compressed into a thin line. 'You didn't do it alone.'

Promptly misinterpreting her remark, he forced a smile. 'Always thinking of the employees, eh? Look, I'm not denying that the kids came up with some great cost-cutting ideas, but we're way beyond that stage.'

'I was . talking about your partners,' she corrected. 'I can remember nights that were nothing but analysis of every little detail. No matter whose idea we were talking about. It could have been yours, or mine . . . or Fritz's.'

Today, mentioning Fritz Diehl's contribution was deliberate.

'You want to talk about what Fritz has done for Sparrow?' Scovil demanded savagely. 'What about bribing Alan Whetmore?'

Eleanor swept on as if he had not spoken. 'I can even remember Jim Vandervoort advancing some criticisms.'

'We had to listen to Jim. He was our money man.'

'He didn't put in a cent more than anybody else. And,' she continued, forestalling his next remark, 'we didn't need his name after we got started.'

She was stopping up the holes, one by one.

'All right, all right. So we were a wonderful, merry team,' he snarled. 'That was a long time ago. Why bring it up now?'

'Because your plan needs some changes,' she said half desperately. 'For heaven's sake, Mitch, calm

174

down and realize I'm trying to help you.'

'That kind of help I can do without. And, for your information, every single item has been okayed by Clay.'

Mrs. Gough opened her mouth, then closed it. Idle recriminations were not on the agenda. She intended to make every painful minute as productive as possible.

'Clay's an expert on the aircraft market, and he's also a first-rate chief of operations. But financial projections aren't his specialty, so that's why he overlooked some inconsistencies in the profit-sharing. After all, you covered it in one short paragraph.'

'Oh, is that what this is all about?' He produced a wry grimace. 'Why the hell didn't you say so, and we could have settled this ten minutes ago.'

He finally circled the desk and sat down. With high hopes Mrs. Gough reached for the relevant document, only to have him lean back, his hands behind his neck.

'You see, Eleanor, if there's one thing I've learned in these last crazy five years, it's to take your jumps one at a time. We're right on the edge of the biggest one ever, and now's no time to rock the boat.'

As he seemed to be straying farther and farther from a balance sheet, she said crisply: 'California will require more people on the payroll. But you don't say anything about increased participation in either profit-sharing or stock purchasing.'

'Now we've got to keep this under our hat for the time being,' he said gravely. 'You see, we're not going to enlarge either plan. The new employees are going to be handled on a more rational basis.'

175

Mrs. Gough watched him in mounting consternation. 'My God, a minute ago you were saying a two-tier labor system was asking for trouble.'

'Well, it isn't going to be two-tier for long,' he reassured her. 'We'll never have a better time to phase out these programs. And once we've got California under our belt, I'll be thinking about a secondary stock offering. We certainly don't want that confused by the remnants of a lot of amateurism. Besides, there'll be more to come and...'

Scovil had almost forgotten that Mrs. Gough was on the other side of the desk. Lost in the pleasure of outlining his goals, he described an airline that not only embraced the United States, but covered the major international routes. Even then he was not done. He dreamily proceeded to innovative tie-ins with resorts and other ground facilities. But she was no longer listening.

He did not notice the lack of response until he had added the last flourish to his elaborate design. Suddenly snapping upright, he leaned across the desk and said:

'I know why you're looking that way, Eleanor. As usual you're letting yourself be overwhelmed by all the minor obstacles. You think Phoebe and her gang are going to raise hell and I should be worrying about that.'

'You don't have to worry about Phoebe, you have to worry about me,' she said with arctic clarity. 'Who the hell do you think you are, Mitch? Wrecking years of work without so much as a pretense of consultation? I will not sit still through one disastrous piece of mismanagement after

176

another.'

He was taken aback. 'I suppose it's been a shock, hearing about Sparrow's future all at once. But just because you're rattled is no reason to go wild.'

'Sparrow doesn't have a future the way you're going. You can't even handle California, let alone the world. The only realistic figures in this whole thing are equipment and hangar costs. Your income projections assume current ticket rates instead of price-war rates. And as for labor!' She sounded as if she were strangling. 'You're so far off the mark, it's pathetic. This great new rational approach makes no allowance for lowered productivity or middle-management salaries.'

Before she could continue her indictment, he pounced. 'Where have you been for the last five years? Sparrow has never—'

'Mitch, it's time you learned there's no such thing as a free lunch. And you'd better learn it fast or Sparrow will be dead on its feet within a year.'

Instinctively Scovil fell back on a tried-and-true technique. 'I thought I could rely on your loyalty,' he said, swallowing his annoyance.

'These days I'm putting my marbles on responsibility. A lot of mistakes have been made, and it's my duty to rectify them.'

The annoyance could no longer be contained.

'And since when have I made so many mistakes?' he asked sardonically.

'Oh, your mistakes aren't important,' she said, with a flick of the hand that reduced Mitchell Scovil to one of the crowd. 'I'm the one who ought to be shot. I've been spending my time protecting Sparrow from the wrong things. I honestly thought Alan Whetmore was a threat, but he was nothing compared to you.'

Scovil's jaw had set and he was gripping the edge of the desk. 'Would you spare me all your droning about duty and responsibility, Eleanor? And I can do without a lot of hot air about how you shoulder your burdens, too. You can forget them. I'm the one who's going to take care of Sparrow.'

'Over my dead body,' she said grimly. 'I don't know where you got this idea of yourself as the Red Baron winging his way through the clouds, but it's got to stop.'

'Whether you like it or not, I'm the CEO of this company,' he retorted. 'And where do you get off, trying to call the shots around here? Sparrow was your only chance at the big time. If we hadn't let you in on the ground floor, you'd still be back at Bayou.'

But a newfound calm had descended on Eleanor Gough. After all the hesitations and equivocations, the stark simplicity of being Mitch's adversary was a relief. In a subdued way, she was almost carefree.

'You didn't just let me in out of goodness of heart. You needed an FAA expert. For that matter, you still do.'

'I can go out and hire one tomorrow,' he said, probing for soft spots. 'They're a dime a dozen.'

She was more than ready for him.

'Everybody's replaceable,' she agreed. 'Including you, Mitch.'

White with rage, he lashed back. 'Oh, so that's what you're plotting, is it? You think you can get support from the board?'

'Don't be absurd,' she said mildly. 'They're all your men.'

'Well, at least you've got enough sense to see

178

that. Face it, Eleanor, there's no place you can go.'

Mrs. Gough could have been correcting a first-grader. 'Yes, there is. I can go to Phoebe.'

He stared at her for a moment, then burst into a contemptuous guffaw. 'That's a good one. I can see you enlisting under Phoebe's banner and becoming her trusty lieutenant. I give it twenty-four hours.'

'But then, your predictions haven't been a big success lately, have they?' she said indifferently as she scraped her rejected work sheets back into her folder.

Now that she was rising, it was Scovil who tried to prolong the discussion. 'We've been through a lot together, Eleanor,' he reminded her. 'You don't want to march out of here and do something silly just because your feelings are hurt.'

His gibes had fallen wide of their mark and so did his cajolery. Her hand was already on the knob when she replied.

'You know, Mitch, you're a bright boy in some ways,' she said judiciously. 'But you have as much business trying to go it alone as an amoeba.'

For a full five minutes after her departure, Scovil sat slumped in his chair, staring straight ahead. Fritz Diehl had stalked through that doorway after a shouting match whose echoes still haunted Sparrow. Jim Vandervoort had passed through it on his way to a fatal car smash. And now Eleanor, inspired by God knew what vagary, had joined them.

As usual, Mitch Scovil saw it all from one point of view.

'I've always been willing to work with them,' he muttered. 'They're the ones who keep leaving.'

CHAPTER TWENTY-ONE

HATCHING OUT

Meanwhile the police, primed by Everett Gabler, had begun fanning out over Boston. Alan Whetmore's address book gave them plenty to start with.

The woman behind the desk at the Orion Travel Agency did not have to send for records. 'Wasn't it awful?' she cried at the first mention of Whetmore's name. 'I could hardly believe it when I read the story.'

'He was a customer of yours?'

'We did all his work,' she said proudly. 'Alan took a trip every five or six weeks. He'd go as far as he could on Sparrow, and we'd ticket him from there.'

The officer's head came up alertly. Could Whetmore have been getting his funds out of town?

'Always to the same destination?'

'Oh no. He went to the in place of the season. It might be Acapulco or Vail or Sea Island.'

She was in her mid-thirites, and her eyes sparkled as she ran down the list. The agency, only two blocks from Whetmore's apartment, was small and seemed to specialize in inexpensive package tours. Alan Whetmore had brought some cachet to Orion Travel.

'And it was always a trip for two,' she continued. 'Alan certainly knew how to show a girl a good time.'

The hint of wistfulness was unmistakable.

180

Whatever this travel agent did after hours, it did not measure up.

'He must have been running a pretty big account here,' the officer reasoned. 'How did he pay?'

Again there was no need for research.

'He always paid in cash,' she said promptly. 'Alan didn't like to run up big bills. He even paid for the hotel in advance.'

The officer hated to puncture this anthem to the departed, but he felt obliged to query her tranquil acceptance.

'Didn't you think that was funny?'

'Oh no. It's great to see someone who's kicked the plastic habit.'

The restaurant on the waterfront was not yet open for business, but that was all to the good. The manager infinitely preferred to deal with the police while his clientele was absent.

'Of course I remember Captain Whetmore,' he said with dignity. 'He was one of our regulars. Maurice usually waited on him.'

Luckily Maurice was on lunch duty and had already arrived. When he was asked about Whetmore's habits, he put first things first.

'He was a good tipper. Of course I always made it a point to call him by name—he liked to be called Captain—and to give him good service. That impressed the lady with him.'

'Was it the same one all the time?'

Maurice shook his head. 'Oh no. In fact we rarely saw the same one twice.'

Asked about payment and size of bill, Maurice was informative. 'He always paid in cash and he never tried to save pennies.' His voice lowered.

'The wine was usually in the middle range.'

It was more difficult with one of the girlfriends.

'Yes, I went on a ski weekend to Vail with Alan,' she admitted readily. 'We had a wonderful time.'

She was obligingly forthcoming about her meeting with Whetmore—at a tanning salon—her relations with him, and even her disappointment when the calls ceased. But about payment she was blank.

'Well, I never paid attention to that,' she said indignantly. 'I don't think that would be very nice, do you?'

Mary Lou, the girl who worked at Kate McDermott's television station, had been more observant.

'I met him on Cape Cod over Labor Day,' she said, 'and then, out of the blue, he called up at the end of October. We had dinner once, and then I took him to a party at Kate's place. You know that Kate's married to the big boss over at Sparrow, don't you? I expect that's what Alan was really after, because that was it.'

'He never called again?'

She grinned cheerfully. 'That's right. But it wouldn't have done him any good. I got engaged the next week.'

'You didn't happen to notice how he paid for dinner?'

'Cash,' she said instantly. 'I remember thinking I'd never seen anybody carrying a roll like that. He should have had more sense.'

The story was the same everywhere. At many

establishments, Alan Whetmore was the last surviving cash customer.

'He gave us a lot of business,' the florist said. 'But even if he ordered over the phone, he dropped by later to pay up.'

The liquor store owner had even dropped hints.

'I told him I'd be happy to run an account,' the owner recalled. 'The less money I have in this place, the happier I am. But he said cash on the barrelhead was his motto. And you can't really argue with that.'

The mechanic who lovingly tended the Jaguar had been surprised to receive crisp, new bills for a set of Michelins.

'But it made a nice change from some of the deadbeats I deal with,' he growled.

After every interview there was a phoned report to Captain Lemoine complete with ballpark figure for Humphrey Belliers.

Finally the accountant looked up from his calculator.

'It isn't chicken feed, Greg,' he said. 'If these numbers are typical, we're talking sixty thousand at least since Whetmore's been in town. It could be double that.'

Lemoine was beginning to wish he had never heard of Sparrow Flyways. 'Did you get on to Nebraska?' he grunted.

'Yes, and Whetmore was normalcy itself out there. He ran up big bills, he juggled three credit cards and always ended up paying whopping interest charges, and'—Belliers, still wincing from Gabler's show of strength, underlined his final words—'and he drew checks to cash regularly.'

183

'When did the break come?'

'Two weeks after he hit Boston. That's when Whetmore canceled two credit cards and stopped getting his cash from the bank. It's also when he moved out of a cheap hotel and took that fancy apartment, to say nothing of buying the Jag.'

Lemoine was idly studying his notes of the last phone call. Now he crumpled them into a ball and pitched it in the general direction of the wastebasket.

'Okay, let's see what we've got,' he said wearily. 'Figuring in the safe deposit box, we're talking about a hundred, a hundred and fifty thousand in the last couple of years. That gives us a rough idea of the amount. The next question is, what did he do to get it?'

Belliers was a policeman first, an accountant second.

'Drugs,' he said reflexively.

'No way! I had the same idea at the beginning. I checked back through every job the guy ever held. He was clean all the way—and in places with fatter opportunities. On top of that, these Sparrow pilots never know what run they'll be on. We can forget drugs.'

'We can also scratch any sophisticated paper crime,' Belliers said disapprovingly. 'In that case, the money would have appeared as dividends from a dummy corporation or something.'

Lemoine stretched himself like a big, lazy tomcat. 'All right, scratch sophistication. There are still a lot of oldfashioned crooks around. I think Whetmore was one of them, working all by himself.'

'It's obvious, isn't it?' Belliers was tiring of the

184

game. 'One pretty stupid guy being paid off for a year and a half and never having trouble with the police? I'd vote for blackmail.'

'Just what I was thinking,' Lemoine said cozily. 'And it all started when Whetmore came to Boston.'

This was undeniable, but Belliers thought they were going too fast. 'That doesn't mean it has anything to do with the people at Sparrow.'

Lemoine cocked a challenging eyebrow.

'Like hell it doesn't!'

The police were not the only ones moving into high gear. Eleanor Gough was making up for lost time with a vengeance.

'W-wonderful,' Phoebe stammered, numbed by Eleanor's abrupt U-turn. 'What convinced you? ... I mean, after all this time...'

As her dazed response indicated, it was no longer glad, confident morning for Phoebe. Ever since rumors of bribery began circulating—and Mitch made absolutely sure they did—Sparrow's solidarity had been collapsing around her head. The nonmilitants, bleating in alarm, leaped to the conclusion that Phoebe had been duped. And, despite her heated protests, she was chagrined to find herself and her platform dismissed out of hand. Between wounded pride and frustration, she was already floundering.

Nevertheless, she tried to deal with Eleanor's bombshell. 'Tell me, what made you change your mind so radically?'

Instead of answering, Mrs. Gough consulted a scribbled pad. 'We're going to be operating on a very tight schedule. There's just enough time to file for a proxy fight.'

'A proxy fight?'

Phoebe had never expected to have her bluff called.

'Of course,' said Eleanor serenely. 'And the annual meeting won't wait. So the first thing is to get the lawyers on to this.'

Gulping, Phoebe could think of no immediate objection. 'I can ask Bryan,' she said unenthusistically. 'One of his friends is bound to do SEC work.'

'No.' The monosyllable was kind, but firm. 'We need a Wall Street firm that knows about the airline industry and specializes in proxy battles.'

Phoebe was flabbergasted to be on the receiving end of worldly wisdom from Eleanor Gough. 'Well, you're the one who's talking about time pressure,' she complained. 'How are we going to find somebody like that in a flash?'

'Oh, I have a few contacts,' said Eleanor, unconcerned. 'I'm expecting Tom Hilyard to call back any minute.'

Dimly Phoebe could recall that, in the early days of Sparrow, Mrs. Gough had spent a good deal of time with a Washington law firm. Phoebe had never known that Mrs. Gough had also been the telephonic voice of Bayou Airlines to Hilyard, Amory, and Smythe. So she was unprepared when Eleanor reported victory fifteen minutes later.

'I told Tom we were in a desperate hurry, so he got us an appointment for right after lunch. The twelve o'clock flight to New York will get us there in time. Will you have to trade shifts?'

With the sensation that she was being towed behind a speedboat, Phoebe found herself racing to consult Mavis, changing her clothes, and hurtling down to New York.

When they disembarked from their taxi in front of a towering skyscraper, Phoebe experienced some unfamiliar qualms. For years she had been proud of her ability to deal with the mighty. Before every quarterly report, she welcomed the outside auditor as one peer to another. When she was in charge of a field team, she sallied into banks without a tremor. But then she had been the embodiment of Sparrow Flyways. Now she was simply Phoebe Fournier.

Her sang-froid was never put to the test. From the moment that Chester Longley, senior partner, hailed Mrs. Gough as an old friend of Tom Hilyard, it was Eleanor who dominated the scene. Scrupulously she introduced Phoebe as the leader of the dissident employees.

'We think of ourselves as employee-shareholders,' Phoebe proclaimed.

As if she were simply rounding out this statement, Mrs. Gough continued smoothly: 'And Miss Fournier holds ten thousand shares herself.'

Longley glanced at Phoebe with more interest as he apologized for not having had time to do his homework on Sparrow. He was, he said, only familiar with the gossip on the Street, then proceeded to take away Phoebe's breath with the extent of his knowledge.

'When Tom told me this was about an inside fight, I was really surprised,' Longley admitted. 'With the stock sliding, everybody expected an outside takeover.'

'I know,' said Mrs. Gough.

'Some people even claimed that Fritz Diehl over

187

at A&P had engineered the trouble at Sparrow. Then, when Mitch Scovil was actually pulled in by the police, nobody knew what to think.'

Eleanor did not spring to the defense of either man. Instead she saw an opportunity.

'Good,' she said briskly. 'With any luck, all the uncertainty about what's going on and who might be arrested should make the raiders back off. If we win the proxy fight in the interim, we have a chance to bring the stock back to a stronger position.'

Rather sadly Longley accepted the fact that Mrs. Gough was not here to supply juicy details about Sparrow's crime wave. And, like all lawyers, he could not resist the chance to deflate a client's expectations.

'That's a damn big "if." You may be right about people backing off, but the proxy fight is something else again. You've got to realize that the odds are against you.'

'Of course,' she agreed quietly. 'But most people starting a proxy fight don't have forty percent of the stock already in their corner.'

'Scovil's got forty percent, too. And the institutional investors aren't going to get involved. They'll stand pat, and you may find your own support isn't as solid as you think.'

This was unthinkable to Phoebe. 'I can vouch for the employees,' she said with something of her old assurance.

Longley shook his head. 'Your people are willing to fight Scovil's policy, but that doesn't mean they're willing to dump him. And that applies even more to the small investors. They figured they were buying a piece of Mitch Scovil with their stock. They can't imagine Sparrow without him.'

Phoebe swallowed. It had taken most of the flight to New York to digest Eleanor Gough's astonishing assumption of leadership. Manhattan's skyline was already visible when Phoebe admitted that she had never expected things to go this far. She wanted a Mitch Scovil willing to confess the error of his ways, a Mitch Scovil no longer imperiling the safety of Sparrow. But she, too, could not imagine a Sparrow without him.

'He could always stay on as president,' she suggested.

'With a hostile board looking over his shoulder?' Longley snorted. 'Forget it!'

'Then maybe he'll come to his senses,' she faltered.

Mrs. Gough was dispassionate. 'I wouldn't bank on it,' she advised. 'I expect it will be a fight to the death.'

One of the wonders of this day of wonders was that Eleanor Gough did not share the general identification of Mitch Scovil with Sparrow. Fortunately Phoebe's bemusement was interrupted when Longley, having completed his formal warning, turned to the business at hand.

'I assume that you and Miss Fournier will be on the slate as inside directors. But some of the current outside directors are Scovil men, aren't they?'

Mrs. Gough agreed that they would have to be replaced and began to consider the claims of a well-known economist.

Phoebe, however, was lagging a step behind. 'Me? A director?'

'Naturally,' said Eleanor. 'Given our kind of horizontal management, it's absurd that we don't already have an employee on the board.'

189

'I never thought of myself as a director. What a title!'

'And what a salary!' Mrs. Gough said with amusement. 'Think about that, too.'

After this Phoebe had to enter into the spirit of things. By the time the ladies had descended to the lobby and Eleanor had stepped aside to make a telephone call, Phoebe was reconciled to the new era in her life and congratulating herself on the caliber of her two allies.

Mrs. Gough was all smiles when she returned. 'We're in luck,' she announced. 'John T Hatcher can give us a few minutes. Let's see, the Sloan is on Exchange Place, so it must be two blocks down there.'

Phoebe came to a dead halt. 'Now wait a minute! We just bought ourselves a high-powered lawyer who told us the institutional investors won't budge. Why did we hire him, if we aren't going to listen to him?'

'That's the same mistake you made the first time you met Thatcher,' Eleanor said reprovingly. 'The Sloan is not an investor. It's a trustee.'

John Thatcher had never lost sight of this distinction. It was the reason he had forced his secretary to squeeze twenty minutes from an already overcrowded docket. Miss Corsa deplored this cavalier imposition on his time, but she had not heard the latest bulletin from Everett Gabler. Now that blackmail had been added to the stew boiling away at Sparrow, Mrs. Gough's request for a meeting could be the harbinger of almost anything.

In spite of this open-minded attitude, Thatcher was surprised to learn that Eleanor was the new champion of the anti-Scovil forces.

190

'Considering the Sloan's very heavy position in Sparrow—and the rumors circulating on the Street—I thought it only right that you be informed before the official announcement of our SEC filing,' she said sedately.

Phoebe was still clinging to the only constant in a shifting world. 'That means forty percent now, with Eleanor's ten.'

Mrs. Gough's methods were not so crude. 'A great deal can happen between now and the annual meeting,' she acknowledged. 'No doubt some stockholders will change their minds and, of course, we hope that there will be a gain in our favor.'

'Naturally,' said Thatcher.

'It would be a help if the police resolve Alan Whetmore's murder, but we may not be that fortunate. In the meantime we'll be preparing a schedule of financial proposals which we'll send to you. Luckily Mr. Gabler will have completed his analysis by then.'

As she continued, Thatcher inspected his guests with burgeoning irritation. They looked as if they were in church. Did they know that a short forty-eight hours ago, both Clay Batchelder and Fritz Diehl had been adding fuel to Wall Street's speculations? Was Phoebe aware that a good deal more than numbers had changed? And most important, did Eleanor Gough realize that, at this very moment, Captain Lemoine was waiting to cross-examine her? Sitting there in an attractive jacket of some rosy purple tweed with a wide silk bow at her throat, she certainly did not seem an appropriate subject for blackmail. But then, Thatcher reminded himself, neither had the last blackmail victim to surface at the Sloan. For the

191

first time in his life he realized that an expression of ladylike attentiveness is the feminine equivalent of a poker face.

'I can certainly promise you that your material will receive very close consideration,' he said noncommittally when Mrs. Gough had finished.

A stranger would have counted three poker faces in the room.

'That's all we can ask,' she said, rising gracefully. 'We realize that institutional investors hesitate to become embroiled in an insider battle. Phoebe and I only hope that the force of our arguments may persuade you.'

Thatcher appreciated the tact with which Mrs. Gough had avoided telling him his business. She was simply making it impossible for him to forget the Sloan's anomalous position.

On the way to the airport, Phoebe felt honor-bound to bestow an accolade. 'You handled that beautifully. I couldn't have done it. You managed to remind him that the Sloan is a trustee without ever coming out and saying so.'

'We don't have to remind Thatcher of much. And he's the only one left who can pressure Mitch into backing down. Just in case you're still hoping for a peaceful solution.'

Eleanor ended on an inquiring note, and Phoebe flushed.

'I'd prefer not to tear Sparrow apart.'

Even to her own ears, this sentiment came poorly from the woman who had polarized Sparrow in the first place. Either Mrs. Gough was too generous to say so, or she was more interested in their meeting with Thatcher.

'Even if Thatcher doesn't oblige, the Sloan can still be very useful to us,' she said reflectively. 'I thought it was worthwhile to stop by, and I'm glad you agree now.'

'Actually I meant more than just your tactics,' Phoebe admitted. 'It's the way you handled both Longley and Thatcher. You went ahead and got exactly what you wanted. I didn't know you had it in you.'

'It's always been there. It just took a while to come out.'

Phoebe was making a discovery. 'You know what, Eleanor,' she said in tones of congratulation, 'you've become liberated.'

Mrs. Gough did not agree.

'Rich women have always been liberated,' she replied coolly. 'Some of them were born that way. The rest of us have to adjust. I've never had any reason to throw my weight around until now. But, if Sparrow is going to be maintained in a form we recognize, it's going to take every ounce we can muster.'

A hideous suspicion dawned on Phoebe. 'Is that why you told Longley about my ten thousand shares?'

'It certainly didn't hurt.'

But Phoebe was true to her generation. 'I earned those shares,' she said rebelliously. 'I didn't have them handed to me on a platter.'

Mrs. Gough, with one eye on the taxi meter, was fumbling in her purse for a billfold. Without looking up, she said:

'Chester Longley doesn't care.'

CHAPTER TWENTY-TWO

SECRETIVE HABITS

Back in Boston, Clay Batchelder wanted to move on to Don Islington's latest concessions. Scovil, however, continued to gnaw another bone.

'Where does Fritz get off?' he demanded. 'I have to lie low because of all the stinking publicity and I haven't done a damned thing. Meanwhile he gets to parade around as if he's Mr. Clean.'

'Take it easy, Mitch. The police are working on it.'

Scovil shook his head angrily. 'We haven't got all the time in the world. You saw what happened to the stock when Lemoine pulled me in.'

'It was just a blip.' Batchelder sounded as if he were trying to persuade himself more than Scovil.

'One more little blip like that and Fritz will have his opening.'

Batchelder was more optimistic. 'Fritz has plenty of problems of his own. He can't have much clout at A&P anymore.'

'I'd like to be sure of that. And what the hell are the police doing? For two weeks they've been all over the place. Now, when they could do some good, they disappear.'

'That's because they've quit concentrating on Sparrow,' Clay insisted. 'They're probably digging away at A&P.'

'Maybe so, but I'd like to see some action from Lemoine.'

The opportunity came sooner than Scovil expected.

After a final round of arithmetic by Humphrey Belliers, Captain Lemoine was back at Sparrow.

'We're going to send in the fraud squad and pull this place apart,' he announced.

'That's crazy,' Scovil retorted. 'I told you where Whetmore was getting his money.'

'For two years?' Lemoine asked ironically. 'Talk sense, Scovil. Whetmore had somebody around here by the short hairs.'

'Diehl was here two years ago. Maybe Whetmore had something on him.'

'Like what?'

Scovil was only sure of one thing. 'Whatever it was, it had nothing to do with Sparrow.'

'Like hell it didn't.' Lemoine hunched forward aggressively. 'That ploy by Whetmore at your meeting was pure extortion. He was on to something so good, he thought the sky was the limit.'

'Well, he didn't get it!'

'No,' Lemoine agreed softly, 'but somebody had to kill him to shut him up.'

For once, Scovil was silenced.

If Mitch was rocked, Clay was belligerent.

'Send your bloody accountants in,' he invited. 'We run a clean shop. You won't find a damned thing.'

'Oh yeah? I suppose somebody forked over a hundred and fifty thousand for the fun of it.'

This was the first time Clay had heard Belliers's final estimate. 'A hundred and fifty thou?' he repeated.

'Starting from two weeks after Whetmore got to

195

Sparrow,' Lemoine said remorselessly.

Batchelder's weakness had passed.

'So? We've got a whole mob of people working here. Maybe he recognized somebody who didn't want to be recognized. Maybe he saw somebody in Boston. It could be anyone.'

'You're forgetting one little detail. The killer could put his hands on a hell of a lot of money. That narrows the circle as far as I'm concerned.'

Batchelder's chin shot forward. 'We're not the richest guys in Boston.'

'Maybe not, but then Whetmore's price got too stiff for somebody, didn't it?'

Scovil and Batchelder had both been willing to lock horns with Captain Lemoine. Mrs. Gough was another proposition altogether. When she finally returned from New York, her thoughts were elsewhere.

'I've been waiting for you for hours,' Lemoine complained.

Mrs. Gough was laying down an attaché case. 'I had to go to New York,' she said unapologetically.

The captain was not feeling reasonable.

'You've been here steadily ever since Whetmore's murder. It's funny that you should go missing the minute we find the real motive.'

She was more pleased than alarmed by his disclosure.

'I always said suspecting Fritz was nonsense.'

Her complacency irritated Lemoine. 'It's a lot closer to home than that,' he said. 'Somebody around here has been blackmailed by Whetmore for two years.'

'Blackmail?' She considered this, then rejected it.

196

'That's absurd.'

And when Lemoine thundered the facts at her, she promptly counterattacked.

'What could possibly be a reason for blackmail at Sparrow?'

He lashed back: 'I don't know yet. But if Whetmore could find out, so can I.'

'You didn't know Alan Whetmore, Captain,' she replied, unimpressed. 'It's inconceivable that he unearthed any company secrets. Even if there were any, he was too stupid.'

'He was stupid enough to back a killer into a corner. There I'll go along with you.' Lemoine was almost yelling at her.

'Besides, we all know what's going on at Sparrow.'

'I wouldn't put it past the three of you to be in this together.'

She shrugged her shoulders with the same exasperating indifference. 'We're not that much of a team.'

'Okay, you're such an expert, you tell me,' he snarled. 'Come on, make a guess. What could there be that's worth that much hush money?'

Her eyes finally met his.

'Absolutely nothing,' she said flatly.

That was not the line they were taking in the employee cafeteria. There speculation was running rampant.

'But everything here is open to our inspection !'

'Inside the company,' said someone shrewdly. 'But what about outside?'

'Such as?' demanded a skeptic.

'Taxes!'

197

'Insider trading!'

'Supplier kickbacks!'

The chorus was a credit to their general knowledge more than anything else.

'Ah, use your heads,' the skeptic said disgustedly. 'Somebody murdered Alan Whetmore after paying him off in a big way. Why do all that if you could waltz down to the IRS and pay back taxes and a penalty?'

There was a brief silence, broken at last by a new, thoughtful voice. 'You're right. Those things wouldn't cause enough grief to be worth killing for. But I'll tell you one thing that would blow this place sky-high.'

Everyone looked expectant.

'What if there was monkey business with the profit-sharing plan?' asked the genius.

The silence was almost reverent.

'Oh, God, we'd be the ones committing murder,' someone said, awe-struck.

Norman Pitts wanted to get everything absolutely clear. 'You mean, if management was skimming a slice off the top?'

'You've got to admit that'd be something worth covering.'

But now the voices of reason made themselves heard.

'I don't believe they could get away with it. We keep an eagle eye on that fund.'

'And Alan Whetmore is supposed to have found out? Act your age. He couldn't even read the financial page.'

'It'd be too big a risk. Why should they do it?'

The genius went that one step too far. 'Suppose it was just one of them? Somebody with a fancy

198

lifestyle to keep up?'

There was instant protest.

'Come on, that's Mitch you're talking about.'

They were still arguing when Everett Gabler, at an adjoining table, quietly left the cafeteria.

Normally, after Captain Lemoine removed himself from Sparrow, the three partners would gather to plan a common defense. When Clay Batchelder appeared on schedule, Scovil realized he had to reveal the breach with Eleanor.

'What the hell can have gotten into her, Clay?' he asked for the third time. 'I think Eleanor's gone bananas. When she left, she was talking about joining Phoebe. If I weren't so fed up with her, I'd feel sorry for her.'

Like most men baffled by the intransigence of a woman, Mitch expected automatic support from his fellows. But Clay had no sympathy to spare.

'You two picked a beautiful time to square off with each other,' he said apathetically. 'Don't we have enough to worry about?'

'That's exactly what I told her,' Scovil replied. He was quartering the room, flinging his comments at Batchelder from every corner. 'Of course, she can't do any real harm. Phoebe doesn't need help to lob her grenades. What can Eleanor add?'

'Ten percent,' Batchelder grated.

Scovil paused in midstride. 'What?'

'Eleanor owns ten percent of the stock.'

'Well, of course, in a manner of speaking...'

Clay summoned the energy to bellow: 'No, Mitch! There's no manner of speaking about it. Her ten percent is counted just the same as yours or mine.'

199

Scovil did not really believe it. 'All right, all right. What difference does it make?'

'A lot. After all, Phoebe's been hinting about a proxy fight.'

Scovil brushed this away. 'That's not really Phoebe's style. She's just letting off steam.'

'Mabye so, but what bothers me is the Sloan's reaction. Thatcher won't make any decision until he sees the final report and Gabler doesn't seem to be in any hurry.'

'There are other banks.'

Clay Batchelder closed his eyes briefly. 'You think they don't read the papers, too? For God's sake, Mitch, Phoebe tied up half the air traffic in the country and your picture with the police made television. Do you suppose the Bank of Boston is going to fall over itself to get our business?'

'Then there's another way out. You said it yourself. The Sloan holds twenty percent. They back us and that more than evens things up.'

'I don't know.' Clay was dubious. 'There's a big difference between a temporary labor grievance and a management split.'

'So what?' Scovil said with undiminished confidence. 'I'll get Thatcher back here and really sell him.'

'God, I hope so. Just see to it that Eleanor doesn't give him an earful.'

Mitch Scovil had been so astonished by Mrs. Gough's defection that he had never considered the practical problems involved. Now he stood staring down at the bare surface of his desk as if there were words of wisdom inscribed on the walnut.

At last he came to a decision. 'I think you should talk to Eleanor, Clay.'

Batchelder gaped at him. It was received truth at Sparrow that Scovil was the one with the magic touch.

'Just what did you two fight about?' Clay asked suspiciously.

'How can you call it a fight?' Scovil temporized. 'I barely got a word in edgewise. You know what it's like when Eleanor gets all windy and uplifted. There was something about not working together.'

The atmospherics were familiar to Clay. When Mitch was revising history, getting the truth was like pulling teeth.

'Employee democracy again?' Clay hazarded.

'Not really. Oh, there was a passing reference, but there was a lot of yapping about shouldering responsibility.'

Clay tried again. 'Was it the Pittsburgh mess?' he said.

'Pittsburgh wasn't mentioned. She was so damned elevated I couldn't tell what she was talking about.' Carefully omitting all reference to California, Scovil retailed some of Mrs. Gough's more generalized statements.

Batchelder was looking more and more uneasy. 'Let me see if I've got this straight,' he said slowly, 'Eleanor made a big mistake, she got Sparrow into a mess, and now she's got to atone?'

'And her idea of how to do it is a real beaut! Splitting Sparrow apart!' For the first time Scovil noticed his partner's dismay. 'Now what have I said?'

'Nothing, nothing.' Hastily Batchelder changed the subject. 'You haven't given me a lot to work on with Eleanor.'

'God knows what'll do the trick. The way she's

201

going, I'm beginning to think she's reached the age when they all go flaky.'

'That could be it.'

Scovil wheeled.

'I was joking, Clay,' he said shortly. 'Why don't you try the old line about pulling together for the good of Sparrow?'

'From what you say, she's not so keen on team spirit right now.'

Like everyone who has passed the dirty work to someone else, Scovil was now brimming over with useful tips.

'Look, I know how you can get to her. For Chrissake, we've got the police back on our necks. Tell her this time they're going after both of us. Tell her they're accusing us of paying blackmail.'

Batchelder shook his head. 'She already knows, Mitch. Lemoine grilled her, too.'

'He did?'

'Why shouldn't he? Eleanor's got as much at stake as we have, and she's a rich woman.' Batchelder produced a wry smile. 'She's probably richer than I am. After all, her kids were off her hands when we started.'

Scovil blinked, then rapidly changed his argument. 'Then we're all in the same boat. We thought we'd gotten rid of Lemoine, and he's after us again. She's got to see that.'

'Sure, she just loved the way you fingered Fritz Diehl. If you ask me, that's probably what set her off.'

Batchelder was rising stiffly as if he had aged twenty years in a day.

'Maybe I'd better just play it by ear,' he suggested from the doorway. 'But, Mitch, don't

202

expect any miracles.'

After he had left, Scovil sat down to the task of organizing his thoughts. He had to establish some priorities. There was the Sloan Guaranty Trust and a potential proxy fight. But above all there was Eleanor Gough.

'Oh my God,' exclaimed Scovil, horrified. 'That can't be it.'

By six o'clock John Thatcher was announcing a decision to Charlie Trinkam.

'There really isn't much choice. I've received pressing invitations to Boston from Scovil, Everett, and Rupert Vernon.'

Charlie had no doubt who counted. 'What did Ev say?'

'He has not only finished his reveiw of the financials, he feels the police investigation is reaching a critical stage.'

'As soon as the cops stopped messing around with alibis and wrenches and started concentrating on money, Ev was bound to get interested,' Charlie observed.

Thatcher recalled Gabler's modest account of his triumph with Alan Whetmore's checkbook.

'More than that, I'm afraid. Everett has become a participant. In any event, he will be making considerable demands on my time. So, while I am at Sparrow . . .'

'While you're dealing with the gloom and doom, I'll be holding Rupert's hand. Good!' Charlie completed the sentence.

Trinkam was a complete professional who could handle any necessary chore, but he made no secret of his preferences. 'I like Rupert's style,' he continued. 'There's always plenty of action when he's around.'

Thatcher also valued Rupert Vernon.

'But you may be getting the short end of the stick, Charlie,' he murmured. 'Murder cases have been known to generate fireworks too.'

CHAPTER TWENTY-THREE

A MODEST FORAGER

The man John Thatcher listened to was Everett Gabler. This might be a humdrum fact of life for Charlie Trinkam, but Mrs. Gough regarded it as a rare opportunity. Her campaign began with lunch the next day.

Predictably, Gabler was still doing research of his own.

'I understand that you have broken with Scovil, but I'm not altogether sure why,' he said as soon as the salad arrived.

'The financials,' she said briefly. 'You've been examining them, too, so I don't have to explain my reaction.'

'You've left it until quite late, haven't you?'

Her apology came in the form of an explanation. 'Yes, but after Fritz Diehl left, Mitch began shouldering me aside, and I actually let him get away with it.' She smiled wanly. 'I thought, because Mitch and Clay had been executives, they must be the experts. When you consider how long I worked for so-called experts, that's pretty silly, isn't it?'

'That would depend on the people you worked for,' Gabler said cautiously.

She laughed aloud. 'I was personal assistant to the president at Bayou when old Mr. Perkins retired and Bill Johnson was promoted. Poor Bill! He couldn't run a corner gas station without help. I ended up doing his job and covering for him. You know the sort of thing I mean.'

Everett did, indeed. Currently, two overpaid incompetents at the Sloan were being kept afloat by their secretaries. He had always accepted the situation as a special dispensation from Providence, without wondering how it seemed to Mrs. Molineaux and Miss Teague.

'Yes,' he said minimally.

Fortunately Eleanor was more concerned with Sparrow than the Sloan.

'Has it ever occurred to you, Everett, how much you don't see when things are going well?' she asked philosophically. 'Mitch was freezing me out, he was alienating the employees, he was turning Clay into a yes-man, and I never noticed because Sparrow was leaping from one success to another.'

Gabler wondered if she were deluding herself. In Thatcher's account of the early days at Sparrow, Scovil and Batchelder had remained behind the scenes, while Jim Vandervoort and Fritz Diehl cast an Ivy League gloss over the partnership. Mrs. Eleanor Gough had not figured in those reminiscences. Of course, this could have been a distortion by Scovil's memory, rather than hers.

Ignoring such thoughts, he resorted to homily. 'Success is no excuse,' he said sternly.

Mrs. Gough had already learned this lesson. 'How right you are,' she agreed. 'I didn't wake up
205

until we ran into snags. Even then, all I did was try persuasion. It took me far too long to realize Mitch is incapable of effective action.'

She paused to sip her wine, waiting to see if Gabler would rise to the bait. Everett, however, seized on something else.

'By snags, I suppose you refer to the major carriers retaliating with price cuts?'

Somewhat disappointed, she began again. 'Yes, Pittsburgh was just a symptom. But Mitch was too stubborn to drop the route.'

'If it was symptomatic, then surely a similar battle would have to be fought elsewhere.'

'Under more favorable circumstances. We can afford to pick where we'll fight, and that should be where Sparrow has an advantage.'

Finally Gabler gave the response she wanted. 'That sounds like an elementary managerial decision. Why didn't Scovil make it?'

Mrs. Gough wanted to ensure that the Sloan understood not only what should be done, but who should do it. 'Mitch has been running in circles ever since People Express collapsed.'

Gabler knew there was more to it than that.

'Isn't he also worried about a takeover threat by A&P?'

'Oh, for heaven's sake,' Mrs. Gough said impatiently. 'Yes, Fritz Diehl said something like that—two years ago. I had forgotten the whole thing, and I'm willing to bet Fritz had, too. Then airlines began folding all over the place and Mitch remembered. That's why he sees Fritz's dark hand behind everything.'

Everett disapproved of runaway emotions. 'That sounds very close to paranoia,' he sniffed.

206

'Mitch isn't paranoid, he's schizophrenic,' she shot back.

'Oh?'

Mrs. Gough was not pulling her punches. 'He's promoted this image of himself as a lone wolf and now he really believes it. Actually Mitch was a lot happier when he had partners sharing the responsibility.'

Scovil's countless public appearances during the last two years flashed before Gabler's eye—television panels, Wall Street talks, magazine profiles.

'He certainly gives the impression of being happy with his lot.'

'Like me, he didn't feel it until recently,' Eleanor said tellingly. 'He's noticing now, all right. That's why he goes through the motions of conferring with Clay about everything.'

'And your defection must be adding to the tension in the office.'

Mrs. Gough was honest enough to admit that she had not been tested.

'Mitch still thinks I'll come around, so he's being very polite. Even under provocation.' Her lips twitched. 'This morning, when he asked me to take care of something, I told him to do it himself. And he even tried to smile.'

Gabler was not surprised at Mrs. Gough's malice. Turn-about, in corporations, is often more than fair play.

'And what does he think will bring you around?'

'He has two strings to his bow. First, he's got Clay Batchelder sweet-talking me. Poor Clay, he's more likely to drive me up a wall. Then there's the police investigation. At the moment we're all suspects. When that's over, Mitch expects things to be normal again.'

Her overview of Sparrow had inevitably arrived at murder. Quite soberly she continued:

'I don't think it's occurred to him that things could be even worse.'

Her realism made it possible for Everett to ask his next question.

'Does the blackmail theory seem sensible to you?'

The answer she had given Captain Lemoine would not do for Everett Gabler. 'Sometimes it does, and sometimes it doesn't,' she said slowly. 'There's been a lot of talk and you've probably heard most of it. But I know what's going on at Sparrow—and so do the employees and the outside auditors.'

Everett had encountered too many auditors mortified by the skulduggery that had eluded their inspection.

'So you think it's impossible?' he asked skeptically.

'Not impossible, but very difficult. Captain Lemoine may think that Alan was saying to Mitch: *Make me a director or I spill the beans.* But I don't believe it for a minute. First, Alan couldn't catch something that the rest of us missed. And Mitch may have his faults, but he doesn't steal from employees. Not now, and not five years ago.'

Unenthusiastically Gabler moved on to a broader arena.

'Everybody has a life outside the office.'

'True. Both my children have phoned to say the police are checking my background. But it's not as if we were three mysterious Cubans who created Sparrow to launder Mafia money. The way we

208

started Sparrow is history, and our lives are open books.'

Gabler, who believed in original sin, retreated.

'Yes, but your proxy fight has introduced a time dimension for Scovil,' he pointed out. 'He has to deal with it before the annual meeting.'

Mrs. Gough was ready to call a spade a spade. 'That's why Mitch wants John Thatcher here, and,' she continued with impeccable precision, 'it sure as hell is why I dragged you to lunch.'

It was, Everett acknowledged, a salient reminder. Before he could agree that the ball was now in John Thatcher's court, his companion's attention wandered.

'Good heavens,' she said, genuinely amused. 'So much for Mitch doing his share of the chores. He's shoveled it off onto Clay.'

Her glance was fixed over Gabler's right shoulder. Resisting the temptation to swivel, he asked: 'A luncheon obligation?'

'Something like that. Clay is towing around Alan Whetmore's brother, and it looks like heavy going. Do you mind if we ask them to join us?'

Clay Batchelder was visibly relieved as he came to rest by their table.

'We're only here for a drink,' he announced. 'Vince has an appointment in town.'

Mrs. Gough competently ran through the social niceties, ending with: 'We didn't expect you back in Boston so soon, Mr. Whetmore.'

'I wasn't planning on it,' Whetmore explained. 'But, when the police told me about Alan's fifty thousand, it was worthwhile getting a lawyer to start probate here. Maybe that sounds callous, but you don't know what it's like when money's tight.'

209

Eleanor Gough had been through this before, and she had no intention of letting Whetmore establish the rest of them as plutocrats.

'Don't be too sure of that,' she said cheerfully, then turned to explain to Gabler. 'Mr. Whetmore is a mailman back in Ohio, but he doesn't know that Clay's brother is a mailman, too.'

Vincent Whetmore shifted tactics.

'Of course I'm thinking of Mother,' he said virtuously. 'At her age she needs all the help she can get. I can't do as much as I'd like because I still have one in college, and you wouldn't believe what that costs.'

Although it had not been his intention, Whetmore had stumbled onto the one topic capable of uniting the group. Clay had been putting a son through college during the first lean year at Sparrow. Mrs. Gough still shuddered at the thought of tuition. By the time Vincent Whitmore had been given a resume of every cent spent by the Batchelder and Gough families for higher education, he was on the defensive.

'It would be great if there was more than just the fifty thousand.' Sheer disbelief took over. 'My God, Captain Lemoine told me Alan got through a hundred thousand in walking-around money. He must have stashed something.'

As a man who had reviewed Alan Whetmore's checkbook, Everett could speak with authority. 'Don't raise your hopes too high,' he said. 'Your brother seems to have regarded money as something to spend rather than to save. He did, however acquire at least one saleable asset. Perhaps you don't know about the car.'

'A car?' said Vincent Whetmore, in tones

conjuring up a rusted-out Ford Escort.

'A Jaguar. Fully paid for. What's more, I think I can give you the name of a man who'll be interested.'

Gabler never threw away business cards. This necessarily meant that he had to shuffle a sizeable deck before he came to Fine Foreign Imports.

'According to them, the car has appreciated since your brother's purchase. But I'm sure you will wish to obtain several offers before you make any decision,' he said, tactfully proffering advice.

When Vincent Whetmore left, he was still clutching the card, bemused by the form Alan's estate was assuming.

Clay Batchelder seized the opportunity to express his thanks. 'That was a help, Eleanor. It wasn't easy finding something to talk about.'

'You should have made Mitch do his own dirty work,' she told him. 'That's what I did, and it could become a habit.'

Clay grimaced. 'It wasn't the ideal time. Lemoine was practically accusing Mitch of murder when the victim's brother walked in on us. I'm too old-fashioned to suggest they go out to lunch together.'

She saw the difficulties.

'By the way, Eleanor,' Clay continued diffidently, 'Lemoine wants to go over our personal finances. I don't know how you feel about it, but Mitch told him to go to hell, said he wouldn't see a thing without a court order.'

Under Gabler's clinical scrutiny, Mrs. Gough flushed, but she never hesitated. 'Certainly not. I don't think Captain Lemoine—or anybody—should

211

be encouraged to go on unlimited fishing expeditions.'

CHAPTER TWENTY-FOUR

GROUND FEEDERS

When Everett Gabler left the luncheon table, he went directly to his hotel, where he found Thatcher and Charlie Trinkam unpacking. They both fastened on Mrs. Gough's rationale for deserting Scovil.

'If she were in politics,' Thatcher said, 'she would simply be following a great tradition. She'd be distancing herself from Mitch Scovil.'

'Before he gets sent up the river, you mean?' Charlie considered this prospect, then went beyond it. 'If that happens, she's sure positioning herself to grab the reins.'

'Yes,' Thatcher agreed. 'But what eludes me is whether she's doing it to ensure continuity for Sparrow or whether she's been waiting for the ideal moment.'

Charlie waved expansively. 'Well, Ev should know. He's just been pumping her.'

Gabler, however, shook his head. Women, in his opinion, were always incalculable. 'That's impossible for me to say. You have to realize that everybody was apprehensive about Sparrow long before Whetmore's murder.'

'That's a pretty shaky bunch there,' Charlie observed. 'One quiver in their P-E ratio and they start falling to pieces.'

'Their uneasiness has a more fundamental basis

212

than that,' Gabler pointed out. 'Sparrow is moving from one plateau to another. Each faction—whether it's Scovil or Miss Fournier or Eleanor Gough—claims to be the only one grasping this. Quite the contrary is true. They all realize what has happened. Where they differ is in their response.'

Thatcher could almost hear the earnest voices ringing in his ears.

'You're absolutely right, Everett,' he said. 'Scovil wants to transform Sparrow into a major carrier. Phoebe's solution, on the other hand, is to hunker down and weather the storm. What is Mrs. Gough proposing?'

'She didn't tell me.' Everett smiled thinly. 'I thought she might have been more forthcoming with you in New York.'

Thatcher recalled the scene in his office. 'Hardly. You see, she wasn't alone with me. My guess is that Phoebe Fournier is simply assuming they agree on the future of Sparrow, and Mrs. Gough is not rocking that boat until she has to.'

'She's a clever woman,' said Gabler, clearly with mixed emotions. 'At lunch she let Sparrow's record speak for itself in order to underline Scovil's shortcomings. Her theory is that he is unbalanced about Fritz Diehl.'

Charlie had always been the Sloan's expert on women. 'That settles it,' he said decisively. 'She's out to snatch the company.'

'Always assuming there's still a company to snatch.' Thatcher turned to Gabler. 'Don't keep us in suspense, Everett. What are your conclusions?'

Scrapping mountains of preliminary material, Gabler answered: 'Sparrow is in a precarious situation, and Scovil is the last man to be in charge.'

213

Charlie whistled. 'That's telling 'em, Ev!'

It never pays, thought Thatcher, to force a prolix man into brevity. 'Perhaps we should turn our attention to the background data for these views,' he murmured.

'Sparrow's financial position is intrinsically sound,' Gabler began. 'Naturally they face the problems associated with spectacular growth. They need to regroup and reorganize their operations. Their earnings will again be disappointing at the end of this quarter, but an executive willing to cut his losses could handle this.'

'That's scarcely as ominous as I expected from your resume,' Thatcher remarked.

If anything, Gabler was pleased. 'Wait! Scovil's plans for a transcontinental route include a fleet of new aircraft and executive-class service.'

'Phoebe doesn't think the public will buy the new image,' Thatcher remembered.

'They may not have the opportunity,' Gabler retorted. 'Before he starts, Scovil will deplete Sparrow's cash reserves and incur substantial interest charges.'

Charlie Trinkam was saddened. 'And I thought he was one of our boy geniuses.'

'He is neither.' Gabler always deprecated hyperbole. 'When deregulation came along, Scovil had the imagination to create a new kind of airline. But he seems unable to adjust to further changes.'

'You shouldn't be surprised at that, Charlie. It's the human condition,' Thatcher observed. 'All revolutionaries become conservatives in the end.'

Charlie always enjoyed the larger view. 'Okay,' he said amiably. 'So we need a Maoist to run Sparrow. Do we import him?'

214

Ignoring all distractions, Gabler forged ahead. 'Even more threatening is the absence of structure at Sparrow. Say what you will, the corporate form has provided American industry with useful guidelines.'

Charlie Trinkam could see the lecture coming. 'I remember hearing something about that,' he said vainly.

But there was no way to hold Everett down.

'Sparrow, with its horizontal management and its stock programs, has blurred the distinction between the stock-holders, labor, and management.'

'Come on,' Charlie objected. 'Lots of companies sell stock to their employees, and the unions are beginning to demand a voice in management.'

Gabler insisted Sparrow was quite different. 'This stock program represents more than a drop in the bucket. As Miss Fournier discovered, it amounts to thirty percent and can be voted as a block. Furthermore, these same young people routinely make management decisions and implement them without any consultation whatsoever. They do not know whether they are working for an hourly wage, a stock bonus, or capital gains. In fact,' he concluded, 'Sparrow has no guidelines and I doubt if it should be called an American corporation at all.'

'Very well, Everett, it can be a miserable mongrel,' Thatcher conceded, 'or anything else you please. The question is, does this hybrid form pose a danger?'

'In one sense it does. Almost nobody at Sparrow understands the accommodations that may be required. Scovil has surrounded himself with thousands of investor-managers. Yet he's incensed

215

when his policies are challenged. Even your Miss Fournier, John, has not assimilated the implications.'

From the tone of Gabler's voice every time he mentioned her, Thatcher had expected, sooner or later, to be held responsible for Phoebe's existence. 'She has some unusual accomplishments to her credit, Everett,' he said mildly.

'Possibly. But I have spoken with her at some length,' said Gabler, suggesting that no investigative stone had been left unturned. 'She signally fails to comprehend that she has been paid with the capital gains on what began as penny stock. She presents herself as a role model without ever wondering if such rewards are still available.'

'Fat chance!' Charlie said. 'The only way you get a return like that is by starting at zilch.'

Thatcher was less interested in truisms than in an earlier remark.

'You said almost nobody at Sparrow recognized the situation, Everett. Is there an exception?'

Gabler pursed his lips. 'Mrs. Gough admits that from the beginning, she had no idea how the system would develop. Her attitude has been that it should remain infinitely flexible. If that woman is to be believed, she is happy with perpetually fluid arrangements.' He did not conceal bewilderment. 'They say there really are people like that.'

'A lady Maoist,' said Charlie, pleased.

Thatcher, thinking of the neat silk bow and the rosy tweed jacket, was kindly. 'She's not exactly what you're visualizing, Charlie.'

But as he spoke, he was foreseeing that if, by any miracle, Mrs. Gough emerged victorious at Sparrow, the ideal person to deal with her would be

216

Charlie.

'Well, Everett,' Thatcher continued, 'you've told us about the financial and institutional land mines lying ahead. What about the criminal ones? Are the police still talking blackmail?'

'No evidence has emerged about any other source of under-the-table money for Whetmore.'

Charlie liked the sound of it. 'That's some mess they have at Sparrow. There isn't a single thing they've missed—murder, strikes, and now blackmail. And the cops have got to be thinking in terms of the three partners. Who else has that kind of cash to put in a brown paper bag?'

'There is no logical necessity for the culprit to be at Sparrow. There is all of Boston too,' Gabler said fair-mindedly.

'Where, according to you,' Charlie riposted, 'Whetmore spent all his spare time with third-rate models, not with millionaires.'

Thatcher pointed out that any policeman in his right mind would dispatch three conspicuous suspects before sifting through an entire city population.

'What bothers me is the underlying cause for blackmail. When it emerges, it could be devastating to Sparrow. Whetmore put a high price on what he knew, and somebody was willing to pay it.'

'It could be anything,' said Charlie cheerfully. 'Let's say that Whetmore recognizes Clay Batchelder as part of the gang that kidnapped Patty Hearst. Or he knows Scovil's marriage is bigamous, because there's a wife and four starving children in Seattle. Or Eleanor Gough's kids are by-blows of the Ayatollah. Or—'

'Thank you, Charlie,' Thatcher interrupted. 'In

217

summary, we seem to have storm clouds threatening Sparrow from every direction of the compass.'

Nature had never intended Everett Gabler for benign and sunny conditions.

'Very true,' he said with quiet satisfaction, 'and therefore I have a suggestion. In view of these circumstances, can the Sloan secure judicial relief from the prohibition against selling the stock?'

Thatcher always welcomed an occasion to show his talented staff that he was far ahead of them.

'Not without the support of the family—which is why I phoned Jim Vandervoort's widow yesterday.'

Everett nodded approvingly. The guardian of the juvenile beneficiary was the appropriate person to consult. 'Did she tell you how strongly her husband felt about Sparrow?'

'No, she didn't tell me anything. In fact, she could barely remember Vandervoort,' Thatcher reported. 'A year ago she became Mrs. Keith Rossiter. More important, two weeks ago she gave birth to triplets.'

Some men can be diverted by trivia; others are made of sterner stuff.

'So?' Gabler demanded.

Thatcher could have described the background noises he had encountered. There had been the clatter of falling objects, there had been questions and counterquestions, and—easily audible above the general din—there had been the piercing shrieks of dissatisfied infants.

'She says she isn't organized yet,' he said evasively.

'The poor girl is probably worn to a thread,' said Charlie with ready sympathy.

218

A reminiscent smile played over Thatcher's lips. Mrs. Rossiter had certainly sounded harried and distracted, but the predominant impression had been exultation.

'I wouldn't say that. But it comes to the same thing, because I have waived my claims to any of Mrs. Rossiter's attention for at least another month.'

'Why didn't you tell her this is essential?' Gabler persisted.

Charlie Trinkam now repaid the lecture on corporate function.

'And you call yourself a trust officer, Everett,' he said reproachfully.

'What does that have to do with it?'

'Trusts are created to facilitate the orderly transfer of property from one generation to the next,' Charlie intoned. 'If they closed the stock market tomorrow, we could still get along. The only absolute essential to our function is a next generation. Without that, where would we be?'

Gabler, who knew that Mrs. Rossiter's efforts could not possibly outweigh his own, glared. 'Do you realize that we have spent the better part of this last hour discussing three women?'

Charlie's mock applause was not intended as balm.

'And you never even noticed,' he said. 'I do believe that somebody has been raising your consciousness.'

'Tcha!' said Everett Gabler.

CHAPTER TWENTY-FIVE

INLAND HABITAT

Humphrey Belliers, who had been so scornful of Alan Whetmore, would have approved of Sparrow's partners. They believed in elaborate strategems for increasing income and lessening taxes. At the first threat of surveillance by Captain Lemoine, they all decided to heap complexity upon complexity.

The Batchelders had succeeded in life beyond their wildest dreams, and usually when Clay produced papers, Mrs. Batchelder silently reached for a pen. Today the act stirred memories.

'Didn't you shift everything around just a couple of months ago?' she asked suspiciously.

Batchelder realized that, for once, the federal government was going to be useful.

'Tax reform, Marjorie,' he said as if that explained everything.

Marjorie never admitted ignorance.

'Oh yes,' she said wisely. 'They talked about it on "Donahue."'

Kate McDermott was more knowledgeable. As she signed, she frowned at Mitch's explanation. 'A new depreciation schedule? You left it pretty late, didn't you? It's December.'

'Just some last-minute details,' he said, pocketing the papers.

Mrs. Gough did not have a spouse, but she did have a family.

Her son, an assistant museum curator in San Francisco, posed no problem.

'Sure, Mom,' he said incuriously.

As a taxpayer she smiled; as a mother she frowned. If Martin ever rose in his profession, he was going to discover that fund-raising was an art form too.

Her daughter in New Orleans was more troublesome. Jennifer had spent several years nursing a new mail-order business.

'But, Mother! I thought everybody wanted to get out of irrevocable trusts.'

'They can't. That's why they're called irrevocable,' her mother said in a tone that brooked no argument.

Fortunately Jennifer was not really interested. She had something else she wanted to talk about. 'Say, Mother, when we all get together at Christmas, I'm bringing someone along. Someone I want you to meet.'

Mrs. Gough had made it clear, years ago, that she was not interested in mere transients.

'Oh yes?' she said hopefully.

The subsequent conversation was protracted and personal.

It took Fritz Diehl over half an hour to get through.

'Eleanor? I was beginning to think your phone was out. I've been trying since two. Thanks a million for your tip yesterday.'

The lilt in his voice told its own story.

'I knew you could straighten things out with the police now that they're concentrating on blackmail, not bribery,' she said.

'I just signed a statement for Lemoine. He's

221

going to call off his dogs in St. Louis, which will make a nice change. How about having dinner with me?'

Mrs. Gough nodded to herself. In line with her new policy, she had plans for Diehl.

'I have a better idea, Fritz. Why don't you come out here?'

Phoebe Fournier was young, but four hours of Christmas shopping can flatten the strongest.

'Ouf!' she said when she returned home and collapsed into a chair.

The phone immediately rang.

She did not welcome Mrs. Gough's suggestion of a trek to the western suburbs. 'I just got in,' she protested.

'I think you'd better,' said Eleanor.

Ever since New York, Phoebe had accepted her role as junior partner. Eleanor was simply better qualified to deal with the world of Wall Street lawyers and proxy fights. But Phoebe was damned if she was going to be outstripped in stamina as well.

'Oh all right!'

Ten minutes after arriving in Newton, Massachusetts, Phoebe decided there was no end to the surprises about Mrs. Gough.

In the first place, there was the house itself. Gleaming hardwood floors, oriental rugs, a Hepplewhite library table—all proclaimed lavish expenditure. And a card table with its mahogany flap against the wall, the ample seating arrangements, and a brick barbecue glimpsed through a window suggested regular entertaining.

222

Eleanor, it seemed, did not creep home to a monastic cell when she left Sparrow.

Even more unexpected, however, were the occupants of the room.

Fritz Diehl, his jacket tossed aside, lounged on the sofa with his hands locked behind his neck. Eleanor was sitting at a grand piano, belting out jazz.

'Hi, Phoebe,' Diehl caroled. 'You a jazz buff?'

Phoebe, whose musical history began with 'The Yellow Submarine,' said that she was not.

'You don't know what you're missing,' he continued. 'I'll never forget the first time Eleanor took me and Libby to Basin Street right after I joined Bayou.'

Phoebe was slowly absorbing the fact that Eleanor and Diehl shared more than office camaraderie. How could this be? It was received truth at Sparrow that Mitch and Clay and Fritz had been as one with their employees. Ma Gough was den mother at best, and fussy schoolteacher at worst.

As Diehl beat time to the piano, Phoebe examined his receding hairline and did some arithmetic. Fritz was older than she had thought.

Mrs. Gough, who had deliberately staged this demonstration, decided that her point had been made. Leaving the piano, she opened a cabinet and dispensed hospitality, while Diehl continued to chat.

'I've been following your campaign, Phoebe,' he said. 'I liked your style in Pittsburgh.'

Phoebe grinned. 'You'd like anything that kept Sparrow away from California,' she replied.

'You'd better believe it. Keep up the good work.'

223

Mrs. Gough placed a glass in his hand and casually changed the subject. 'What a shame you had to come all the way to Boston to make your police statement. Although, of course, I'm delighted to see you.'

After a quick glance at her noncommittal expression, Diehl laughed.

'All right, Eleanor, I surrender,' he said ruefully. 'I heard a rumor that you're filing with the SEC. Satisfied?'

'I thought that might be it.'

Now that the cat was out of the bag, Diehl relaxed. 'When I left Sparrow I wondered if you'd ever really go to the mat with Mitch. Well, it took you long enough, but you're doing it with class.'

'And, as Phoebe just remarked, in a way that vitally affects your interests.'

Diehl nodded. 'If Sparrow goes to California, I'll lose my job. Of course, I may be out on my ear anyway.'

He did not receive a rush of womanly sympathy.

'Yes,' Eleanor said, settling herself midway between her guests, 'and you understand the position here, Fritz. If Phoebe and I lose this fight, we'll be out on our ears.'

This conclusion was axiomatic to Fritz Diehl, but not to Phoebe.

'What makes you think that?' she gasped.

Eleanor regarded her sternly. 'Why do you think Mitch hasn't already fired you? He doesn't want to force the issue. But once we do exactly that, he has nothing more to fear. And there won't be any place for us at Sparrow.'

This explanation should not have been necessary. But Phoebe had lived so long with special privileges

224

that she had forgotten pink slips. Suddenly hereditary fears surfaced. Where could she find another job like this one? What employer would provide scope for her talents? Could she be blacklisted?

'In fact, Fritz,' Mrs. Gough said decisively, 'if the proxy fight goes against us, and we want to perpetuate the principles of Sparrow, we'll have to found another airline.'

Phoebe could only goggle. Fritz Diehl, however, burst into a loud guffaw.

'You've come a long way, baby,' he quoted merrily.

Unmoved, Mrs. Gough continued her Napoleonic tactics.

'And, if things go sour at A&P, you might do worse than join us.'

'I've got to hand it to you, Eleanor. This is the last thing I expected.' Suddenly he sobered. 'But if I can go to the top at A&P, I'm staying.'

Mrs. Gough nodded. 'If we can go to the top at Sparrow, we're staying,' she rejoined. 'And I'm not denying that the difficulties would be greater now than five years ago.'

She knew her man. When other people saw problems, Fritz Diehl instinctively searched for solutions.

'What do you mean? Sure the competition's tougher, but remember the trouble we had raising the seed money. This would be a piece of cake. And we've got a proven track record.'

It was no part of Eleanor's plan to disagree. 'I was thinking in terms of available routes. On the other hand, there are possibilities in the Northwest that haven't been exploited.'

In spite of herself, Phoebe joined the game.

'And we'd have a head start on key employees. I know Joe Cleveland is itching to head his own shop.'

'If Mitch starts swinging an ax, you could pick and choose,' Diehl remarked. 'But you'd still need an equipment man. Were you thinking of Clay?'

Eleanor now sounded more like a reluctant follower than an instigator. 'I hardly think that's possible. Clay is standing behind Mitch every inch of the way. In fact, that's why I invited Don Islington to join us for a drink.'

Diehl eyed his hostess appreciatively. 'Got any other tricks up your sleeve?' he inquired.

Bit by bit, Phoebe was catching up. 'Islington is the one who's trying to unload that overpriced fleet on Mitch,' she said. 'Why should he come out here?'

'Because aircraft sales are slow. He'll be affected by what we do, too,' Eleanor explained absently.

An hour later Fritz Diehl was expanding on this topic to Islington.

'It's a funny situation, Don,' he mused. 'If Sparrow goes to California, I'll be unemployed and you'll be on velvet. But if Eleanor and Phoebe squash the deal, then you're the one in trouble.'

'That's why I've got a real interest in how things turn out.' Islington looked expectantly at Eleanor.

She did not give him a satisfactory answer. 'It's too early to say. California may not be out of the question. Our main goal is to rationalize Sparrow's operation. The only firm decision is termination of the Pittsburgh route.'

Islington waved Pittsburgh aside.

'What I'm interested in is your schedule. If you

folks are going to horse around for months, it's not going to do me much good. My people are just about ready to scratch the possibility of this deal, and when they do that, they'll probably scratch me, too.'

Mrs. Gough cocked her head. 'I hadn't realized you were that close to the edge,' she said untruthfully. 'If we can't be any help with the sale, I suppose we might help in a different direction.'

'There isn't anything else that's going to help.'

Blandly she swept on. 'This will be public information in twenty-four hours anyway,' she began as if just reaching a decision. 'Phoebe and I are filing for a proxy fight with Mitch.'

'There's been talk,' Islington admitted as he drained his glass.

Mrs. Gough rose and began to fix him another drink. Her subsequent remarks were tantalizingly dropped as she busied herself with bottles and ice.

'The fight could go either way,' she announced, reawakening Phoebe's misgivings. 'If we get bounced, we'll be starting up on our own and we'll be looking for an equipment man.'

Islington could hardly believe his ears. Involuntarily he looked at Fritz Diehl.

But Fritz shook his head, smiling gently. 'I just heard myself. Aren't they something?' he asked with ironic admiration.

Don Islington clearly did not share this sentiment, but he confined himself to his own predicament. 'Even supposing you get this thing off the ground, you'd never pay me the kind of money I'm making now.'

Executive relocation calls for tact, but it calls for realism as well. Fritz Diehl decided to make

227

amends for his earlier withdrawal.

'Will anybody?' he asked baldly. 'Like you said, no one's buying airplanes.'

Islington swallowed. 'Probably not. So I take a cut in income. I don't say I'm crazy about it, but at least it's not pie in the sky. Hell, if I have to, I can go into business for myself as a consultant. With new airfleets costing a small national budget, every line in the world is going to need equipment counseling.'

The art of persuasion does not lie in forcing people to the wall.

'You can always get by, you have a good many options,' Eleanor said soothingly. 'But most of them don't lead to anything bigger. Actually I wasn't talking about hiring an executive. I was talking about finding a partner.'

Islington recoiled. 'You mean you're looking for an investor? No way! I'd have to be out of my mind.'

'Thanks, Don,' Fritz said cheerfully. 'For that frank appraisal of what we did when we started Sparrow.'

'You were a bunch of kids without responsibilities.'

'Like hell!' Diehl retorted. 'I had two children at the time.'

'So you had some babies,' Islington said dismissively. 'That's different from me. I've got kids who go to orthodontists and drive their own cars. You think I'm going to scrub my salary, throw away my savings, and hope for a miracle? Forget it!'

Phoebe was drinking in every word. Until today she had believed that success like Sparrow's was due to inspiration, intelligence, and dedication.

Miracles should have nothing to do with it. Fritz Diehl and Don Islington were both mirroring astonishment at the audacity of Mrs. Gough's proposal. And Phoebe had a sneaking suspicion that they were the voices of prudence—which led to the most disconcerting insight of the day.

Eleanor Gough was willing to gamble recklessly when she saw something she wanted.

CHAPTER TWENTY-SIX

PREFERS COASTAL WATERS

For all Americans, December involves a shopping blitzkrieg and the end of the tax year. Breadwinners face something else as well. Like it or not, Sparrow Flyways was saddled with its annual Christmas party. This year there were no triumphs to report, and employee morale was at a record low. To make matters worse, formal notification of Mrs. Gough's proxy battle had reached Mitch Scovil that very morning. With prospects like these, everybody would have liked to cancel. Instead, they rushed around, looking for dilution.

Mitch Scovil ran into Fritz Diehl on State Street. Midway through an awkward apology for his misguided accusations, Mitch suddenly saw a way in which Diehl could be useful.

'Oh, come on, Fritz,' he urged. 'To show there's no hard feeling. It'll be like old times.'

Diehl, who recognized the motives for this invitation, smiled enigmatically. 'When you put it like that, how can I refuse?'

229

Relieved, Scovil punched him in the upper arm. 'Great!'

'To show there are no hard feelings,' Diehl murmured.

Eleanor Gough also realized that outsiders might be what she needed that evening.

'Just the men I'm looking for,' she announced, when she came across Everett Gabler conferring with Humphrey Belliers.

Police accountants rarely receive invitations in the course of their duties. Humphrey blinked, then accepted immediately. Gabler, an old hand at company hospitality, agreed on the condition that John Thatcher had not made previous plans for him.

'Well, that's blown it,' Thatcher said philosophically when he heard. 'I told Batchelder we'd come if you hadn't made other plans. He was so pressing, they must want every neutral body they can find.'

Needless to say, this reading of the situation did not encourage optimism. When they returned to their hotel at the end of the workday, Thatcher headed firmly for the bar.

'If we are attending the social donnybrook of the year, I need all the fortification I can get,' he said.

He was not the only prospective guest whose thoughts had taken this direction. No sooner had they passed through the archway than Fritz Diehl waved them over to his table and explained that he, too, was attending the festivities.

'It may be better than we expect,' he declared happily. 'The way things are going, somebody may clobber Mitch.'

Gabler was not prepared to encourage fisticuffs.

'Even if such an eventuality occurs,' he said stiffly, 'we will be long gone by then.'

Thatcher was with him every inch of the way.

'Courtesy may require us to put in an appearance,' he reasoned, 'but we can circulate a modest length of time and then discreetly leave.'

Diehl's spirits were rising higher and higher. 'You mean the bastards didn't tell you where the party is?'

Gabler, an ascetic in private life, was accustomed to the perquisites of visiting firemen.

'What difference does that make? They're sending a car for us.'

Diehl was now grinning broadly. 'Not exactly. The car only takes you to the pier.'

'The pier?'

'Then you board a harbor cruiser and take to the sea. The idea is to spend the evening dining and dancing and admiring the city lights.'

Gabler stared at him in stark disbelief.

'In the middle of December!'

'The kids always love it,' Diehl assured him solemnly.

This was no recommendation to Everett. 'So we can look forward to an interminable evening of pitching decks and open dissension. What else, for heaven's sake?' he snorted.

'Quite a lot,' said Thatcher. 'If the radio in the cab was accurate, you can include falling temperature, gale winds, and driving sleet.'

Thatcher's words were not wasted on his companions. When they foregathered in the lobby to await their driver, Fritz Diehl was dashing in a cossack hat and fur mittens, while Gabler had

231

supplemented his gray overcoat with buckled galoshes and a scarf of conspicuous length and brilliance.

'Princeton colors, Everett?' Thatcher inquired after absorbing the orange and black.

Gabler, a loyal son of Haverford, was not abashed. 'The shop had a limited selection and, this evening, I feel that warmth outweighs other considerations.'

Any fears that Gabler might be a sartorial eyesore were laid to rest when their limousine deposited them. The young people mounting the gangplank had enveloped themselves with enough winter gear to scale Mount Everest. There were down parkas and après-ski boots, foam-thickened gloves, and knit headwear of all descriptions.

The red pom-pom bouncing along in front of Thatcher suddenly swiveled to reveal Phoebe Fournier.

'Oh, Mr. Thatcher, I'm so glad you're going to be here,' she cried with unmistakable sincerity.

Things must be bad indeed, Thatcher reflected, when even Phoebe was daunted by the prospect of a Sparrow gala.

'We're looking forward to it,' he replied without a quaver.

A moment later he was regretting his powers of dissimulation.

'I'll tell you what,' she caroled over her shoulder as she passed on to the deck, 'I'll save you a dance.'

To a man of Thatcher's generation there was only one reply when a pretty girl offered a space on her crowded card.

'Splendid,' he boomed, inwardly resolved to flee whenever she was in the offing.

The beginning of the evening, however, proved painless even by Gabler's exacting standards. The cocktail hour was brief and without peril. Although hard liquor was available in the usual serried ranks, the drink of choice with the young people seemed to be an innocuous wine cooler, and they were more than ready to charge the dining room as soon as the doors were flung open.

Conviviality at dinner was encouraged by the use of small tables. Thatcher and Gabler were sitting with Clay Batchelder. He was not an accomplished host but his deficiencies were offset by the warmth of another old acquaintance.

'Hi, Mr. Thatcher,' said Joe Cleveland. 'This is a lot better than our last meeting, isn't it?'

When Batchelder had difficulty getting the party going, Joe swam smoothly into action with an explanation of the Chinese waiters.

'It all goes back to the first Christmas at Sparrow,' he said. 'Mitch wanted to have some kind of celebration before the holiday rush, but I guess he was pretty broke. So he took all twenty-five of them to the local Chinese hash house for chow mein. Now we get catered by the ritziest gourmet restaurant in Boston. Here, try some of these black mushrooms.'

Gabler, after one bite, agreed that it was a welcome change from the usual soggy fare.

'Well, some lobster and a few scallion pancakes are a small price for him to pay,' said Joe, who combined a healthy zest for the good things of life with an understanding of how they were acquired. 'After all, everybody here has busted a gut for the company.'

But one of his colleagues did not wish to fly

under false colors.

'Actually I'm not a high achiever,' Norman Pitts said conscientiously. 'They have a dozen rookies at the party every year, and I drew one of the lucky tickets.'

'Then I assume you have not been with Sparrow very long,' Thatcher said kindly.

It was like opening the floodgates.

'I got out of orientation four weeks ago, but I already feel at home. Everybody's great at letting you into the action but, of course, I haven't been on a team or come up with a cost-cutter yet.'

Batchelder roused himself to do his duty.

'There's plenty of time for that,' he encouraged. 'You've barely gotten your feet wet. You're in reservations, aren't you? Well, there's room for improvement there. Maybe you'll be here again next year.'

Batchelder was simply being a leader of youth, but Pitts had succumbed to the Sparrow virus more than most. 'I've already got an idea,' he said instantly. 'Most of the time we wouldn't have to make the reservation at all.'

This was riveting enough to freeze Batchelder as he was helping himself from the waiter's tray.

'What's that?' he said, spoon in midair.

'It's the old home-computer gimmick,' Joe Cleveland said disparagingly.

Norman was indignant. 'Why do you call it a gimmick?' he demanded. 'Travel agents tap into the computer bank for airline reservations. There's no reason why our customers can't. If you think that's impossible, you're just not keeping up with the times.'

'I never said it was impossible.' Cleveland was

234

immensely tolerant. 'When you first told me about it, I said you had to put some meat on its bones and then write up a proposal.'

'But the thing speaks for itself. Sparrow must be spending a lot of money on reservations. And home computers have been selling like hotcakes. A big percentage of those sales are probably to yuppies who'd be on to something like—'

'Hold it right there!' Cleveland directed. 'You say we must be spending a lot. You've got to find out how much. And what percentage of home computers have this capacity? Above all, how many people use them to do anything but play games? You can't expect to get credit for a proposal like this unless you're willing to do the gut work.'

Thatcher was amused by the exchange. It reminded him of an experienced herd dog training her puppy, while the herdsman idly looked on. But, when he glanced at this particular herdsman, it was apparent that Clay Batchelder had other preoccupations. Of course the scene could scarcely hold much novelty for him. Nonetheless Thatcher thought that Sparrow's management should be leaping at any opportunity to emphasize those aspects of their system that worked. They were few and far between these days.

If Batchelder was blind to these considerations, Joe Cleveland was not. For the next hour he did the honors for the company, leading the discussion to the special achievements of his colleagues at the table. With the arrival of dessert, Batchelder's abstraction was explained.

'Now, if ever, is the time to support Mitch.' He turned apologetically to his guests as he rose. 'He has to give the financial projections for the year and announce the bonus. I know he's not looking forward to the next fifteen minutes.'

But Mitch Scovil, loyally flanked by Batchelder and Mrs. Gough, did a very creditable job. He was forthright about the situation, while managing to convey an air of sturdy optimism. His only departure from business was an obligatory reference to Alan Whetmore's death. He deplored the murder and the convulsions it entailed but looked forward to a speedy police resolution. In finale he announced that the band was already warming up and invited everybody to have a good time.

An hour later Thatcher cast a surreptitious glance at his watch and congratulated himself.

'This isn't half as bad as I expected, Everett,' he commented. 'And we only have another hour or so to go.'

His comfort was largely due to the physical layout of the party. The dining room was approximately midship. When Mitch Scovil had concluded his remarks, the young people had surged forward to the dance floor. Their elders had made their way more decorously aft to the lounge. The usual small talk was occasionally punctuated by a blast of music as a couple, red-faced with exertion, entered and fell on the refreshment tables. Thatcher had even been beguiled by Mrs. Gough into a brief excursion to the deck where he had peered through the scudding sleet to view the lights of the waterfront before hastily returning to shelter.

'The evening is not yet over,' Gabler replied automatically, but he, too, was so off guard that he absently steered a course past the bar without first checking its occupants.

'I wish you'd tell Fritz he's got rocks in his head,'

Mitch Scovil genially invited the newcomers. 'He's trying to claim that there's no difference between being a cog in a mammoth corporation and running your own show.'

Thatcher would have evaded the issue, but Gabler fell prey to his passion for accuracy.

'I would scarcely describe a vice-presidency at A&P as being a cog in a machine,' he said severely.

'Call it what you like,' Scovil said with an expansive wave. 'You've still got a lot of other people trying to second-guess you.'

Thatcher felt that, of all the subjects available, it was unfortunate that Scovil should have hit upon one that struck a spark from Everett.

'Surely that is unavoidable in any substantial enterprise,' Gabler said with that heavy reasonableness guaranteed to provoke resistance.

'Not at Sparrow,' Scovil insisted grandly. 'This is my baby, and what I say goes.'

'That's a fine line coming from you,' Diehl retorted. 'You've got the Sloan living in your accounting department, and your employees launching a proxy fight.'

Scovil was unimpressed. 'Ah, but you've missed the real difference,' he said as if uncovering a hidden subtlety. 'In your position, you've got to listen to the kibitzers. I don't.'

'Why don't you wake up, Mitch? You're still trying to bowl over the grown-ups by being a young hotshot. It's about time you realized you are one of the grown-ups.'

Scovil shook his head with a pleased expression. 'You're jealous, that's your problem, Fritz. Face it, you're not a born entrepreneur, you have the soul of a wage slave.'

237

By this time, Thatcher realized that both disputants had had too much to drink. Fortunately neither of them was displaying symptoms of pugnacity. Scovil was encased in complacent superiority. Fritz Diehl, blinking owlishly, was becoming more judicious by the moment.

'The trouble with you, Mitch, is that you don't realize we could call the tune the first couple of years because we were the only ones with anything at stake. As soon as you become big and successful, that's over. A lot of other people have something riding on Sparrow now.'

'Sure they do. I'm carrying them all, just the way I have for five years. That's why I make the decisions.' Scovil squared his shoulders, either as a symbol of his burdens or as a sign of departure. 'I promised the gang I'd be on deck by nine-thirty. I've got to go now.'

A few minutes earlier the blast of discordant percussion had announced the arrival of yet another group of dancers, but Thatcher had been too intent on the discussion to identify them. Now he saw Phoebe Fournier advancing.

But Phoebe had things on her mind other than dance partners. 'I heard that last crack,' she said, watching Scovil's retreating figure with simmering disapproval. 'Mitch isn't listening to anybody these days. He's put in earplugs for the duration.'

'Can you blame him?' Joe Cleveland had loomed up behind her, carrying a saucer of sushi. 'Half the company is saying Whetmore blackmailed Mitch for skimming the employee profit fund.'

His remark was not overly loud, but it reached Eleanor Gough, who was bearing down on Everett for the mandatory trek outside.

238

'Joe, how can you make an accusation like that?' she demanded sternly. 'That fund is the core of Sparrow's operations. Mitch would never attack it.'

'You don't have to jump down my throat,' Joe defended himself. 'Hell, you could look on it as an improvement. Two weeks ago they were all saying Mitch was a murderer.'

'That's not funny,' she snapped. 'It's bad enough to say Mitch lost his head in his anxiety to protect Sparrow. But it's simply insane to think one of us could have been deliberately undermining Sparrow for years.'

Her fervor made everybody uncomfortable, but Joe rallied.

'Look, Eleanor, I don't really think anybody is playing games with the profit fund. After all, Phoebe monitors that fund and nobody's putting anything past her.'

This tribute left Phoebe unmoved. She was still concentrating on Scovil's intransigence.

'God damn him. He's got no right to behave like this,' she muttered.

Fritz Diehl was amused. 'Calm down, Phoebe. Right now, Mitch is being his own worst enemy.'

'Like hell!' she shot back. 'If he pushes us into a proxy fight and wins, he's forcing us out into the cold where we have to start a new company. That makes him my worst enemy.'

For Thatcher, this reference to a new company put a different light on Mrs. Gough's expectations from the Sloan.

'You know, Phoebe, Mitch would say you don't have the soul of an entrepreneur,' Fritz Diehl said teasingly. 'You're not willing to take the risks, so you're not entitled to anything.'

'Big risk he took,' Phoebe scoffed. 'Mitch got a lucky win on the lottery. It was easy for him.'

Diehl was not prepared to have his own contribution undervalued. 'Well, it was damn hard for some of us. I couldn't have done it if my father hadn't died then. And I still had to go into hock.'

'All right, I'm not saying it was as easy for you as it was for Mitch. But at least you were older than I am. You'd had more time to save.'

This outrageous statement was too much for the bankers.

'Increased age usually brings increased responsibilities and expenditures,' Thatcher informed her.

Everett was more statistical. 'On the whole, you will find that discretionary income falls after the twenties, virtually disappearing until after the children are grown.'

Phoebe, thrown into momentary disarray by this introduction of unborn children, was silent, and Fritz resumed the attack.

'You remember what Don Islington said? He couldn't take a cut in income, let alone fork out assets.' Diehl turned to Thatcher. 'Don's an equipment man that Eleanor and Phoebe were sounding out in case they go it alone. But he's got a slew of adolescent kids, and obligations from here to eternity.'

Mention of Mrs. Gough embarrassed Phoebe. 'Oh, Eleanor, I realize you took an almighty risk when you sold your house to invest in Sparrow. I suppose,' she said, taking her hurdles bravely, 'I should stop complaining about how hard it will be for me. No matter how I slice it, it was worse for you.'

240

Mrs. Gough seemed to be having second thoughts.

'You always think you have a right to take your own risks,' she said somberly. 'But half the time, what you do affects other people. When you're building something together, you have a moral responsibility to each other. Because, win or lose, everybody is stuck with the consequences.'

Phoebe was taken aback. 'Eleanor, I didn't mean I'm not willing to go through with it. But it's all so needless, if only Mitch would see sense.'

'Why should Mitch see things any more clearly than the rest of us? In spite of what he thinks, he's not infallible. He's ... oh, hello, Clay.'

Batchelder had materialized at Mrs. Gough's side, his wristwatch conspicuously to the fore.

'It's nine-thirty,' he began briskly, then stopped as he saw she was still elsewhere. 'We said we'd be on deck by then.'

She shook herself briskly. 'I almost forgot. I'll get right up there.'

The spell had been broken and she bustled off, leaving Clay and Phoebe with puzzled frowns.

'I don't know where Eleanor picked up this guilt-and-atonement talk, but I could sure do without it,' Clay groaned, before he hurried to catch up with her.

Diehl burst out laughing. 'That's Sparrow all over. Mitch pretends he's in charge of things. Then he'll end up leading a cheering section while Clay and Eleanor get things done. You want to see the show, Phoebe?'

He linked his arm with hers, but Phoebe stood stock-still.

'We weren't talking about the same thing at all,'

241

she said in a gust of discovery. 'Eleanor's still trying to find some justification for Alan Whetmore's murder. That's what she meant by other people getting involved.'

'Eleanor's always windy at these affairs,' Diehl said impatiently. 'Do you want to come or not?'

Slowly Phoebe began to move. 'I'm coming, I'm coming. But I wish I understood Eleanor better. I don't like the way she sounds.'

'Phooey!' Ruthlessly Diehl bore her off, shouting an invitation to Joe over his shoulder.

'In a minute,' said Joe, providently turning to reload his saucer.

Everett Gabler was beside himself with indignation. 'Do you realize what that young woman was doing? Now I am the first to admit that Mrs. Gough may have some peculiarities, but she is a woman of principle! More principle, I daresay, than anybody Miss Fournier's age has ever heard of. I consider—'

It was well known at the Sloan Guaranty Trust that Everett Gabler, once launched, could continue indefinitely. But few monologues are proof against a sudden explosion overhead.

'Good Lord, what was that?' he exclaimed.

Joe Cleveland was chuckling as he left them. 'We're passing Logan,' he explained. 'We always fire off rockets to salute the staff on duty.'

He grinned mischievously.

'You've got to admit, we do things differently at Sparrow.'

His remark stirred to the surface too many disturbing images.

'You certainly do,' Thatcher rejoined.

242

CHAPTER TWENTY-SEVEN

A PLAINTIVE WHISTLE

Thatcher and Gabler were not talkative as they made their way ashore and waited for their limousine to nose its way along the pier. But once the doors were safely closed, Gabler was prepared to voice his concerns.

'I have been thinking, John,' he began.

Since Gabler had fallen into a brown study at the bar and remained mute for the remainder of the evening, Thatcher had surmised as much.

'I noticed,' he said.

'Of course you remember what Miss Fournier said just before she left us. That girl was making a deliberate and not particularly subtle attempt to direct suspicion toward Mrs. Gough. In my case, at least, her tactics have backfired. Her uncalled-for innuendos opened up an entirely different possibility for me.'

'I agree about the tenor of Phoebe's remarks, but I'm not so sure they were uncalled for, Everett,' Thatcher objected. 'Mrs. Gough's discourse about the unforeseen consequences of one's own actions was certainly odd.'

Gabler was close to snarling.

'There is not one jot of evidence to suggest that she was referring to herself as the perpetrator of these consequences,' he retorted. 'Her reaction would be identical if any principal at Sparrow were responsible.'

'Perhaps,' said Thatcher, who was anxious to

proceed. There had never been any doubt which of the two ladies Gabler would choose to support. With Mrs. Gough, Everett mounted only the same wariness he extended to any Sloan customer. With Phoebe, he acted as if he were dealing with Che Guevera. 'You said something about a new possibility?'

But now that Gabler had discharged some of his steam, he reverted to type. With a silent nod toward the limousine driver, he said darkly: 'Later.'

'Oh, very well.'

Enemy ears, for Gabler, included room-service waiters as well as chauffeurs. When Thatcher ordered coffee and sandwiches, Everett could barely contain his impatience.

'I very much fear that both I and the police are guilty of overlooking an elementary fact,' he said the moment they had been served. 'Simply because of the size of the sums paid to Whetmore, we have focused our attention on the three partners, forgetting Phoebe Fournier's net worth.'

Thatcher frowned. 'Just a second, Everett,' he objected. 'It's improbable that Captain Lemoine has the slightest idea how wealthy Miss Fournier is.'

Gabler ducked his head in agreement. 'In a very real sense, Sparrow has four principals, not three.'

'I'll pass on that one, but of course you're right about the resources Phoebe has.'

'Or *had*,' Everett said emphatically. 'Has it occurred to you that her reluctance to invest in a new venture is entirely out of character? She is always portrayed as leading the way, not lagging behind. Isn't it possible that, after major disbursements to Whetmore, she could have difficulty raising the money? Particularly when she can't afford to let anyone know she's short? And, to my mind, she presents the most easily explained target for blackmail.'

Thatcher nodded slowly. While Gabler had fastened on Phoebe's remarks at the bar, he himself had been riveted by Joe Cleveland's. 'It's Phoebe who's supposed to oversee the profit-sharing fund for the employees, theoretically to prevent hanky-panky by management. But nobody seems to keep an eye on her.'

For a moment both bankers contemplated this violation of basic security maxims.

'There is far more to it than that,' said Everett, returning to the matter at hand. 'You don't know how these Sparrow field teams work, John. They set up everything needed to implement a new facility, which means that the possibility for kickbacks from contractors is self-evident. Good heavens, she could have created her own supply company.'

'She wouldn't be the first,' Thatcher agreed, rather startled at the sweeping opportunities presented to Phoebe.

'Wait!' Gabler instructed remorselessly. 'I'm not finished. She is also the in-house liaison with the independent auditors. It cannot be denied that she has had temptations on every side. I also think it striking that her chosen second-in-command should be Joe Cleveland.'

Gabler was conducting a shameless, no-holds-barred, defense of Mrs. Gough. But now Thatcher, himself, experienced a wave of partisanship. Joe had made tonight's dinner endurable. Furthermore, he was the only participant at the ill-fated meeting with Whetmore whose contributions had been valid

245

and cogent.

'What about Cleveland?' Thatcher growled.

He was promptly disarmed.

'On the whole, a young man with very sound instincts for his age,' Gabler said indulgently. 'He is clear-sighted about the goals of the employees, sensitive to the needs of people, and inclined to stick to the point. But...'

With Gabler almost any commendation ended in *but*. Thatcher waited to hear what the fatal flaw was this time.

'But he is entirely lacking in any financial or accounting skills.'

Now that they were both degenerating into champions, Thatcher thought it right to reestablish some impartiality. 'You just said that Mrs. Gough's remarks could be interpreted in different ways. So could Phoebe's choice of adjutant. Maybe she wanted a balanced employee representation.'

'Or maybe she wanted someone incapable of double-checking her work. What's more, her selection of Alan Whetmore as committee spokesman defies justification. It was so strange that when his safe deposit money was found, Cleveland and others jumped to the conclusion that she had been unknowingly manipulated by a competitor.'

By this time Thatcher was interested enough to lay down his half-eaten chicken sandwich. 'You're not maintaining that Phoebe thought she could pay off Whetmore by negotiating his idiotic demands, are you? Because, believe me, she is far too knowledgeable about Sparrow to think she could have succeeded.'

'Exactly,' said Everett. 'But Whetmore was not knowledgeable. She could have maneuvered him onto a collision course with Mitchell Scovil. Even more compelling, it explains that meeting. You said yourself, John, that Whetmore was thunderstruck when his list was brushed aside without a hearing. Perhaps he was waiting for Phoebe to throw all the weight of the united payroll behind him.'

'I admit that might explain Whetmore's behavior at the meeting, but what about before?' Thatcher murmured. 'He deliberately changed his schedule to evade Phoebe, and he certainly made no pretense that his list had been endorsed by other employees. Quite the contrary.'

Everett was so engrossed by his argument that he absentmindedly helped himself to a potato chip.

'John, why don't we stop speculating and look at what has actually happened?' he suggested. 'Scovil's control over his work force has almost disappeared. Things have reached such a pass that a proxy fight seems inevitable and, wonder of wonders, Phoebe Fournier is now on the insurgents' slate of directors—a position she repudiated in front of Alan Whetmore. To sum up, everything has worked out to her advantage.'

'Not quite, Everett. The leadership of the anti-Scovil forces has passed to Mrs. Gough. You're not forgetting that, are you?'

Now Gabler sounded like a hanging judge.

'Far from it. But now that Mrs. Gough has emerged as a power factor, Miss Fournier is casting her in the role of murderess. Viewed in one light, all these events make a coherent picture of Phoebe Fournier advancing her own interests at any cost.'

After some consideration, Thatcher shook his head decisively.

'You may be right in your reading of Phoebe's

character. She may be a cold-blooded thief and killer. Or she may be aiming for Sparrow's front office. However, you cannot combine the two. I can believe that Whetmore was blackmailing someone who finally decided to kill him. I can't believe that the murderer was also thinking about corporate advancement.'

Everett Gabler had a long and successful career in the art of persuasion, but his tactics were always of the water-dripping-on-stone variety. He was still going strong when Charlie Trinkam rolled in from a night on the town with Rupert Vernon.

'I've got to hand it to Rupert,' he said cheerfully, tossing his coat over a chair. 'When it comes to enjoyment, he's got the right approach. Someday I'd like to see him in a place worthy of his talents.'

'In Rupert's book, that's probably Edinburgh,' warned Thatcher.

'Don't you believe it. I'll bet it's a toss-up between Paris and Hong Kong.' Charlie surveyed his companions with bright interest. 'So how did your bash go? Did they start swinging on each other?'

'Remind me to introduce you to Fritz Diehl, Charlie,' Thatcher said dryly. 'You both seem to have the same yardstick for the success of a social event.'

Gabler was impatient with these diversions. Instead, he tried to enlist Charlie in his cause by a careful recapitulation of his suspicions.

'There!' he concluded. 'You have to admit that it covers the main facts.'

Charlie's response dashed Gabler's hopes.

'The trouble with you, Ev, is that you don't understand girls like this Phoebe,' Trinkam said authoritatively. 'I haven't met her, but I'm willing to bet that she comes from a background where she didn't know a damn thing about money.'

'She taught elementary school for a year after college,' Gabler admitted.

Charlie nodded sagely. 'And she was bored stiff. Then she was lucky enough to get a job with a company just getting off the ground, and found herself doing things she'd never dreamed of doing. Before you know it, she thinks she's the smartest thing that ever came down the corporation pike. She doesn't realize that she got the rewards of other people's risk taking.'

Gabler was swift to point out that this appraisal did not cover everything.

'If Miss Fournier had simply been reluctant to join a new venture, I would have accepted your explanation,' he said. 'After all, true entrepreneurs are relatively scarce. But why the sudden attempt to cast suspicion on Mrs. Gough?'

This, too, posed no insuperable problem for Charlie Trinkam.

'How old is this lady?' he asked, hitching himself forward like a consultant reviewing the patient's medical history.

Everett sniffed. 'I have, of course, not inquired. But she has two grown children, a married son and a daughter.'

'Mother-of-the-bride stuff. I thought so.' Charlie had spotted the symptom that explained everything. 'You've got to realize that these girls all think they're a new breed, striking out where no woman has ever gone before. Your Phoebe's burned up that some dame in pastel chiffon and a little flowered hat has got more of the right stuff than she has.'

Floundering in deep waters, Gabler thought he saw an opportunity to score. 'When last seen, Mrs. Gough was far from wearing the clothes you describe.'

Specialists are accustomed to interjections from the untutored.

'When her daughter's going down the aisle, she will be,' Charlie said simply.

'So you think Miss Fournier is acting from some form of jealousy?'

'Not exactly.' Trinkam pondered briefly. 'Your Phoebe has been knocked off her little pins. She thought she knew all about good old Mrs. Gough. It turns out she hasn't even scratched the surface. So she's beginning to wonder how much more is lurking down there. As far as she's concerned, it could be anything—including murder.'

Everett was a past master of minimal retreat. Instinctively he surrendered outlying ground to maintain his center.

'You may be correct about Miss Fournier. I agree that Mrs. Gough's performance these past few days has been sufficiently unexpected to startle any colleague,' he conceded. 'But I still believe that the Whetmore meeting must have been contrived. That is the only explanation for its incongruity.'

Thatcher always enjoyed the spectacle of Charlie instructing Gabler in the way life is lived outside an accounting ledger. While his subordinates clashed, he quietly demolished the remaining edibles on the tray. He was about to pour himself another cup of coffee when Everett made his final declaration.

As the words penetrated, Thatcher froze. The pot remained suspended, the cup stayed dry, while vignettes from Sparrow flashed before his eyes.

250

There was Eleanor Gough stubbornly insisting that Scovil could not evade the employee meeting; there was Clay Batchelder hustling Joe Cleveland away from contact with Alan Whetmore; there was Fritz Diehl comparing Phoebe to Don Islington.

'You've put your finger on it, Everett,' he said. Then, with mounting conviction: 'Good God, it's been staring us in the face all along.'

CHAPTER TWENTY-EIGHT

SIGHTED IN LOUISIANA

The solution to Alan Whetmore's murder was staring far too openly for Eleanor Gough's peace of mind. Late as it was when she returned from the party, she began packing a suitcase immediately.

Phoebe Fournier, on the other hand, enjoyed a night of untroubled repose, waking to sunny blue skies and a feeling of buoyant optimism. Her misgivings of the previous evening did not survive the light of day. Eleanor had simply been reacting to the strain of simultaneously confronting Mitch Scovil and maintaining Christmas cheer. Today would be business as usual, Phoebe promised herself, and the first item on the agenda was a lunchtime huddle with Eleanor. Mitch had already been shaken by the official notice from Chet Longley. This afternoon he would be meeting with John Thatcher and Everett Gabler. After these two body blows, he should be ripe for compromise.

This happy mood lasted until Phoebe's coffee

break took her to the cafeteria, where she found the central table crowded with the early morning shift. From their midst rose the despairing accents of Joyce Wrigley, who was notorious for the lamentations that accompanied her well-intentioned career of mistakes, miscalculations, and mishaps.

'You know what a madhouse the 6 A.M. shuttle was,' she keened.

'It always is,' a fellow sufferer groaned.

But Joyce was merely painting in the background. 'So there I was, snapping the head off this poor schnook who hadn't made out his boarding pass. And wouldn't you know it? Eleanor Gough was next in line!'

She paused dramatically while her colleagues gasped in pleasurable dismay.

'What did she do?' they asked.

'She just had time to board. But she won't forget, not our Eleanor. When I think of what she'll say to me when she gets back, I could just die.'

It was nothing new for Joyce to prepare to meet her maker. While everybody else produced rival episodes, Phoebe thumped down her coffee mug and stalked over to the table.

'Are you saying Eleanor's gone to New York?' she demanded, cutting across anecdotes about other lapses.

Joyce was puzzled. 'Of course she was going to New York. That's why people take the shuttle.'

'Dammit!' said Phoebe as she saw her hopes of seizing the psychological moment fade.

But there was worse to come. Two hours later she was preparing to go out to lunch when the locker room was inundated with a flight crew coming off duty.

252

'Hi, Stephanie!' she said, moving over at the mirror where she was brushing her hair. 'Through for the day?'

'Finally,' said Stephanie triumphantly. 'These morning shuttles during the Christmas season are living hell.'

Phoebe looked at her with new interest. 'Say, I hear you had Eleanor on board the dawn flight.'

Stephanie was leaning forward to apply her lipstick with pinpoint accuracy. Only when the operation was complete did she reply. 'That's right. And was she ever in a tizzy when we had to circle for twenty minutes at La Guardia. She was so uptight I thought she'd scream.'

'She probably had an appointment in New York.'

'Not New York,' Stephanie corrected. 'She was afraid of missing her connection with Delta. You know she always flies with them when she visits her daughter in New Orleans.'

'New Orleans?' Phoebe stammered.

Clicking her cosmetic case closed, Stephanie turned for a final word. 'And if you ask me, something's wrong down there. Eleanor looked really grim.'

'Oh no!'

'A family emergency, for Chrissake,' Phoebe reported indignantly. 'That's all I need.'

Joe put down the ketchup bottle and looked reproachful. 'It probably isn't what Eleanor needs, either,' he pointed out.

'Oh, I know it's not her fault,' Phoebe grumbled. 'But it couldn't have happened at a worse time. From the look on Mr. Gabler's face when he finished the books, Mitch should be pulverized by

253

their meeting.'

'Have a heart, Phoebe. It must have been pretty bad if they called Eleanor in the middle of the night. She could be sitting around some hospital by now.'

'Just coffee, Eleanor? Sure you don't want to try the pastry cart?'

Mrs. Gough was not maintaining a deathbed vigil. Instead she was lunching, a good deal more grandly than Joe and Phoebe, in one of New Orleans's renowned restaurants. Her host, in another world and another life, had been her boss.

Unlike her colleagues at Sparrow, Eleanor Gough had never lost touch with New Orleans. There, Fritz Diehl and Mitch Scovil had been itinerant executives, holding down their first jobs after business school. Clay Batchelder had been an outside consultant, destined to live intimately with Bayou Airlines for several months and then disappear forever. Mrs. Gough, however, had spent twenty years sinking roots into the community. It was not unusual for her to be catching up on company events with Bill Johnson, and he never suspected that this time his reminiscing was being artfully steered. Like all stay-at-homes, he assumed the returned traveler was as engrossed by local gossip as he was.

'That was Ramon Estevez, Eleanor. You must remember him.'

Eleanor's face was a polite blank.

'He ran our charters to Mexico,' Johnson amplified.

Now her expression correctly mirrored dawning memory. 'A little, dapper man? Rather flashy?'

254

'You could call it that. The customers ate up his gallant hidalgo act.'

She nodded. 'Of course. I just didn't place the name.'

'How could you forget him? He and Whetmore were our men of the world. Everybody else at the club played golf, but the two of them were always toweling down after squash and telling us how they'd chartered a boat to go out after the big ones. You must . . .' Johnson's voice died away in a tide of embarrassment. Then he coughed and began again. 'Of course you weren't at the club in those days.'

'No, I didn't move in those circles,' she agreed calmly, then continued with a twinkle, 'and I still don't. No power on earth would get me out on the Gulf in one of those boats.'

Johnson smiled gratefully. Trust Eleanor not to take offense at a little slip. She was still the same, he thought. Just as unassuming and comfortable as ever.

The men of the Sloan were not quite so content with their lot. The previous evening John Thatcher's dazzling insight had been subjected to a punishing critique by his subordinates. This had failed to reveal a single flaw. But where, they asked, was the proof?

'Nowhere that I can see,' Thatcher had admitted ruefully. 'What's more, there's still one unanswered question. How does a stupid, uninformed man like Whetmore discover things that have eluded everyone else?'

This was no mystery at all to Charlie Trinkam. 'Somebody tells him.'

'What difference does it make?' Gabler had snapped. 'We are still left in an untenable position.'

As the hour for their meeting with Scovil approached, Everett became more militant.

'It is inconceivable that the Sloan should support either of these factions at Sparrow until this entire matter is resolved,' he trumpeted.

'If it ever is,' Thatcher said. 'We're talking about five years ago.'

Gabler snapped his fingers at this bagatelle and narrowed his eyes. 'With sufficient persistence and the cooperation of relevant financial institutions, an investigator could surely produce evidence.'

Things were bad enough without Everett Gabler disappearing from the East Coast on a search for the Holy Grail.

'Given enough time, the police can probably do it,' said Thatcher, sternly directing his colleague's attention to their primary interest.

'But Mrs. Gough, you may have noticed, has carefully arranged a scenario that forces the pace.'

'And no wonder!' Everett snorted.

It took two cheeseburgers for Joe Cleveland to reason Phoebe into a realistic frame of mind, and his good work was almost immediately undermined.

'How should I know when she's coming back?' demanded Sally, the receptionist. 'I didn't even know she was leaving.'

'But she always calls in,' Phoebe protested, her voice unconsciously rising.

Over the years it had been well established that, during any emergency, the phone might ring forever in Mitch Scovil's apartment, it might be answered by an unhelpful adolescent in the

256

Batchelder home, but Eleanor Gough was always available.

'If you ask me, that's just it,' Sally grinned. 'I'll bet she's told Mitch and Clay that they can carry the can for a change. She sure enjoyed telling Mitch to run his own errands the other day. Anyway, until she tells me different, I'm holding her mail here.'

It did not help that Phoebe, automatically following Sally's gesture, spotted an envelope bearing the letterhead of Chester Longley's law firm.

Phoebe was outraged. This was no time to be playing games. If Eleanor was simply twisting Mitch's tail, the least she could do was keep her partner informed.

With her jaw set and her spine stiff, Phoebe stalked into the corridor just as Mitch Scovil rounded the corner, ushering John Thatcher and Everett Gabler to the executive suite.

'Oh, Mitch,' she blurted. 'Did Eleanor tell you when she's due back from New Orleans?'

She regretted her impulse immediately. The smile was wiped from Scovil's face and he stopped in his tracks, leaving his guests to forge ahead.

'New Orleans?' he repeated, his eyes wide and fixed.

'That's right,' she said impatiently. 'I want to reach her.'

Scovil merely shrugged his shoulders. 'How would I know?' he asked, then added tauntingly: 'If you're having trouble figuring out what Eleanor's up to, Phoebe, there's a lot of that going around.'

Bent on extracting information from Scovil, Phoebe never noticed the startled glance exchanged by his visitors.

Two hours later, even Mitch Scovil could not convince himself that he had succeeded in winning the Sloan's support. Characteristically his report to Clay Batchelder placed the blame on other shoulders.

'I never thought Eleanor would play so dirty. How the hell can I get the Sloan to see reason when she's letting off one land mine after another?'

Clay was still one day behind. 'We always knew that it might come down to a proxy fight.'

Actually Mitch had never believed it for a minute.

'It wouldn't have, if Phoebe was still running the show,' he grated. 'Eleanor's the one who's charging around like a wild bull. Yesterday we hear from her lawyers and today she lights out for New Orleans without a word to anybody. How do you think it looks to Thatcher when we can't even keep track of our top management?'

'What the hell did she go to New Orleans for?'

'I don't know. I suppose it's something to do with her daughter.' Catching sight of Batchelder's expression, Scovil went on less confidently. 'Well, it has to be something like that, doesn't it?'

'Sure,' said Clay too quickly. 'That's bound to be it.'

'What else could it be? It's been five years since we moved to Boston. She doesn't have anything left down there except family,' Scovil persisted.

Clay had his second wind by now. 'We don't know what kind of interests she's got down there, and we're not going to find out by talking to each other,' he said firmly. 'Besides, nine chances out of ten, it's her daughter, just like you said.'

The ensuing conversation was not much comfort

to either man. Scovil was unwilling to break down and admit that the Sloan had blasted his grandiose plans. Batchelder was determined not to voice his forebodings about Eleanor Gough's disappearance. Both men wanted unqualified reassurance and sympathy for anxieties they refused to specify. Neither of them got it.

In an attempt to end their session on a positive note, Scovil had to cast far afield. 'At least there's one good thing,' he remembered. 'The stock has inched up to thirty and change.'

'Great,' said Clay dully.

'Well, now we know where the evidence is located,' Thatcher said as soon as they rejoined Trinkam. 'It's at Bayou Airlines.'

'Or *was*,' Charlie rejoined. 'That's one enterprising lady you've got there.'

She was even more enterprising than Charlie gave her credit for, as Phoebe discovered the next day. Upon being told by the Sparrow switchboard that there was still no word from Mrs. Gough, Phoebe realized there could be only one logical explanation. Eleanor planned to spend the day in transit. Fortunately Phoebe was in the right business to verify this conclusion. It was the work of a moment to dial a number in Delta's New York office and make her request.

'G-O-U-G-H?' her acquaintance double-checked. 'First name, Eleanor? Sure, Phoebe, I'll have someone on the reservations computer find out and get back to you.'

'I owe you one, Hilary,' Phoebe acknowledged.

'Forget it.'

Hilary's performance was flawless. It was not her fault that computers are remorseless in their display of data.

When Phoebe answered the phone twenty minutes later, she heard an unfamiliar gravelly voice.

'You the party inquiring about Gough, Eleanor?' it rasped.

'That's right,' she said eagerly. 'I want to know if she's reserved space back yet.'

'And just where is back?'

It was a measure of Phoebe's confusion that she had descended to amateurism. 'Boston, Mass.,' she corrected herself crisply. 'She flew down to New Orleans and I want to know when she's coming back.'

'Something's wrong somewhere.' The voice had become perceptibly more cheerful. 'New Orleans was just a stop-over. Gough, Eleanor, transferred to Aero Mexico. She left the country on their two forty-five flight yesterday afternoon.'

CHAPTER TWENTY-NINE

ENDANGERED SPECIES

Phoebe was so stunned that she distinctly heard a click and renewed dial tone before her frozen lips produced an automatic acknowledgment. Every subterranean suspicion of the last twenty-four hours revived. Eleanor had discarded the behavior patterns of a lifetime. Eleanor had been talking about guilt and responsibility for days. Was this her atonement? Was her flight supposed to be Sparrow's salvation?

Wildly looking around the accounting department, Phoebe was not reassured. Instead of old friends, she saw too many members of Captain Lemoine's fraud squad. Heads bent, fingers poised over calculators, they were sandwiched into every square inch of the already crowded facility.

Like a zombie, she rose to seek more neutral surroundings. As her thoughts stopped whirling, she decided this was no time for old cronies. It was too late to share discoveries under a pledge of secrecy. For once, Phoebe yearned to shift her burden to other shoulders. Somebody would have to inform the police, but it was not going to be her. Not on your life! Management pulled down the big money. Let them do the dirty work.

This effectively directed her to one man. Clay Batchelder had been disturbed about Eleanor even before the party. More important, Clay would instantly confer with Mitch. After that, it was out of her hands. Mitch, as they already knew, was perfectly capable of pointing the finger.

Phoebe finally ran Batchelder to earth in one of the storage sheds, barely noticing in her progress across the compound that the skies had darkened and were filling with pendulous gray clouds.

The weather, however, was uppermost in Batchelder's mind.

'They're forecasting freezing rain tonight,' he grumbled upon her entrance. 'I just hope it holds off until after dinner.'

Phoebe made no pretense of replying. Instead she baldly repeated Delta's announcement.

'I'm worried, Clay,' she concluded.

261

But he was unwilling to meet her halfway. 'Come on, Phoebe. I admit Eleanor's been acting weird these past couple of weeks. But that's no reason to think what you're thinking. There are probably lots of explanations.'

'Name me one.'

Clay winced. 'How do I know? Sure, I'm worried about Eleanor. But only because I think the strain's getting to her. She hasn't been at all like herself. That's why she walked out on Mitch.'

'That's got nothing to do with bolting to Mexico.'

'Maybe not.' Clay sounded almost desperate. 'Look, Lemoine wants to comb through our personal finances. Eleanor stopped in New Orleans first. Maybe she's moving some investments out of the country.'

Phoebe eyed him stonily. 'Don't treat me as if I'm a child. I'll bet you and Mitch are moving assets, too. Neither of you has to leave the country to do it. You just call your broker or lawyer.'

'Eleanor's got family down there,' Batchelder said doggedly. 'She may need their signatures.'

'There's another explanation,' Phoebe said.

Batchelder was not encouraging. 'You're full of them today. And I don't like any of them.'

'You know the way we're always hearing that story about the start of Sparrow? I mean, Fritz getting his inheritance and then Mitch hitting the lottery just when he needed it?'

By now Clay was deeply suspicious. 'That's just part of Mitch's PR.'

'And then Eleanor tells us how she sold her house to get her stake?' Phoebe pursued relentlessly.

'So?'

'Well, she has to say something. But does

262

anybody really know that's how she came up with a hundred thousand? From what you all say about Bayou, Eleanor was in an ideal position to pull off some quick embezzlement.'

Batchelder had sunk onto a stool to listen to Phoebe. Every time she made a point, he shifted as if he were squirming under a physical onslaught. The look he flashed from under his heavy eyebrows was not friendly.

'You're making this up out of thin air, Phoebe,' he charged. 'There's nothing to support it.'

'Oh yes there is,' she insisted, determined to voice every one of her fears. 'The fraud squad hasn't come up with one single irregularity in Sparrow's books. There's not a damned thing anybody could be blackmailed about. But Alan Whetmore was in New Orleans when Eleanor was supposed to be selling this famous house. He had friends and contacts, he could have heard a lot after the rest of you left. Maybe the police are looking at the wrong company's books.'

Clay was heaving himself to his feet. 'Your trouble is an overactive imagination, Phoebe.'

'I could go on.'

But he was already on his way to the door. 'Well, I don't want to hear it.'

'Then give me one good reason why Eleanor's in Mexico,' Phoebe challenged his back.

'I don't know, and I don't care!'

A distant onlooker could easily have decided that Eleanor Gough had come to Acapulco to work on her tan. Like any other vacationer, she was sitting on a patio, gazing at the sea, with a marina spread immediately before her and the world-renowned cliffs to her left. Wearing a short-sleeved blouse and a cotton skirt, she reclined at ease with a cigarette in one hand and a glass of iced pineapple juice in the other. To Ramon Estevez, sitting directly across the small table, she did not seem so relaxed. Her voice was tight with control and the knuckles grasping the glass showed white in the unforgiving sunlight. But, even at close range, certain telltale signs escaped him. He did not know that the cigarette was the first after a three-year abstention, and he could not see the lines of tension concealed by wide wrap-around sunglasses.

'I never thought it would come to this,' he snarled.

'You've been well paid.'

Her indifference flicked him on the raw.

'It was peanuts. By rights, this should all be mine.'

He waved his arm angrily in a gesture that encompassed the bar, the clubhouse, the marina.

Mrs. Gough fastened on only one aspect of the scene—a sign suspended from a cross post, reading: ESTEVEZ MARINA AND YACHT CLUB.

'In one sense it does,' she pointed out.

'Don't give me that. The bank owns ninety percent and they're nervous about the payments.'

'It's not my fault if you've botched things.'

Ramon would have liked to deny this, but it was all too clear where the fault lay.

'My one regret is that Whetmore did not die by my hands, preferably wrapped around his miserable throat. He could have saved us all much trouble.'

'That wasn't Alan's big aim in life. Forget him!' she directed. 'He is no longer a factor.'

Despite himself, Ramon agreed. Magniloquent

264

threats of vengeance are not really satisfactory after the corpse has been buried.

'It is curious, is it not?' he mused. 'In the old days, who would have expected this? Then, Alan and I were friends and men of substance. You were a menial nobody.'

He peered at her, hoping that she would be stung. But he was disappointed; she was not even interested.

'The only important thing about the past is that it does not prejudice the future,' she said. 'But that's very easy to forget, when the past is still the present.'

Ramon, like Mitch Scovil and Clay Batchelder, found Eleanor tiresome when she soared into loftier realms. He himself was equally unmoved by past and future. The present had always been difficult enough.

'I have not made as much out of this as I should have,' he said, reverting to his original grievance.

Eleanor merely murmured something about a plane to catch and put down her glass. As she reached for her capacious straw bag, Ramon's eye rested on it speculatively. Possibly there was still hope of further profit from his association with Mrs. Gough.

'When will I see you again?'

As the only occasion on which this was likely to occur was a joint courtroom appearance, Eleanor checked in her preparations for departure and involuntarily grimaced.

'With luck, never!'

Ramon did not share her desire to put distance between them. Frowning against the brilliant light, he let his glance follow her receding figure until a clump of palm trees obscured it.

Inevitably the police fraud squad had reached the conclusion already arrived at by both Everett Gabler and Phoebe Fournier.

'The place is so clean it squeaks!' Humphrey Belliers reported at the conclusion of the audit.

When Captain Lemoine remained unresponsive, Belliers feared that his past blunder was rising to haunt him.

'That's not just me,' he hastened to add. 'That's the fraud squad and even Gabler, too.'

Finally Lemoine roused himself from his trance. 'I know. Thatcher and Gabler were just in here. They've got a theory that explains everything. But to get the evidence means going back over five years.'

'Sparrow wasn't in existence then,' Belliers protested.

'Not Sparrow. They're talking about personal finances.'

'Well, the court's already rejected a fishing expedition with the three of them.'

'It's just one now. But the court's still going to say no when all I have is a theory.'

Belliers would have liked Lemoine's confidences to be more specific, but he had other grounds for dissatisfaction. 'What difference does it make? If you were just doing one, there wouldn't be anybody to arrest when you were finished. These people run an airline. They know all about hopping a plane to leave the country.'

'I thought the same thing,' Lemoine said placidly.

Common sense was Belliers's outstanding

characteristic. 'I'll bet the old curmudgeon could do it under the table,' he suggested. 'The Sloan swings a hell of a lot of clout with other banks.'

The captain recalled his recent visitors. Everett Gabler had been wearing his usual expression of stern disapproval. But under the disapproval there had been disappointment.

'He not only could do it, he wants to do it,' said Lemoine, thoughtfully examining his fingernails. 'But Thatcher is calling the shots. He intends to shovel the whole mess into our lap and go home.'

'Ha!' Belliers snorted. 'The Sloan is in the hot seat, too. Why don't you apply for another court order? When you get thrown out, Thatcher's not going to like it at all.'

But Lemoine was sinking deeper and deeper into his thoughts. 'Somehow I don't think it will come to that. I think those crazies at Sparrow are raising such a head of steam that they'll blow themselves to bits.'

On the whole Phoebe was satisfied that she had done the right thing. She had not failed to note the signs of Clay's discomfiture. In front of her he might profess skepticism, but by the time he had analyzed and reanalyzed her suspicions with Mitch, they would both be convinced.

For that very reason she took care to stay beyond their reach. The next three hours she spent penetrating nooks and crannies of the Sparrow compound whose very existence she had forgotten.

It did not lighten her mood of sober resignation that the day's roster included too many people who had been on duty when Alan Whetmore was murdered. As the weather worsened, she overheard many people draw the same comparison.

'God, will you look at that fog rolling in. It was just like this the night Alan got killed.'

At the third repetition, Phoebe's defenses crumbled, and she finally admitted what she had been avoiding as late as her conversation with Batchelder. The fraud squad might examine books, and she could use words like embezzlement and blackmail; but the crime that had convulsed Sparrow was not a wrongful transfer of money. Alan Whetmore, however contemptible, had been a living, breathing entity until he was lured to that desolate, fog-shrouded spot and battered into a bloodied shell.

Shivering, she continued to wander until she found herself in the outpost that received fresh laundry. It was here that a persistent caller, who had been trying to reach her for some time, finally succeeded. The voice was unmistakable.

'About Gough, Eleanor,' it began.

'You mean you're still tracking her?' Phoebe gasped.

She could have bitten her lip in vexation. She did not want to follow Eleanor to Costa Rica—or Havana, for that matter.

'You're the one who asked about her return,' he reminded her.

'Are you saying she's coming back?'

'She's probably there by now. Her ETA in New York was three fifty-five. If you ever answered your phone, you would have known sooner.'

This time, at least, Phoebe managed to beat the dial tone with her dazed thanks.

She could not begin to imagine what Eleanor was up to now, but this unexpected return did not allay her suspicions. She was, she realized, honor-bound to report the development to Clay. With dragging steps, she made her way back to the main building, oblivious to the fact that night had fallen and the first spitting showers of icy pellets were delicately rebounding from every surface. Her determination carried her to Batchelder's office, but he was not there.

'Clay's left,' Sally answered her question.

'He's already gone home?' Phoebe echoed, wondering what to do next.

'Well, actually, not home. He was asking Francine the quickest way to get to Newton.'

Phoebe made no attempt to conceal her dismay.

'But he mustn't do that!' she cried.

Blind to Sally's amazement, Phoebe castigated herself. After the twin debacles of the employees' meeting and the Pittsburgh shutdown, Joe Cleveland had said she was good with numbers and lousy with people. And he was right! In spite of a week learning that she had failed to read Eleanor Gough entirely, she had had the colossal arrogance to assume that she could predict Clay's actions. Deliberately working on his earlier fears, she had been so sure that he would rush straight to Mitch. Instead he must have checked Sparrow's passenger lists and now, out of some stubborn sense of loyalty, he was going to give Eleanor a chance to explain. The ghost of her belated realism about Alan Whetmore's murder rose to haunt Phoebe. It would never occur to Clay to be on his guard.

'And it's all my fault,' she said bitterly, completing Sally's confusion before she dashed away.

She was heading straight for those police

269

accountants she had been so anxious to avoid a few hours ago. None of this would have happened if she had gone to them in the first place.

But, unnoticed by Phoebe during her soul-searching, the magic hour of quitting time had come and gone. Both the police and the Sparrow regulars had departed, leaving only two men in the office. John Thatcher, already in his overcoat, was waiting while Everett Gabler shoveled stacks of notepads into an ancient buckled briefcase.

Thatcher looked up at Phoebe's tumultuous entrance and smiled. 'You'll be glad to hear you're getting at least one desk back, Miss Fournier,' he said. 'We're leaving on the next shuttle and—'

She never let him finish. In a torrent of words, Phoebe relieved herself of her suspicion, fear, and guilt.

'I'm going out to Eleanor's house right now,' she ended on a surge of nervous desperation. 'They think they're old friends with nothing to be afraid of, and that's dangerous. But if somebody else is there, I don't see how anything can happen.'

Even as the sentences tumbled out, Phoebe realized she was not provoking the reaction she had expected. Thatcher and Gabler did not reject her ravings out of hand; they did not plead with her to reconsider her plans; they did not even seem to be surprised. Instead they nodded as if she were merely confirming what they already knew.

There was, however, the beginning of a frown on Thatcher's face. 'I had not considered the possibility of additional violence,' he confessed. 'You may be right about that. In any event this seems the ideal moment to try to wrap this whole thing up. What do you say, Everett?'

But Phoebe, like Captain Lemoine, had no doubt who was calling the shots, and she had no intention of waiting for pro forma consultations.

'My car's right outside and we don't have any time to waste,' she said, urging them toward the door. 'Clay left half an hour ago.'

Following her lead, Thatcher and Gabler were grateful for a guide across the parking lot. The overhead lights were almost useless, each one a pale nimbus regularly obscured by drifting tendrils of fog. At ground level every object—cars, railings, stanchions—was weeping with moisture, and the metallic ping of ice crystals had swollen into a steady background accompaniment.

'This may take longer than you think,' Thatcher warned as he closed his door.

The words popped out of Phoebe's mouth before she could stop them.

'It was just like this on the night Alan was murdered.' Shaking her shoulders angrily, she gunned the motor into life and continued firmly: 'We'll leave the fog behind as we head inland.'

In one sense, she was accurate. As they swept westward along the Massachusetts Turnpike, they passed through the unseen barrier of the freezing mark. Fog and icy rain gave way to increasingly heavy snow. By the time Phoebe circled onto the Newton exit and headed into a maze of side roads, the windshield wipers had created two semicircles in a thick mantle of white.

Outside, houses and shrubs were fast losing their individuality, and every turn seemed to reveal the same vista. Phoebe was muttering over and over, like an incantation, the directions from her earlier trip to Mrs. Gough's home.

271

'Third right, then second left, then fourth right.'

Her memory was all that stood between them and total disorientation.

Everett Gabler was sitting in the inadequate backseat, his bony knees hunched under his chin. With the side windows blanketed and the rear defroster fighting a losing battle, he could have been squatting in a black cave. Always distrustful of any competence other than his own, he stared past the two shadowy silhouettes ahead of him and despaired of ever reaching their destination.

Thatcher, on the other hand, was congratulating himself. He had expected the normal nighttime suburban phenomena of invisible street signs and nonexistent house numbers. But now, with even major landmarks obliterated, he was grateful they had not entrusted this expedition to a city cab driver.

His confidence was vindicated when the fourth right brought them to a short cul-de-sac permitting no further progress. Gabler sighed fatalistically and Phoebe, peering intently beyond the wipers, emitted a grunt of satisfaction.

'That's Clay's car!' she cried, swerving sharply into a driveway behind a Lincoln.

With the agility of practice, she wriggled out of the car and began crunching up the walk before her passengers had extricated themselves from unfamiliar seat belts and door locks. Driven by the fear that their trip had taken too long when every second counted, Phoebe was in no mood for formalities. Finding the front door unlocked, she ignored the bell and tumbled into the hallway, crying loudly:

'Eleanor! Clay! It's me, Phoebe.'

Her boot heels clicked on the waxed floor as she made straight for the living room, marching boldly into the silence until she was brought up short by the scene before her.

Mrs. Gough was directly ahead, her back to the fireplace, her arm outstretched along the mantel, her fingers touching the base of a heavy silver candelabra. Unresponsive to the intrusion, she continued looking downward at the chair facing her.

Then Phoebe heard an agonized groan and her horror-stricken gaze fastened on Clay Batchelder, slumped forward, his hands cradling his head as if shielding it.

'What have you done to Clay?' she demanded.

Mrs. Gough finally looked up and Phoebe gasped. This was an Eleanor never seen before. Like an avenging fury, she stood erect, her shoulders back and her head high. But it was her face that had undergone a transformation. The dead skin was so taut that the deep lines and hollow shadows seemed chiseled from some gray, unyielding stone. Mrs. Gough had not aged; she had desiccated.

With incredible relief Phoebe heard footsteps behind her, then a reassuring voice at her shoulder.

'Batchelder's all right, he's just sobbing,' John Thatcher explained. 'Confession doesn't come easily to some men.'

CHAPTER THIRTY

A WELL-FORKED TAIL

'I should have realized that it was unnecessary for us to race out to Newton,' Thatcher said to Phoebe Fournier, two days later, when they were all waiting for a plane to New York. 'Mrs. Gough was capable of handling Batchelder in any showdown, and she knew exactly what she was dealing with.'

Phoebe was even more apologetic. 'I had it the wrong way round. When I saw the two of them in that living room, I thought Eleanor had just bashed Clay.'

Everett Gabler snorted.

'No doubt I should have explained more clearly,' Thatcher said hastily, to forestall a clash. In reality, he still did not understand how she could have been so mistaken.

'You shouldn't have had to,' Phoebe echoed his unspoken thought. 'I guess what really bugs me is that I was the one who brought everything out in the open at the Christmas party, and I never realized what I was doing.'

'Well, I didn't either,' Joe Cleveland said handsomely.

'I wouldn't expect you to,' Phoebe replied with more candor than tact. 'But what the hell happened to me?'

Joe was more than ready to tell her. 'You got thrown off balance when Eleanor was willing to tear up more of the pea patch than we were.'

'I really didn't mind Eleanor's being gung-ho.'

274

Phoebe insisted. 'But she was capable of so much more than I bargained for that the possibilities began to include murder.'

'You talking about the murder?' demanded Fritz Diehl, as he and Mrs. Gough returned from the newsstand. 'Good. The papers haven't told me a thing except that Clay confessed. Why in God's name did he do it?'

Phoebe reddened with embarrassment at this indication that her words had been overheard, but Thatcher, ignoring her social gaffe, answered Diehl's query as succinctly as possible.

'Whetmore was blackmailing Batchelder. So Batchelder killed him, using the employee dissension as a smokescreen.'

'Are you telling me that Clay had some dark secret in his past?' Diehl found this the hardest part to believe.

'He certainly did. You could all have saved yourselves a good deal of grief if you had asked, five years ago, where Batchelder got a hundred thousand to invest in Sparrow.'

'It never occurred to me.' Diehl scowled as he tried to reconstruct ancient history. 'Back then, when Mitch and I were scratching around for some seed money, Clay was very sympathetic. He never acted as if it was a problem for him and, of course, we didn't know much about him. He wasn't a paid hand at Bayou, he didn't live in New Orleans, and he had his own business.'

Eleanor Gough was rueful. 'These days we know more about the Don Islingtons of this world. We weren't surprised when Don refused to consider investing in a new company because he has expensive family responsibilities. We should have

275

remembered that Clay had the same kind of obligations when we started Sparrow, and he went right on meeting them.'

'Catch that wife of his letting him cut costs in the home,' Diehl chuckled. 'But if Clay didn't have a cent, what did he do?'

Mrs. Gough's equanimity vanished. 'The same thing everybody at Bayou did who wanted easy money,' she said caustically. 'He agreed to a drug run.'

'The goddam idiot! I always knew Clay was limited, but I didn't realize he was a jerk.'

John Thatcher shook his head sadly. 'I expect he was consumed by envy at seeing two young men miraculously enabled to live a dream. Batchelder wanted to share the golden opportunity.'

'Didn't he realize he'd have it hanging over him forever?' Diehl protested.

'Clay's strong point is daily operations. He's not very good at anticipating long-term developments,' Mrs. Gough said temperately. 'According to Clay, he only considered the immediate risk. The drug-enforcement people keep an eye on repetitive patterns. So he thought a one-shot effort would be safe, particularly as his partner in crime was just as deeply involved. Once the run was over, Clay never gave the matter a second thought. That is, not until Alan showed up at Sparrow, having found out all about Clay's past.'

'God, for a minute I thought you were going to say Alan had been the partner,' Joe Cleveland exclaimed. 'And I knew he didn't have that kind of moxie.'

Mrs. Gough's pride at not employing pilots in the drug business had suffered a setback. 'No, Joe,' she

276

agreed, 'Alan didn't believe in taking risks.'

'Then he should have been more adept at recognizing them,' Gabler remarked. 'Blackmail can be a dangerous pursuit.'

'Clay says Alan was greedy from the start,' she reported, 'but it was the physical exam that put the fat in the fire. Alan knew his days as a pilot were numbered.'

Thatcher was all too familiar with this line of reasoning. 'So he decided to emerge as a senior executive with a seat on the board and access to the firm's assets. Whetmore thought it would be easy for Batchelder to arrange, and Batchelder knew it would be impossible. That's why he kept everyone in the dark before the employees' meeting and sat back to watch the sparks fly.'

'And we obliged,' Phoebe groaned. 'Imagine playing patsy to Clay Batchelder!'

'Remember that you were a disappointment to him,' Thatcher said hearteningly. 'He wanted you all to go for Whetmore, not each other.'

Gabler was barely able to contain himself. 'What good did all that nonsense at the meeting do? As soon as the money surfaced, the police knew they were dealing with a more complex situation.'

'I think Whetmore's legendary stupidity was to blame for that,' Thatcher argued. 'Batchelder probably didn't dream that the cash was being dissipated on simple bachelor thrills. If it had been steadily absorbed into normal investments, the police might never have noticed. After all, Everett, you were the one who established the magnitude of the under-the-table payments.'

It is difficult to be critical of praise, but Gabler came close.

'My intervention should not have been necessary,' he said ungraciously.

'Even the emergence of the fifty thousand was no real threat to Batchelder,' Thatcher continued. 'Whetmore's outlandish behavior at the meeting could easily be attributed to an inept *agent provocateur*, and Batchelder snatched at the theory of Diehl's responsibility.'

Eleanor was obliged to demur. 'Clay wasn't that quick to agree when Mitch first raised the idea.'

'Perhaps not in front of you,' said Thatcher, who could imagine Mrs. Gough's reaction to such an accusation. 'But in New York it was quite a different matter. He did everything but name Diehl directly to me. And when I checked back yesterday with some of my men, they said that a Mr. Werner from A&P contented himself with describing police activity in St. Louis. It was Batchelder who was filling in chapter and verse for all comers.'

'Between the two of them, my old pals Mitch and Clay did a real job on me,' Diehl said unforgivingly.

Thatcher refused to pander to this single-minded view. 'Not for long. As soon as Everett went to work, the list of suspects narrowed to a handful,' he said, skillfully eliding Gabler's preference for Phoebe as First Murderer. 'By that time Batchelder was desperate, and he fastened on Mrs. Gough as the only acceptable scapegoat.'

Phoebe still did not realize how docilely she had danced to Clay Batchelder's piping. 'I agree that he made all Eleanor's talk about guilt and atonement sound suspicious, but he was just using the material at hand.'

'Not precisely. Mrs. Gough spoke in terms of duty and responsibility. As soon as she left, he paraphrased her remarks to give them a more sinister gloss. What's more, from Scovil's uneasiness about Mrs. Gough during our last meeting, I suspect he may have been subjected to the same subtle poisoning by Batchelder.'

Mrs. Gough was more interested than disturbed. 'I noticed that Mitch was leery of me, but I felt the same way about him. You see, I knew there were no irregularities at Sparrow. If Captain Lemoine was right about blackmail, something had happened when we were all at Bayou, something that Alan could have found out about. I wondered if it could have been as simple as a drunken-driving accident with Alan sitting in the passenger seat. It wasn't difficult to visualize Mitch just stepping on the accelerator and speeding away. When disaster strikes, he does tend to ... to...'

'To panic,' Diehl said baldly. 'Face it, Eleanor, Mitch can't take pressure.'

But Eleanor had no trouble with the concept. She had simply been searching for the right word.

'To go hysterical, is what I was going to say,' she corrected calmly. 'It wasn't until the party that everything straightened itself out. Only twenty-four hours earlier, I'd been talking to Don Islington about his financial problems. Then Phoebe started in on how we all got our stake money, and I realized that Clay had never told us where his came from. And if I was looking for a little irregularity at Bayou, I didn't have to think twice. The only logical course of action was to go to New Orleans and make sure.'

It did not seem quite that simple to Thatcher.

'But how did you get results so quickly? We had been thinking in terms of a laborious financial resurrection,' he admitted.

'That's because you didn't work for Bayou,' Eleanor retorted. 'I merely encouraged Bill Johnson to tell me anecdotes about who had been picked up for drug-running after we left. When he told me that the biggest bust involved one of Alan Whetmore's buddies, I knew I was on the right track. Then all I had to do was locate Ramon Estevez and go ask him.'

'And he just told you?' Thatcher made no attempt to hide his skepticism.

Mrs. Gough smiled. 'For a price. Ramon was having trouble meeting the payments on his marina. I wrote a check and he confirmed what I already suspected. Shortly after Ramon came out of prison, Alan turned up in Acapulco on one of his fancy weekends. In the course of a long, boozy reunion, Ramon told him about Clay's solitary fling. At the time it didn't mean anything but, when Alan came to Sparrow, he realized it was a gold mine.'

'He was right,' said Thatcher, speaking as an expert. 'Ramon didn't know about Batchelder and Batchelder didn't know where Ramon was. In effect, Whetmore was offering protection.'

'That's certainly how Ramon saw it. When I told him Alan had gotten a hundred and fifty thousand, he went wild. As far as Ramon was concerned, it was his personal property that Alan had exploited. He was still trying to find some profit for himself when I left.'

All of Gabler's confidence in high-minded ladies was proving to be justified. Beaming, he said: 'When it was learned that you were in New Orleans, there were fears you might be engaged in a cover-up. I knew that was out of the question.'

280

'Clay didn't. That's why he came out to Newton, to persuade me to keep quiet. And, if I'd found out two years ago, I might have been tempted,' she confessed, proving that she had more of the old Adam than Gabler recognized. 'That kind of publicity could have killed Sparrow. But after Alan's murder, silence was unthinkable. Clay didn't understand my moral objections at all. He didn't give up until I reminded him that I was now a prime suspect. That's when he started crying.'

Fritz Diehl was still riding his hobbyhorse. 'I'm surprised he didn't suggest serving Mitch up on a platter.'

'Oh no,' said Eleanor instantly. 'He needed Mitch to run Sparrow. Clay even tried to ensure that Mitch had an alibi for the time of the killing. And he never would have touched that wrench if he hadn't assumed I'd brought it to the office. In fact, Clay had the nerve to be quite indignant with Mitch for nullifying these protective efforts and getting himself hauled off to the station.'

'He should have remembered that Mitch always hogs the limelight.' Joe Cleveland reviewed his own statement, then added a rider: 'But that doesn't mean Clay hasn't been central at Sparrow.'

Phoebe burst into derisive laughter. 'Now that you're taking over some of his work, it's going to be the mainspring of Sparrow,' she jibed.

When Thatcher raised an eyebrow, Mrs. Gough explained.

'While Clay is out on bail, he's giving us as much help as he can for the California expansion. Joe and I are going to New York to see about some secondhand planes, with Joe taking care of the technical end.'

281

Thatcher was carefully expressionless. 'Then you've agreed to Scovil's proposals.'

'No, Mitch has agreed to mine,' Mrs. Gough replied without batting an eye. 'We're canceling Pittsburgh and going transcontinental on our tried-and-true system—used aircraft, economy facilities, and no frills. Phoebe has been right to insist on that, as I am sure you see.'

Thatcher saw more than that. On the surface it appeared that everyone had gotten something. The truth, he suspected, was quite different. Eleanor Gough had gotten everything she wanted.

'So everybody's happy. Right, Phoebe?' Fritz Diehl asked challengingly.

But Phoebe was beginning to learn. 'I didn't realize Eleanor saw so much merit in the California idea,' she said sedately. 'And if I find space at the right price, that makes a real difference.'

They were saved further constraint by the public address system, which burst into life. A voice, distorted enough to be almost unintelligible, informed them that Flight 235 was ready for boarding. Galvanic unheavals began at every bench as passengers crammed themselves into overcoats and snatched up shoulder bags and carry-ons.

'Don't bother,' said Mrs. Gough as the first ripples began in her own group. 'I've told them to keep seats for us. It will be easier to let the others fight their way through.'

Even at economy rates, Thatcher thought, it paid to travel with the management. It also gave him more time to satisfy his curiosity.

'You say that Batchelder is out on bail?' he asked.

'Yes, Clay has agreed to plead guilty to a lesser charge of unpremeditated murder. With time off for good behavior, he should be out in seven or eight years.'

'Wonderful,' Diehl said ironically. 'What you mean is that your lawyers worked their tails off to avoid a public trial featuring drug smuggling and blackmail. So Sparrow gets off the hook, the DA's office gets a conviction, and poor old Clay pays the price.'

It was Joe Cleveland who took up the cudgels. 'What's with this poor-old-Clay business?' he rapped out. 'Clay bashed in Whetmore's brains with a wrench. That's way out of line in my book.'

'And he put the rest of us through the wringer,' Phoebe chimed in. 'For three weeks we've been wondering if we had any company left.'

At this point Everett Gabler was inspired to air his own uncompromising views. 'What you say is very true. It is outrageous that a comparatively light sentence should be the judgment for a cold-blooded murder which was motivated by sheer self-interest.'

'You both make me tired,' Eleanor Gough said trenchantly. 'Fritz thinks it's deplorable that Clay should go to jail at all. Everett wants an eye for an eye. You're both enjoying the luxury of demanding the impossible and being affronted when you don't get it. What happens to Clay isn't all that important. What is important, is minimizing the fallout on innocent bystanders. As Phoebe says, we've been put through the wringer, and we don't deserve to have Sparrow fall apart under us.'

'Attaboy, Eleanor!' Joe applauded.

John Thatcher was not far behind him. Defining absolutes has always been easy. Thatcher reserved his approval for those willing to forge a decent compromise between things as they are and things

283

as they ought to be.

'I certainly agree that Batchelder's sins should not be visited on others.'

Fritz Diehl was more than ready to change the subject. 'Sure,' he said, and continued without missing a beat: 'But what I'd really like to know, Thatcher, is how an outsider like you tumbled to Clay. It can't have been just Phoebe's review of how we all got a hundred thousand.'

'No, that simply provided the missing motive. And, after Everett had given Sparrow a clean bill of health, we needed one. Of course we had no idea what crime Batchelder had committed at Bayou to obtain his original stake. But we started at the opposite end from Mrs. Gough. For weeks I had been puzzled by that extraordinary meeting with Whetmore and its consequences.'

'Oh, that!' Joe flapped a nonchalant hand. 'We're different at Sparrow.'

'Not to the point of lunacy,' Thatcher said dryly. 'When Everett insisted the meeting must have been rigged, I realized there was only one person who could have done it. Why, for instance, didn't Scovil read the list beforehand?'

All four of them tried to explain at once, but Fritz Diehl's baritone easily prevailed.

'Because Mitch is such a lazy S.O.B. he never reads his in-basket.'

'Exactly.' Thatcher was willing to accept any phrasing that took them in the right direction. 'But his shortcomings were not allowed to interfere with the operation of Sparrow. You yourself pointed out at the party that Mrs. Gough and Batchelder would both go on deck to make sure the rockets were fired properly. Similarly, when there was anything important, they thrust it on Scovil's attention. But, in spite of the fact that Whetmore could easily have been scotched before the meeting, Batchelder did nothing. His tactics almost backfired when my arrival jeopardized Scovil's attendance. Then Batchelder had to abandon passivity and weigh in with the deciding vote.'

Mrs. Gough was shaking her head at her own blindness. 'I never even thought of that,' she admitted.

'As soon as you looked at Batchelder twice, the situation was obvious,' Thatcher insisted. 'Once the hostilities at the meeting started, he tried to prevent you and Miss Fournier from attacking each other and encouraged you to go after Whetmore. He wanted as many people as possible to tangle with his intended victim.'

Joe Cleveland thought he saw another nice touch. 'I suppose that's why Clay pretended I was about to deck Alan.'

'Only partially. The most damning thing of all was the timetable.'

'Now wait a minute,' Diehl objected. 'Nobody had an alibi. Mitch himself was roaming around Logan.'

'And while Clay may have been running all over the Sparrow compound before dinner, so was I,' Mrs. Gough added.

Not to be outdone, Phoebe made a contribution, too. 'And Joe and I were both stuck in the tunnel.'

Thatcher regarded them all severely. 'You're looking at the wrong time period. Consider Whetmore's movements before the murder. He left the conference room, consulted the work roster for his next flight, then took his car to a restaurant

285

several miles away. While there, he checked his watch and rushed off so as not to be late for something. As he was never seen again, it's safe to assume that something was his meeting with the killer.'

'So?' Diehl asked, puzzled by Thatcher's air of completion.

'That appointment must have been arranged before Whetmore left the Sparrow compound. When and where was it made? Scovil was closeted with Islington, and Mrs. Gough was making a speech at the water cooler. But Batchelder was alone with Alan Whetmore.'

Joe Cleveland looked thunderstruck. 'You mean when Clay pretended he had to hustle me out of the building, it wasn't just to throw suspicion on me?'

Relieved that someone had grasped his meaning, Thatcher nodded. 'Alan Whetmore had just received a nasty disappointment and might easily have said something rash. Batchelder started to soothe him while we were still there, by attributing Mitch Scovil's rage to lack of preparation. As intended, Whetmore interpreted that as a suggestion there was still hope. Then Batchelder had to get all of us out of the room—under the pretext of keeping the peace—and set up his victim for murder. He was the only one who had the opportunity to do so.'

'Imagine Clay doing all that,' said Phoebe. 'When I chose Alan as our spokesman, I gave him just the scenario he needed.'

Unwittingly Thatcher probed a sore spot. 'Batchelder was ingenious in some ways, but he made critical miscalculations about people. First there was Ramon Estevez, chatting too freely about the past. Then Mitch Scovil wandered into the line of fire. But worst of all was the money. Batchelder obscured the payments at his end without troubling to learn if Whetmore was exercising similar caution.'

'Clay made a real balls-up of the whole thing, didn't he,' murmured Diehl. 'He should have stuck to what he knew about.'

'Well, that's what he's doing now, insofar as he can without leaving the jurisdiction,' Eleanor replied. 'If we can just defer this court date for four or five weeks, our proposals for California will be ready. And that, of course, is why Fritz would like to see us all embroiled in a messy trial.'

'It would help,' Diehl acknowledged cheerfully. 'But don't overrate the innocents in St. Louis. When I explain how Sparrow will be running a real cheapie, they'll think the threat has receded. Some of them still haven't grasped that price is a competitive factor. Hard to believe, isn't it?'

His insouciance led Thatcher to infer that Fritz Diehl could not yet be counted out in the power struggle at A&P.

'And now, I've got to be off,' Diehl continued. 'Have a good flight, everyone.'

'You're not traveling with us?' Thatcher enquired, for once forgetting reality.

'Are you crazy?' Diehl replied with mock ferocity. 'I do my flying on A&P. I just dropped by to get the dirt.' Having shaken hands with everyone else, he bent to peck Eleanor Gough's cheek. 'I'll give you a ring sometime this week, Eleanor, and let you know how things are.'

'Fine,' she said absently, 'if I don't get to you first.'

287

The frenzied mob that had been filing through the gate was now reduced to a tail of eight or nine people. Automatically everyone began to check belongings.

'I gather from this agreement with Scovil that the proxy fight is a thing of the past,' Thatcher ventured, 'and we won't be seeing you back at the Sloan.'

'Only for financing,' she replied calmly, 'after we decide what aircraft to buy.'

Thatcher blinked at this indication that the impossible had, indeed, happened and Mrs. Gough was supplanting Mitch Scovil without a battle royal. Perhaps this was the moment for the Sloan to send in its own designated hitter. That is, if Charlie Trinkam could ever be extricated from his current assignment, now that Rupert Vernon was offering to make Boston the winter home of the Edinburgh Festival.

Meanwhile, she was sweeping on: 'And there's one more item in our agreement that will interest you. Mitch needed no persuasion to see that Phoebe was the ideal replacement for Clay on the board.'

Phoebe unsuccessfully tried to smother a giggle. 'Alan must be turning in his grave,' she finally yelped.

During the congratulations, Joe directed a conspiratorial wink at Thatcher.

'That's just great, Phoebe,' he said artlessly. 'Now, whenever anything comes up, we can get together and tell you how to vote.'

The merriment vanished from Phoebe's face like dew before the desert sun.

'Like hell you will!' she snorted.

Seizing her duffle bag, she marched toward the plane. Joe Cleveland instantly fell into step beside her, initiating what was bound to be a spirited debate.

Thatcher was delighted to have Mrs. Gough to himself. 'Has Scovil retired from active participation in Sparrow?' he asked bluntly.

'Of course not. Mitch just has some other problems right now.'

'You mean, beside Batchelder?'

'Kate McDermott, his wife, has been offered a spot as anchorwoman on a network morning show,' she explained, obscurely amused. 'It's a wonderful opportunity, but, of course, it's based in New York.'

Tucking a portfolio under her arm, Eleanor Gough rose and briskly shook herself. The gesture was a simple act of physical adjustment but Thatcher, overcome by a sudden fancy, saw her as a tigress waking from a long sleep and stretching luxuriantly. With a chill prickle at the nape of his neck, Thatcher realized how many potential big cats there were in his own life. He did not want to be around when his secretary, Miss Corsa, and his daughter, Laura, began to flex their muscles.

Oblivious to his premonition, Mrs. Gough gazed at the boarding desk where Joe and Phoebe were still at it, then at the corridor down which Diehl had disappeared. Thatcher knew without being told that she was considering Mitch Scovil and his marital problems, Phoebe and her new status at Sparrow, Fritz Diehl and his struggle at A&P.

Eleanor Gough, rapt in some sibylline overview

of the past few weeks, took several seconds to achieve the summation Thatcher was waiting for.

'These young people,' she said with affectionate scorn. 'They don't have a clue!'

Photoset, printed and bound in Great Britain by
REDWOOD PRESS LIMITED, Melksham, Wiltshire

ABOUT THE AUTHOR

Emma Lathen is the non de plume shared by Mary Jane Latsis, an economist, and Martha Henissart, a lawyer. The authors met at Harvard, where they were doing graduate work. Miss Henissart went on to practice law for twelve years, and Miss Latsis worked as an agricultural economist for the United Nations and the United States government. Their first book written together, *Banking on Death*, was published in 1961. *Something in the Air* is the twentieth novel by Emma Lathen.